Dredging Up Memories

A.J. Brown

Dredging Up Memories
Published 2016 by
Stitched Smiles Publishing
Copyright ©2016 A.J. Brown
Front cover design by Lisa Vasquez
Stock by Shutterstock and Marcus J. Ranum
Edited by Amanda Shore

Disclaimer: The works in *Dredging Up Memories* are works of fiction. Names and events are creations from the author's imagination except where noted.

ISBN: 978-1-945263-01-9
ISBN-10: 1945263016

Dedicated to: Logan, better known as The Boy.

TABLE OF CONTENTS

Forward

Walking in mud with butterflies above. Sounds dirty, painful, but with its payoff. You'll have moments, I'm sure, where this story will be thick; it'll push you, and it may just hurt, but you'll battle on. Why? Because of the simple, honest feelings it displays. The payoff.

Hank Walker is your friend, father, brother, and son. And he is a good Ol' Boy. You will connect. And not just with Hank but also to a teddy with a boy's name and girl's voice. You'll meet his family and friends. You've met people like them before. There'll be bad guys and good guys. Scary and hopeful.

A.J. Brown has a knack for the feels, of making it personal and real. If he's your ride through the end of the world, be prepared to get a little dirt on you.

Follow Hank, walk through the apocalyptic mud with him, dredge up those fluttering memories.

—Justin Dunne
Co-Author of the novel *Tales of the Nothing Man*

Five Weeks After It All Started...

The rifle was light. Unlike Pop's shotgun; that thing was heavier than any firearm should be, and the kickback could knock you on your ass if you weren't ready for it. Pop called it Ox—I guess it was an appropriate name for something so powerful. It always reminded me of Babe the blue ox, Paul Bunyan's companion. I reckon that's how Pop saw his shotgun—more as a companion than a weapon or hunting tool.

One time my brother, Leland, thought he was man enough to wield old Ox and took him out of the gun rack in Pop's shop. He handed it to me, and I almost dropped it. The wood stock was cold, the barrel like ice, and my nerves were frazzled. You see, Leland was the oldest of the four of us, and I was his sidekick little brother. He played jokes on all of us and did things that the rest of us wouldn't think of doing. Like pulling Ox off the gun rack.

"Come on," he said and took the shotgun from me. I had never been so relieved in my fourteen years.

"I don't think this is a good idea, Lee."

He shook his head, and his hair—which was down to his shoulders—moved from side to side. "Don't be a wuss face, Hank. Dad will never know. We'll go out to the fence behind the barn and shoot a couple of shells and put it back. Easy as pie, little brother."

Easy as pie? Nothing is ever easy as pie.

I set up a can on one of the old fence posts by the chicken coop and then got behind him. Leland took aim, the shotgun in the crook of his shoulder, right in the socket where the

1

collarbone and shoulder come together. He squeezed the trigger with no hesitation.

A bomb went off in my head, and my ears rang for most of the rest of that day. Leland went backwards and ended up on his back, unconscious. Seven hours later, he came home from the hospital, arm in a sling, shoulder dislocated and collar bone broken. He had a lump on the back of his head where it hit the ground, resulting in a concussion that gave him headaches for months after.

"Did I hit the can?" he asked me before he went to bed that night.

"Nope. But you did take out one of the fence runners."

Memories. It's the hardest part of this whole…end of the world thing? If that's what it could be called. That's all I have now: the memories of loved ones and friends passed on and, in many cases, rose up. How odd does that sound? Rose up? Like anyone thought the dead really could get up and walk.

I guess it was possible after all, wasn't it? Shows how much we knew.

I stood from my pickup, slung my pack over my shoulder, and closed the door, leaving the keys in the ignition. Just in case. I shouldered my pack and walked to the center of the street, rifle in both hands. An old, blue sedan sat off to the left, its wheels up on a curb, its front end crumpled by the light pole it had hit. The left front tire sat at an odd angle, a dead person beneath it. I moved to the front of the vehicle. Another dead man slumped over the steering wheel, his skull ruptured. Hair and bits of tissue clung to the windshield, the glass spider-webbed from where his head struck. Flies buzzed about, zipping through the broken window and lighting on the man's head and shoulders and probably the rest of him as well. The stench of death hung in the air and reminded me of roadkill after three days in the summer sun: a cloying, heavy odor that turned the stomach and lingered with a reach much further than anything—rotten or pleasant—should.

I let out a long breath. Recognition could sometimes bring you to tears, but not in this case. It only brought back old memories. "I'll come back for you in a little while, Mr. Martin. Get you out of there, okay?"

He had been my baseball coach in another time, back when it was safe to play games. Back when there was no fear of something dead coming out of the woods or around a corner to rip you apart. From the looks of him, he wouldn't be getting up and joining the ranks of the undead.

The man underneath the car was a different story. His head twitched, a movement that was so insignificant but so startling at the same time. One of his hands moved, then his eyes opened. No matter how many times I've seen it, I still can't get used to seeing the dead move, get up, and walk around. I certainly can't get used to seeing them eating people. His mouth opened, and he hissed, a deep, throaty sound.

I didn't recognize him. He could have been a neighbor or a friend or just another dead head that shambled into our little town. It didn't matter; he was a rotter even if he was a person at one time. I took aim with my rifle then stopped. Instead of shooting him, I brought the heel of my boot down on his forehead. His head slipped beneath my foot, and he groaned. I brought my heel down again, this time in the center of his face. His nose shattered, and my heel broke through rotten skin. A third time, and there was a hollow crunch that made me shiver. My stomach rolled, and for a moment, I thought I would throw up. The man stilled.

I scanned the small neighborhood—an odd cul-de-sac, not quite a square but nowhere near a circle either. The six houses formed a U of small homes and overgrown yards. A few skeletal remains lay about here and there. The one lying in the second yard to my right was a woman at one time, and from the flower print skirt she still had around her decomposing hips, I guessed she was still fairly young, maybe not even thirty yet.

Jeanette entered my thoughts. I tried to shove her back into the deepest corner of my soul. Swallowing hard, I shook my head and hoped she and Bobby were okay, that Jake had managed to get them to a safe zone before the dead managed to swarm our small town. I closed my eyes and saw her, the fear on her face, the look of disbelief as Jake pulled her away by her arms.

"Go!" I yelled.

Go.

I had stayed behind with Leland and Pop and Davey Blaylock. Someone had to fight. The military wasn't going to be coming to Sipping Creek, South Carolina. Like thousands of little do-nothing towns all across the country, it existed just to exist.

A slight shuffle brought me from my memories. I looked past the back of Mr. Martin's car. Mrs. Crenshaw shuffled along in a slightly bent over manner, her body a gray mass of ugly. White puffs of dirty hair hung along the sides of her face; one eye dangled by the optic nerves. A bloom of blood clung to the front of her nightgown. Her feet were bare, and pieces of skin and meat hung off the sides, and her toes were

4

nothing more than bones. There were scratches on her arms and neck and face, deep grooves that bled before she died.

"Morning, Mrs. Crenshaw," I called and waved, knowing full well the only answer I would get was...

She groaned, turned her whole body toward me. Not just her head like a living person would but her entire dead, stiff body. She picked up her pace, one hand extending outward, the other one appearing as useless as teats on a bull. I guess she tried to straighten, but Mrs. Crenshaw had suffered from Osteoporosis in her old age and had that hump on her back — the Dowager's Hump, she once told me — that kept her from being fully upright while alive, much less in her rotting, dead state.

It pained me to see my sixth grade teacher like this. She had been a cantankerous old bat, especially when I was a kid, always fussing about not spoon-feeding her students. If we wanted to learn, we would earn it in her classroom. Not many of us passed. I scraped by with a low D—not great but passing. She wasn't loved by many, and most of us thought she was the meanest teacher we ever had. Even so, she didn't deserve the fate dealt her.

Raising my rifle, I took aim. Brown drool trickled from her mouth, slinked its way down her chin. I waited as she drew closer, her moan echoing in the cul-de-sac. A tingle of dread crept into my stomach. What if others heard her? I still didn't know if they could hear, really truly hear in the way that you and I can, or if they felt vibrations from voices, or maybe words sounded like echoes in their ears, just a reverb of slow motion sounds that were no more than a *wah wah wah wah wah wah*. I didn't know if they could actually see either, or smell, but what if they could?

I shrugged. The rifle would be louder than any moans she could make. And if they could hear, then the gunshot would attract more of them.

"A little closer, Mrs. Crenshaw," I said and drew a bead on her forehead. I pulled the trigger. Mrs. Crenshaw's head snapped back; she stumbled on impact and tipped backward. She landed on that fleshy hump and rolled slightly to one side. I let out a long breath, held my rifle on her as I approached. I nudged her foot, then her arm, then the side of what remained of her head. "I'm sorry, Mrs. Crenshaw," I said and lowered my gun.

Just as I thought, others came out of hiding, their rotting bodies lurching along. Flies buzzed about them as if dancing around mobile, all-you-can eat bars. Two of them came at first, then three, four more from around the backside of one of the houses. Mr. Mitchell stumbled over a Radio Flyer sitting in a driveway, crashed to the ground with a thud and a clatter as the wagon toppled over. His fat stomach burst, sending brown sludge and rotting organs onto gray concrete. He tried to stand but could only manage to roll over. His intestines spilled out.

Biting back vomit, I took aim at the nearest corpse, a woman, and squeezed the trigger. The top of her head disappeared, and she dropped to the ground. The next shot took the man closest to her. The third one missed, and I back pedaled to the front of Mr. Martin's car. They closed in quick, their moans escalating. I crawled onto the hood of the car then onto its top. It gave slightly but held my weight.

The next three rounds dropped the nearest of the dead. The others clambered over their fallen comrades. I slid the pack from my shoulder, reached inside for a pistol. Easier. Faster.

Four shots, and only one undead remained. My hand shook for a moment. Killing the ones I knew was always harder, more painful. Tommy Banks was no different. His son played with my son, two eight-year-olds with heads full of dreams and lots of mischief left undone.

"Deep breaths, Walker," I said to myself. "Slow and steady." Like that tortoise that raced the hare. Slow and steady, and I should win the race. But what was I racing against? The dead? Time? I didn't know.

Tommy scrambled over several corpses as if they were just speed bumps in the way. He teetered to one side and almost fell when he did so. His black hair was still dark but matted down on one side like he just woke up from a two-day sleep and forgot to do a comb through before going out. He wore a uniform, and his nose was crusted with what looked like brown snot. He must have been really sick the last time he arrived home from work. Like Mrs. Crenshaw, there were scratches on his face. His arms reached across the hood of the car, his mouth snapping, his teeth clattering together. I swallowed the lump in my throat. I took aim, pulled the trigger. Tommy Banks' head snapped back, then he slumped against the car, his head dragging down the passenger's side door as he fell, leaving a smear of blackish red in its wake.

My shoulders sagged, and I lowered my head. Forcing back tears, I slid onto the hood and jumped over the bodies. I wasn't done. A clean sweep of the neighborhood was needed, and I hadn't even reached the first house. A few feet from the car, I turned back, stared at the mass of rotting flesh surrounding Mr. Martin's old, blue sedan. It was a nightmare. It was all just a nightmare. It had to be.

I pinched my arm then my face. I was wide awake.

Mr. Mitchell was still moving, crawling toward me, his blackened intestines dragging behind him, his hips and legs left back where he had split in half. His bald head bled where he had struck it against the sidewalk. Still he crawled on, his fingers slapping the concrete hard as he tried to move faster.

How did I forget about him? I raised the rifle. A second later, he stopped moving, the bullet taking off the side of his head.

I walked back toward my truck, stopping at Mr. Martin's car. I looked at him. It would be a pain in the ass to pull him free, but it needed to happen.

"Soon, Mr. Martin."

At my truck, I slung the rifle into the bed and grabbed the pickaxe and shovel. I was already tired, but they were good people, these folks from Sipping Creek. I couldn't leave them to rot or to let the elements wear away what remained of them. And the animals...I didn't know if eating their flesh could kill the animals, most of them dogs that used to be well-fed and loved, but I didn't want to ever have to find out.

In the old world, we buried our dead. It was closure for those left behind. Stones marked graves, sometimes witty or profound statements on the markers. At that time, I wasn't concerned with phrases or even closure. Respect held me in that neighborhood.

Three feet in to digging a mass grave, I stopped. A faint groan held my attention. Staggering from the Banks' open door was Thomas, Tommy's son. His jaw sat slack, his hair stuck up in cowlicks as if he, like his dad, had just woken up from a long nap. Drooping, white-filmed eyes sat in deep sockets. He stepped off the side of the porch and fell straight down. One leg struck the ground first, and then he somersaulted and landed hard on his back. I cringed. If he had been alive, that fall might have killed him. It would have knocked the breath out of him and then sent him into a screaming fit when he was able to breathe again. I wanted to run over to him, to see if he was okay. I didn't.

Instead, I watched. It took him a couple of minutes, but he managed to roll over and get to his feet.

Daddy, can I go to Thomas' house?

How many times had Bobby and Thomas played together? How many times did they have sleep-overs? How many times had Tommy and I taken them to the nearest race or to one of the ball games over at the University in Columbia?

Spiderman clung to the front of Thomas' blood-stained shirt. A chunk of flesh was missing from his neck. I wondered if he was awake when he had been killed, if there was terror in his eyes, fear in his heart, and a scream cut off from his throat. I wondered if Tommy had been the one to do it. Dead and on autopilot and seeking fresh flesh to satiate an insatiable hunger.

We watched each other, me in the hole, Thomas at the base of the front steps. I tossed the shovel to the edge of the grave and climbed out. Thomas shambled toward me, his groan so much like a child in pain. Honestly, I guess he may have been. Maybe the rotting dead weren't so dead after all. Maybe they could do more than stumble and eat. Like think and feel.

I braced myself, glanced toward my truck. I could run, grab a gun long before he could reach me. Instead, I held my ground, shovel in hands, eyes fixed on my buddy's kid.

"He's not Thomas," I whispered over and over, trying to calm my nerves. It didn't help.

The shovel shook in my hands as he approached. Ten or fifteen feet from me, he lifted his arms, his face changed from a once loving little kid's to a horrible semblance of what he used to be, lips turned down in a sneer, brows furrowed. He bared his teeth as I backed away.

"I'm sorry, Thomas," I said and swung the shovel with every ounce of strength I had. The hollow, metal-on-skull sound echoed in the silent neighborhood. My hands stung from the blow. Thomas staggered sideways and fell, but he wasn't done. Blood seeped from the nasty gash on the left side of his head. On his belly with his legs pushing and arms pulling, he crawled toward me, unfazed by the blow he had taken.

I raised the shovel above my head and brought it down. His skull cracked, and mercifully—for both of us—it was over.

I dropped the shovel, backed up until my butt hit my truck. I climbed in, locked the door. For the first time since the world went to hell, I cried. Straight up and down bawled. Images of my family scampered across the front of my mind, Jeanette and Bobby, my brothers, Pop. It was all too much to swallow.

"Get a grip, Walker," I said and wiped my eyes. Several deep breaths followed.

Most of the rest of that day, I dug holes. Three of them: one fairly large and two smaller. The dead are heavier than folks might think they are, especially Mr. Mitchell with his trailing insides. It's dead weight—no pun intended—and it's like carrying tree logs or boulders. I laid them in the big hole, like human matchsticks all in a pile. Mr. Martin and the dead body beneath his wheel and whatever remains of folks littered the street went into the second hole. The bones and body parts that had been scattered about went in there as well. Tommy and Thomas Banks went together in the last one. I couldn't bring myself to separate them. But I didn't bury them right away; was Karen still alive? Was she dead? Was she somewhere around the neighborhood, in her house?

Though we were raised in the church, I had never been much on praying. But I prayed this time—I had come to praying a lot by then. I said some words out into the air, hoping the wind would carry them to the right ears, the right heart.

Night was well on its way. There was no time to sweep the houses like I had hoped to. The day's events had drained me, both heart and soul. I went back to my truck, locked the doors, and loaded my pistol and rifle. Behind the seat sat Pop's old shotgun. I still have never fired it, not having the luxury of a broken collarbone like my brother. Maybe one day, I would. But not that day, the day I took down an undead child and his father. The children, they're always the hardest to kill.

I closed my eyes, pistol in hand. Exhaustion claimed me as night settled in…

Five Weeks and a Day After It All Started...

The rap on the window snapped me from dreams of Jeanette and Bobby sitting in the warm sun at Brayland Park. Bobby squashed tiny ants as they scurried onto the blanket Jeanette had laid out. She wore a sundress, yellow and white striped that came to just above her knees. He was in a baseball uniform, Junior Jaycees on the front of his garnet shirt, his number 9 on the back along with his last name, WALKER, in white lettering. I was there, watching everything through a video camera lens. I wasn't very good at holding the camera steady, but thankfully, in the dream, I held it just right.

Jeanette looked up at me, waved. She got Bobby's attention, and he glanced up, taking his mind from the destruction of the ant family long enough to flash me a toothy smile and yell, "Cheese."

I woke. Not to a cop knocking on the window wondering why I was parked in the middle of the road and why there were a number of guns in the cab but to a woman, her dead fingernails scraping glass, brown stains on the front of her once blue shirt. Her skin sagged along her face. I could see gray tissue beneath her drooping bottom eyelids. She had no eyes, just a sense that something living sat beyond her reach.

I cranked the truck up, let it idle for a moment as I watched the vaguely familiar woman. She mashed her face against the window, her nose bending to the left, her lips squashing on the glass. Her moan was muffled, but it was enough to kick start my instincts. I backed up. Her lips left a smudge of brown behind. She fell forward, gravity pulling her off balance and to the ground. I shifted the truck into DRIVE. Her skull popped beneath the tire. My skin crawled. My stomach flipped. I closed my eyes and listened to the rumble of the truck's engine.

I drove the length of the street. It ended in a cul-de-sac. I circled around, glancing at the houses. In the distance, I could see the graves I had dug the day before. No undead shambled from open doors or fell over damaged fences. The woman lay dead for good in the middle of the road, her head nothing more than a pulpy mass of tissue and bone.

Before getting out of the truck, I grabbed my guns. In the rearview window, I saw Ox hanging on its hooks. Maybe one day, I would use Pop's shotgun. Until then, I have my rifles and pistols and all of Leland's ammo. Pop's as well.

"Don't think about them," I said and stood from the truck.

A hundred feet away lay the woman. I went to her and nudged her with the toe of one boot. I had to be certain.

The houses loomed before me, the U-shaped cul-de-sac appearing more and more like a death trap than the homes of loving families and good country folk. The houses felt larger than they were. In my mind, they were like abstract paintings, distorting the reality of the world, making things stretch out higher to the sky. I wasn't looking forward to going inside any of them. These sweeps made my stomach knot in anticipation. Or dread. Probably a little bit of both.

I inched into the first house, a yellow, two-story ranch style. The door remained open. Inside, the place was in shambles. Furniture was tipped over, windows broken. Blood had been spilled on the floor and spattered on the walls. There's always a lot of blood. Pictures of happier times hung on walls. A woman, a man, a little girl all smiling wide. The girl clutched a tan teddy bear wearing a bunny suit. I wanted to smile at the innocence, but I knew that purity was gone,

13

and if that little girl were still in the house, there was a good chance she was dead—either really dead or risen up.

Before heading up the stairs, I closed the front door, made sure the back one was shut as well. I didn't need any rotters coming in while I was upstairs. They could be sneaky like that. I learned that lesson the hard way during one of the first sweeps I had done a few weeks earlier. It was in one of those Victorian houses on the edge of town. Not many folks lived on Route 11, so I thought nothing of leaving the door open. The problem? The owners had probably been old or disabled—there was a ramp that led to the porch. I should have known better, but at the time, I don't think anyone still alive knew much about these things.

I made the sweep, found no one in the house. On the way down the steps, three rotters greeted me. One of them—an older man with a bald head—was missing an arm and looked like the rot was catching up with him a lot faster than the other two. He was slow and bumbled about, running into the walls and the banister before he fell down. His head ruptured when it struck the hard wood of the floors, ending things for him before I could.

The other two...

The other two weren't quick like a living person, but they still moved with something akin to grace, making a straight line toward the steps. I leveled my pistol at the first one and waited. He managed to get a foot on the first step before teetering back and bumping into the other one, another male, this one younger, maybe a teenager or in his early twenties. I watched, wanting to see if they could actually climb the steps, if their stiff muscles and bones would allow them to lift those legs higher than an inch or two off the ground.

Again, the one male tried to go up the stairs but couldn't seem to get his leg high enough. I took a couple of steps down, aimed, and pulled the trigger. The blast was deafening. My ears rang. Only the teenager remained, his brown hair somehow still neatly combed.

"Sorry, kid," I said, squeezed the trigger again. He toppled over, landing on the old guy with the ruptured skull. My hands trembled for hours after that.

I shook my head, pushing aside the memories, and went up the stairs. There were three rooms: a bathroom and two bedrooms. Only one door was closed. I checked the two open rooms first, finding the mother in a bedroom, her head smashed in, her mouth bloodied, a chunk of someone's flesh still clenched tight in her teeth. I lifted her lifeless body over my shoulder, carried her outside, and set her down next to the woman who had woken me. Back inside I went, up the stairs to finish the sweep. The bathroom was empty. The other bedroom had to belong to the child. This I knew before pushing the door open.

Unlike in the horror movies, the hinges didn't scream. I was stunned when I stepped into the pink room. Nothing looked out of place. It was as I thought a little girl's room should be: dolls and a play house in one corner, a mirror on the wall, stuffed animals on a blanket that held pictures of cartoon characters. The only thing that might have been odd was the stuffed bear lying on the floor, the one in the bunny outfit from the picture on the first floor. I picked the bear up. It was soft, plush.

I've never been an overly emotional man, but the events of the weeks leading up to that point in my life had changed things considerably. Tears tugged at the corners of my eyes as

15

I thought about the stuffed animal, about the little girl, and what probably happened to her along the way. I hugged the teddy bear close, smelling little girl soap or shampoo or maybe just her natural scent. I smelled the innocence I saw in the picture.

It took me back to Bobby, back to a little blanket he received when he was born. It was black and white. One end laid flat over his infant body; the other end had the head of a puppy and two front legs that looked more like arms for hugging. I remembered how he held it tight to his chest when he got older and "Doggy" no longer covered him. He took Doggy with him when…

Turning on my heel, I hurried out of the room, teddy bear in hand. I closed the door behind me and made my way down the stairs. Outside, I set my pack on the porch. I opened it up and pulled out a red spray can, put a big X on the door, and placed the can back in the pack. I tucked the bear inside as well, zipping the pack on both sides so only its head poked out.

"So, what's your name?" I asked, knowing the silence I would receive.

As if on cue, a thought popped in my head.

Humphrey.

The thought didn't feel right. It didn't feel like it was mine but someone else's, as if I had stolen it from the mind of the little girl in the picture.

"Humphrey?" I nodded, pushing away an uneasy feeling. "Humphrey it is."

The other houses were similar: a couple dead folks, a rotter or two that had been taken down by someone else before they moved on. Or at least I hoped they were able to move on. The bodies were taken outside and laid together.

The afternoon sun was directly overhead by the time I had finished all but one house. That house I would leave for later. Another three hours and another mass grave—this time for seven people—had been dug and filled in. I was tired but not finished.

I didn't want to go into the Banks household. I guess I didn't really have to, but I knew if I didn't, I would always wonder if Karen were in there, if she were dead or alive or shambling about, not quite resurrected but something that was a perverse form of it.

At the porch, my mind replayed Thomas' tumble from the day before. I closed my eyes, shook my head, and then reopened them. A deep breath, and I went toward the house. My body moved on autopilot. Legs went up the steps, one hand pushing the door further open, the other hand clutching to my pistol. Again, legs moved throughout the house, room by room, eyes scanning, taking in the ruins of the inside of the house, hands pushing doors open until I had gone through the entire house, and Karen was nowhere to be found. I exhaled, thankful she wasn't there.

That was a short-lived feeling. Passing the back door, I peeked out the window. In the center of the yard was a grave, a cross jutting out from the freshly turned dirt. I knew it was Karen even before I walked into the yard to see Tommy had painted her name on the cross: *Karen Banks, Loved Forever.*

I didn't think about it so much as I just did it: I dug another hole, this time next to the grave of Karen Banks. Back at the front of the house, I dug again, this time digging up the bodies of my friend and his son. Tommy and Thomas went into the other grave, right next to their wife and mother. I found the small paint can in Tommy's shop. On the cross Tommy had placed on Karen's grave, I painted Tommy and Thomas' name and then put the can away.

Back at my truck, I looked back to the small neighborhood. I needed to leave for a while. No, I wasn't done with my hometown, but the memories were so strong they hurt.

"Time to go, Humphrey," I said and pulled the little guy from the pack. His brown eyes sparkled; his pink, stitched lips were in the shape of a smile. His paws held pink pads on them, and his nose was a slightly lighter pink. I strapped the bear in the passenger's seat with the seat belt and cranked the truck up. I pulled away from the U-shaped cul-de-sac and glanced down at Humphrey. "She took good care of you, didn't she?"

He said nothing though I imagined he spoke one simple word. *Yes,* and the voice was that of a young child, a female…

Seven Weeks and Two Days After It All Started...

"Sometimes, life kicks you in the teeth." It was one of Pop's sayings. It was how he referred to dealing with everything, good or bad. Either it kicked you in the teeth or it picked roses for you, and even then, those roses held thorns. "It's how you respond that makes you who you are." It was also one of the last things Pop said before...

I can only shake my head and close my eyes and pray there was a better place on the other side of this mess.

It had been a little under two months since folks started dying and rising, but Pop's words still rang loud in my ears. By then, the sweeps had led me through most of Sipping Creek. I don't know how many hundreds of people I killed.

Killed? That's laughable. If things were normal, I would have probably never been able to take aim at another human being. But things were far from normal—still are. The only place left to sweep was the street I had lived on. I reckon you could say my world ended on that street—at least the world I knew, the one I had lived in, had a family in.

I drove the short distance to where home had once been, having not seen a living person since...since too long. More and more, Jeanette and Bobby were on my mind, and more and more, I wondered if they made it to the cabin or if they were now walking among the dead.

Why was I still there? Why was I still sweeping our little town? Why did it matter anymore? If anything, Pop is why. Leland is why. Davey Blaylock is why. Every single person I ever knew was why I was still there. The dead were dangerous. They may have been our friends and neighbors

19

and family at one time, but once they changed, once death had hold of them and turned that key in their brain that made them rise again, they were no longer people. They were monsters. But deep down inside, I still thought of them as people with souls and feelings and probably just as scared of me with a gun as I was of them.

Kill or be killed. Isn't that the famous saying? Kill or be killed? Yeah, that's the way it is now. But the living are losing the war. There are only a few of us left. Maybe even just me. I don't know. What I did know — do know — is there are so many more rotters, and wiping them out seems to get harder and harder each day.

I think of Jeanette and Bobby and hope they are still among the living. Why did I send them away? Why didn't I go with them? Why didn't all of us just stick together? In my nightmares, I see them shambling along a street, their faces slack, eyes staring off into nowhere, mouth open. Blood is on their clothes and skin. I pushed the thoughts away, refusing to think of them as decaying corpses.

At the corner of Elaine Street, I stopped the truck and stared at the carnage left behind. Somewhere along that street, I was going to run into neighbors, folks closer than most of the dead I had encountered, and I would have to put a bullet in their brain to end their misery. It was on that day as I sat in my truck, the motor idling, that I wondered if the dead *knew* they were dead; if they could feel and think. If I was careful, I could find out, but one mistake, no matter how small, and I would know the answers a little more intimately than I wanted.

I slid out of my seat, shouldered my pack, and looked down at Humphrey. "Hey, buddy, you keep an eye on the truck, okay?" He didn't answer, only stared straight ahead at the dashboard he was too small to see over. I would have to remedy that if he was going to continue to tag along. I checked my guns, slid the machete into its sheath, and strapped it to my back.

It was as if the Heavens knew I wouldn't be able to handle putting the folks in my own neighborhood down. The eight houses along the right side held none of the undead—none of the living as well. There were no bodies anywhere. Sure, there was some blood, and most of the houses had been ransacked, windows smashed and doors kicked in. Like most of Sipping Creek—most of the world I guessed—people had left in a panic, taking only what they could carry and leaving memories behind. I crossed the street and made it four houses in the direction of my truck.

I stopped there.

The gray trim looked the same, accenting the red brick structure. The grass had turned gray in some places, brown in others. The garden that lined the brick fence on the left side of the yard had wilted, the stems of elephant ears lying on the ground, withered and black. The front door was closed. Around the back of the house was much as I remembered. A swing set, a playhouse, an old Fairlane under a dark blue tarp, its engine in various states of repair in the garage off to the right.

Bobby's toys lay strewn about the yard, left where he had last played with them, forever forgotten. I went back to the front, looked down the street, then in the other direction. Nothing. No one. Just a soft wind whistling on a dead street to keep me company. I walked to the next house—the Baxters'—bypassing going inside mine. I remembered telling

21

Max what was happening, asking them to go with Jake and my family up to Table Rock, that the mountains might be safer than the small towns or the big cities. Inside told me all I needed to know. There were bodies—four of them—but it didn't look like the dead had gotten hold of them. The boys— both in their early teens—lay in their beds, sheets pulled over their heads. The brown stain where their heads were relayed the story. I found Sarah in Max's bedroom; she, like her sons, still lay in bed, the sheet pulled over her head.

On the couch in the den sat the body of Max Baxter, one of my longtime friends from high school. The pistol lay on the floor at his feet. The bullet had entered under his chin and left a crater in the top of his head. The ceiling above and the wall behind him were spattered with dried masses of brain matter, hair, and blood. One hand clutched tight to a piece of paper. It took a minute, but I managed to pull it free. Two words were scrawled in black marker; two words that showed the desperation of the situation: *I'm sorry...*

"Yeah, me too," I said and dropped the paper to the floor. Pop would have said Max's response was that of a coward's. Me, I'm not so sure I agree. Maybe it was the only way he could protect them. Maybe he saw them in his head as the rotting dead, the same as I saw my family in my nightmares, and hated the very thought and did what he thought was best. I don't know.

Wrapped in sheets, I pulled their bodies into the front yard. Before all was said and done, I would need to bury them.

There was nothing in the final three houses, their owners having fled like many others. That left my house—the only one of sixteen in the neighborhood without a bright red X on its door. I won't lie and say it was a piece of cake. I won't say I walked right in and checked the place out and got out of there, X in place, the past behind me without a struggle at all. No, I stood in my front yard for the longest time, terrified to go inside. Not because I thought I would find someone—I knew I wouldn't—but because of the memories stepping inside would bring back. Just standing in the yard was bad enough, but going inside…going inside meant facing the almost certainty that I would never see my family again and that I was truly alone in this world gone insane.

My legs shook as I took the steps and stood in front of the door. Funny to think about it now—I even laughed a little then—the door was locked. From my wallet, I produced a key, slid it in the knob, and turned it until I heard that familiar click. The door opened, and I fought back the urge to run. Though we had left in a rush, the house was not a mess like so many others. Sure, there were a few things out of place, but all in all, the house looked as if someone still lived there.

I stumbled through the living room and down the hall, my legs not wanting to work, my mind screaming for me to just go away, to never come back unless I want my heart broken all over again. The kitchen held a couple of beer cans—the ones Leland and I had emptied the night the dead came to town. The bedrooms were mostly neat, the only thing really not right being the beds were not made. Bobby's room was the typical boy's room: not really a mess but not really clean either, kind of an organized chaos. I could hear his laughter, see him playing with cars and trucks and Legos and marbles…but he wasn't there. It was all a trick of the mind, memories surfacing, waving hello, and dipping back under the blackening waters of life. I closed his door, went back up the hall, and stopped short of the front door. The attic door was in the ceiling in the center of the hallway. I pulled the drop chord and lowered the stairs.

It was dark and dusty, but the lights from the ventilation on each side of the house made it easy to spot the blue and gray car seat sitting next to a bag of old winter clothes. I reached for it and then stopped. A sound came from the corner of the attic. It wasn't much. Just a little rustling, like a squirrel had gotten in there somehow. I waited, holding my breath, focusing on the corner. If it wasn't a squirrel, then maybe someone had managed to get into the house and hidden up there. In more certain times, that would have been an irrational thought. But the times weren't so certain, and sometimes, rationale goes right out the window.

I slipped the pistol from my waistband and held it out in front of me.

"Who's there?"

The rustling came again. It sounded like it was by several bags of Bobby's old stuffed animals. Maybe the big, white rabbit with the bowtie that I won for him at the state fair in Columbia when he was only two.

"Come on out now."

My mind told me it was just a small animal. *A squirrel, Walker. That's all, old boy.*

I was in full squat mode, duck walking across the dusty attic floor. I was only a few feet from the white trash bags. I could make out the lumps of stuffed animals all crammed together, a head here, the length of a leg there. Was that a snout trying to push through the plastic? I moved the bag. A rat darted from behind it and across the room.

I screamed and fell back. It wasn't my most graceful moment. I took aim and fired the pistol. A piece of wood splintered in the floor, but I missed the rodent. I saw its tail slither behind some boxes.

A few months earlier, Jeanette would have been on me about getting some traps or some D-con or call an exterminator for crying out loud, and I would have told her I could handle it, Babe. And I would have tried to catch that rat. That was then.

Instead of pursuing the vermin, I duck walked backwards to the dropdown door. I grabbed the car seat, looked it over. No rat goodies left behind.

I took the seat and made my way down the steps, closing the attic door behind me and hoping I had trapped the rat inside. I doubted it. It had gotten up there somehow; it would find its way out as well. Outside, I locked the door and placed an X on it. Sipping Creek was done. All the undead that I could find were dead again, and all except for the Baxters had been given the proper burial they deserved.

At the truck, I moved Humphrey, strapped the car seat in, and then stuck him in his new chair—one high enough to see out the windows just in case he got bored of the trip. "Hang tight, buddy," I said.

My imagination spoke for him.

Sure thing, Mr. Walker, it said.

Before leaving, I buried the Baxters and placed a marker over the grave. It wasn't much—a cinderblock with their last name spray painted on it. The sun would be setting soon, and I hoped to find higher ground before it did, somewhere I could park the truck and get some sleep.

I drove along, Humphrey quiet, the world rolling beneath the wheels. The sun was beginning to sink in the horizon. Another hour or so, and it would be dark again.

Then I saw the woman crossing Grover's Field just outside of town. By the way she lurched, I knew she was one of the dead.

Sleep would have to wait.

I pulled the truck to a stop, staying in the road. I got out, leveled my rifle at her, and then lowered it. She was an older lady, her hair gray, the sags along her chin and arms normal for a living woman, not for a body rotting away like the dead were supposed to. Her face and arms held scratches on them. The front of her shirt and pants were red, and she wore only one shoe—a light blue slip-on.

"Stay here, Humphrey," I said, stepped to the front of the truck, and set the rifle on the hood. I pulled out one of the pistols—a do-nothing .22 caliber thing—and took aim at her.

She shambled into the road, almost fell along the shoulder. She stopped, not more than thirty yards from where I stood. Her head rose as if she were smelling the air. *The dead can't smell,* I thought. Then she turned toward me, her milky eyes catching mine. The expression on her face changed from one of slack-jawed boredom to maniacally hungry. A moan escaped her, and she lifted one arm toward me as if she were pointing. Her bumbling gait became more of a panicked hurry as she approached me.

I leveled my pistol toward one shoulder and squeezed the trigger. Her arm jerked backward, and the groan that came from her…it sounded as if she were hurt, but it didn't stop her from advancing on me. I squeezed off a second shot. One of her outstretched fingers snapped off. She moaned louder. I set the pistol on the truck's hood, picked up my rifle, and aimed it at one knee. She was less than ten yards away when I pulled the trigger. Her knee disappeared, sending her to the ground. The moan, the groan…the scream…it filled my ears. I still hear it to this day.

"I'm sorry," I said, my heart aching for the pain I had inflicted on her. Somehow, she managed to get onto her back. Black blood oozed from where her knee had once been. My stomach rolled over, and my body tingled with sadness. I drew a little closer to her as she struggled to stand, reminding me of a turtle on its shell, doomed to die in that position. Through her insatiable hunger and those milky eyes, I saw her pleading with me to…to do what? Feed her? No. I didn't think so. I saw in those pained eyes the desire to be dead — completely dead — and free of existence as a walking corpse. It reminded me of the way Jeanette's brows would teepee over her eyes and her bottom lip would poke out slightly when she wanted something she thought I would say "no" to. This was different though. This woman didn't want a fancy meal or flowers or a trip to wherever. She wanted a release. I couldn't begin to imagine the feeling of being trapped in a decaying body, completely unable to control what I was doing, unable to tell someone I was in there and I was still alive, that I could still feel and smell, and the hunger…

I thought I had been slowly losing my mind over the previous few weeks, but the insanity that must creep in on the dead, the helplessness…I have no words to explain how it made me feel just to think about it.

Again, I apologized to the woman. When I took aim the next time, it wasn't to wound her; it was to test a theory I thought was true. Her struggles ended with the sound of my rifle going off. I went back to the truck, grabbed the pistol off the hood, and shoved it in my waistband. I had another grave to dig, another person to bury. My thoughts centered around the many rotters I had put down. Up to that point, I had refused to see them as rotters, but that was really what they were: slaves to the hunger, trapped in dead bodies, longing to be freed. The undead knew they were going to die again every time I pointed one of my weapons at them. Maybe they welcomed it like I thought that woman did. Maybe the reason they hurried toward me when I raised the gun wasn't so they could feed but so that I would hurry and put a bullet in their brain…hurry, for crying out loud.

I buried the woman, spoke a prayer over her, asking for mercy for her soul…and for mine as well. If murder is a sin, then I'm Hell-bound. I asked for forgiveness I wasn't so sure I deserved.

The sun was almost gone as I got back in the truck. I closed the door, put the window all the way up, and looked over at my riding partner. I started to speak then only shook my head, preferring to let the silence ride along with us. I put the truck in gear, flipped the lights on, and drove off, my thoughts lingering with the woman a while longer before turning back to Pop. Up to that point, life had kicked me in the teeth, but unlike Max, I didn't choose to exit the story stage left. I stuck around for whatever the world would bring me.

Eight Weeks and Three Days After It All Started...

Humphrey sat in his seat, his head slightly higher than the edge of the door. He could see over the dashboard and the road ahead of us. My little stuffed traveling buddy. We sat atop a hill overlooking a small town—Harkers, South Carolina. It wasn't much of a hill, but it gave me a clear line of sight in all directions. The town wasn't much of a town either—a couple of buildings that looked as if they belonged in the fifties, some cars lining unmetered parking spots. There was a red vehicle stopped at a streetlight. The light itself had long since expired. A few houses off in the distance ran along a cracked blacktop that was in serious need of repaving.

There wasn't much to see.

I lined the perimeter of my truck with cans and wire— enough to raise a loud clatter if someone or something were to try and cross it. I had made the makeshift alarm system after that lady tapped on my window a few weeks earlier. If anyone approached, I would know.

Night settled down. A slight breeze blew in, ruffling the leaves of trees a hundred feet to our right. I needed gas for the truck but had no desire to pilfer the tanks of the cars below in the dark. I could wait until morning. It's not like the world was passing me by.

I leaned across the seat, made sure Humphrey's door was locked. His glass eyes reflected in the moonlight, a shimmering image that made him look alive.

"Do you remember what it was like, Humphrey?" I asked. "You know, before...all of this?"

I waved an arm like a game show host revealing prizes to be won. *All of this can be yours if the price is right…* Humphrey said nothing.

"Do you even know what happened?" I looked down at my lap, the pistol sitting between my legs. A bottle of water sat beside me, half full. I took a long swig, swallowed. "Of course you don't. You can't be all that old, can you? Maybe six, if that?"

Four.

I glanced down at him, startled by his voice. I nodded. "Okay. Four it is."

I thought of my boy when he was four. Star Wars and Legos and Hot Wheels cars—he loved them all.

"Daddy, I'm going to be R2D2 for Halloween." The beeps and boops and whirrs that came from his mouth made me smile as he pretended to glide across the kitchen floor. By Halloween, he had changed his mind. Instead of being R2D2, Luke Skywalker's trusty companion, he went for R5D4, the rusty bucket of bolts that barely worked well enough to roll five feet. Bobby popped and clunked as he pretended to move like a robot. Then he would wheeze as he broke down. He was a great little R5D4. And he let people know when they called him the other robot. I shook my head, tried to push Bobby from my thoughts for a while.

Humphrey stared ahead, unmoving, his stitched-on smile never wavering. Always the optimist.

"You know, it started with a slight fever," I said as I stared down into the darkness of Harkers, a small town as dead as any other in America. Humphrey said nothing, not even a whisper in my brain. He just sat…and listened to this lonely man talk. "A kid in North Carolina got sick, his fever not rising much above ninety-nine degrees. His name eludes me at the moment. It's something normal, like Robert or James. The fever was just enough to make him uncomfortable. His body began to ache as if the fever were much higher. The doctors said he had the flu, maybe even some new-fangled viral flu. They actually said that—new-fangled, like it was doctor speak." I shook my head. The night sat still beyond the cab of the truck.

"Let it run its course, they said. Give him Tylenol and Ibuprofen, alternating doses every four to six hours, they said. If he's not better by the end of the week, bring him back, they said.

"The kid…was his name William? I can't remember. Something like that. Anyway, he got sicker. His temperature never went up though. Gray sacks formed under his eyes. His hair became matted, as if caked with mud. Breathing became irregular gasps. The doctors sent him to the hospital, said something about pneumonia. His skin began to gray. The doctors then cried his kidneys were failing.

"Internal bleeding, they said when he began to vomit blood. They didn't have a clue.

…

"He cried a lot."

Didn't they all? I thought. All those sick children, crying, wanting their mommies and daddies.

"What was his name? Jessie? Larry?"

I shrugged. "His momma sat in the hospital bed with him, cradling her little boy in her arms—the same arms that held him when he was born, comforted him when he was hurt, hugged him just to hug him. She wept as he slept, held onto her strength in those few moments he was awake before…"

I hated myself for not remembering his name. I should've never forgotten. How could I have?

Carl with a C? Or Karl with a K? I couldn't remember. I should have.

I continued my story. Humphrey remained silent, his ears as perked up as they would ever be. "His name was in the local papers as doctors from MUSC and other places within the region went to see him. Duke Medical Center could do nothing for him.

"The kid lost weight, and by the time he breathed his last, he had become nothing more than an emaciated stick figure, skin on bones, if you will." Skin on bones? That's the best I could do for the kid? Describe him as skin on bones? The thought haunts me. What if that kid had been my Bobby? What if any one of those millions of kids had been my Bobby? What if, since I last saw my wife and boy, Bobby had suffered the same fate? My breath hitched as I thought of the boy—a boy whose name I couldn't remember, whose name I should have never forgotten.

"By then his momma—her name was Nancy, this much I'm sure of—had gotten sick. Like her boy, it started with a slight fever that never reached a hundred and progressed to the vomiting blood, graying skin, and loss of weight. She began to itch and scratch at her skin, tearing it in some places. Her death came quicker than her son's, accelerated by lack of sleep and food. Her body just couldn't hold up under the grief and illness.

"The kid's pediatrician and a couple of nurses got sick as well. Who knows how many kids and parents were in the office the day the kid—was his name Jeffery—was there? I guess most of us know how it goes from there. Fever.

32

Stiffness. Throwing up blood and graying skin. Loss of weight. Itching and scratching and…death.

"A not so funny thing happened a few hours after Wilson—Wilson! That was his name." Tears stung my eyes as I thought about the dark-haired kid with green eyes, his pale complexion a trait inherited from his momma, from Nancy, whose husband was Richard Walker, my second youngest brother. How could I have forgotten Wilson's name? How many times have I said I'm sorry into the air, begging my brother, his wife, and Wilson to forgive me for such a horrible thing?

I could shrug it off if I wanted to. Richard had left home angry when he was eighteen and really never returned, not in the sense that he belonged. No, Richard was never the same after leaving, but he was in the wrong. I don't care what he may have thought. Stealing is wrong, but stealing from your family… It was an addiction that caused him to be the way he was for a while. I reckon after he got clean, either Pop or Richard just didn't get over things.

I never met Wilson and only met Nancy on two occasions, so I guess it's forgivable, right?

I laughed and cried at the same time, a contradiction of emotions welling up and exploding from within. I reached down and took Humphrey from his seat, hugged him tight. I could still smell the scent of little girl on him. I sat holding that bear, whispering into his ear and staring out into the darkness of a dead world.

"His name was Wilson. Was. You see, when he died, a few hours later, he woke up. The doctors—you know, those guys who said he had a viral flu and then kidney failure and whatever else—those doctors said he must have slipped into a

33

coma or something and came out of it. Hallelujah, they said. It's a miracle, they said.

"But it wasn't a miracle." I pulled the bear from my chest and stared into his glass eyes. "Do you understand? It wasn't a miracle. It was just the opposite. It was a disaster. You see, the doctors...they went to check his vitals, and it turned out he didn't have any. No heartbeat. His lungs weren't working. No blood pressure. But Wilson sat up on that gurney right after the orderlies moved him, and no sooner than his momma was taken away to her own bed where she died a couple hours later. And you know what Wilson did?"

I waited for an answer that didn't come.

"He bit one of the doctors on the hand, tore off the flesh from between his thumb and pointer finger. The doctor, he cursed up a holy hell—at least that's what Lee told me when he arrived at my house a couple of days later, scared and half out of his mind. His wife and boys were in the car out in the driveway, waiting for us to hurry up so they could go away, go as far as they could before the sickness reached us.

"By then, it was too late. By then, it had been a week since Wilson had gotten sick and visited the doctor that first time. Do you know how many people he came in touch with during those first three days? And how many people did those people come in touch with?"

I rambled. What else was there to do? Everything that had happened in those long few months, every word I hadn't spoken or even thought, came rushing out.

"Lee said Richard was in shock—more from the deaths of Nancy and Wilson than from the sickness he had come down with. His face had taken on that gray pallor. He was as good as dead, but the doctors wouldn't go near him. Lee argued and yelled for them to help him, but they wouldn't. They were scared. Everyone was scared. Nancy was in the morgue, her once lifeless body staggering about. No one was brave enough to go in there to see her. Not after what Wilson had done.

"That doctor...that doctor Wilson bit got his hand bandaged and got a tetanus shot for good measure, but the wound spread out; his skin turned black around it. Within a day, the doctor was dead. Like Wilson and Nancy and soon to be a bunch of others, he didn't stay that way long."

It's said that the Bible is not completely comprehendible, that the mind could not handle the depth of knowledge and truth within its words. I believe that applies to these...events...as well. The mind can't fully comprehend what is going on until it's entirely too late. I set Humphrey down, wiped my eyes with the back of one hand.

"Richard really couldn't do much, you know? They quarantined the hospital. Cops surrounded the place. No one was allowed to leave. Lee had managed to get out of there before the cops came, said he was going to get something to eat and would be back soon. When he arrived back, there was no going in, and he sure wasn't telling the cops he had already been there. He said a few folks tried to escape, and they were shot. Can you believe that, Humphrey? Scared folks were killed by the police because, well, they were just as scared. People started panicking, and things went south pretty quick. Just like the movies.

"You know, Lee was the only one Richard talked to all that often. I guess he still looked up to his oldest brother. I don't know. I do know I wish he and I would have squared things away. After all, it was my money he had stolen... I guess I failed to mention that, didn't I?

"Lee and I shared a couple beers, him drinking one down fast before popping the top off another one—this is after our families were on their way to Table Rock. Brothers having a couple of beers like the old times, but things were never going to be like the old times again. You know?"

I set Humphrey back in his seat, straightened out his bunny costume. "Hey, what do you say we get you some new clothes? Maybe some traveling clothes or biker jeans. What do you say? Would you like that?"

Yes.

I nodded. "Yeah, I think that's a good idea. Maybe we can find a mall or a Wal-Mart or something and get you some new clothes. You don't want to be seen in public in your pajamas, do you?"

No.

Humphrey was talking again in his girlish voice. I never thought much about me calling him a boy but hearing his voice as a little girl's. Maybe I should have named him something else, given him a female name. But then, Humphrey is what he said he was called.

"You know," I said and looked down at Harkers. "Leland, he came with us to try and save some folks in town. He sent Jessica and the boys on up to the hills, up to Tablerock, with Mike Simmons, his best friend. I guess I already said that, didn't I?" I continued to stare at the small town as I talked. "They...umm...were in a red car—the four of them, you know?"

He had grown silent again. Maybe he knew what I knew.

"Yeah, me too, buddy," I said.

36

I checked my pistol and the rifle between us. Fully loaded with plenty of rounds on the floorboard if needed. Inching down in my seat, I patted Humphrey on the head. "Get some sleep, little guy. Long day tomorrow."

But sleep...she's a mistress who long since divorced me. I sat staring at the night. The stars still shone their brightness on the world. The moon still hung high, a blue hue to her white surface, a ring of yellow around her. I wondered if she had any clue what was happening down here, and if she did, did she care?

I prayed what we taught Bobby, I think more for the comfort the words brought. "Now I lay me down to sleep. I pray the Lord my soul to keep. Let angels watch me through the night and wake me in the morning light."

I wasn't so sure about angels, but calmness swept over me, and I closed my eyes to the fleeting day...

Eight Weeks and Four Days After It All Started...

Dawn came, the sun casting its blinding rays on us. Nature's alarm clock. My joints ached as they did every morning. Sleeping in the truck just wasn't good on the body. I missed the comfort of a bed and sheets and a pillow. I missed the sound of a real alarm clock telling me to get out of bed, that yes, this was all a nightmare, and welcome back to reality. I missed the smell of brewing coffee and cooking on the griddle. I even missed the old job—what I would give to be able to go back to those days.

I glanced around our surroundings. Things were much the same as the night before. The world still spun, the sun still came up...time, however, no longer sped along at a breakneck pace. It had dropped down to extra slow motion, each second like minutes, each minute like hours. Survival and loneliness are wearisome bedfellows at best, and I had them both as companions.

"You awake, Humphrey?"

A yawn and a yes followed.

"Ready to head down there?"

Silence.

"Me neither."

I cranked the truck up, and we pulled onto the road. I could have made it to the next town over, maybe even further if I really needed to, but I had no desires to push my luck. I drove slow, scanned the area for anyone, living or dead. There were a few areas of blood near the fifties style buildings. The skeletal remains of a person lay scattered about near the entrance of what was the town police station—a building no bigger than a convenience store. The door stood open, a bloody shoe a few feet from it. Not for the first time did I wonder what terror a victim went through, if the person were ripped apart or killed themselves before the dead got to them.

Up ahead, I could see the red car sitting at the parking light. My stomach quivered at the notion of who could be in it. I turned the truck around, pointed it back toward I-26.

"Stay here," I said to Humphrey.

I stepped out, pistol in hand, slung the rifle over my shoulder. A handful of bullets later, and I eased away from the truck, the door closed, keys in the ignition. I've never quite gotten over the jitters; each day, it's the same thing. Nerves on end. Quick breaths. Dry eyes from a lack of blinking. Knots in my stomach. Sweaty palms. Not quite like a first date but pretty close to speaking in public in only your underwear.

The blood on the sidewalk had dried, paled over time, becoming more of a washed red color. The shoe in the door of the police station was a Nike. A bone jutted from a blood-crusted sock. I peeked in through the door, not wanting to go in like a gangbuster and get myself killed. Shadows played along gray walls, making it difficult to see anything not directly in the sun's light. My hand shook as I placed the palm down on the cool door and pushed it open. There were a couple of desks, papers and computers atop them, chairs nearby. A coat rack sat near the door, a gun rack on the far wall, steel bars keeping anyone from taking the weapons. A body lay in the center of the room, flies buzzing about—a cop, his gun still in hand.

Against the wall closest to the door lay another body, a hole in its head. On the other side of the closest desk was a third person, a woman with jeans and a bloodied shirt. The top half of her head was missing. She was closest to the cop, probably the one who took him down. But he got the shot off, or maybe someone else did.

I pushed the door open further, letting it hit softly against the wall. A hall led away from the central room. I inched past the corpses, checked the cop to make sure he was dead. He had put a bullet in his own head. I thought back to the Baxters, the way Max had mercifully killed his family before they could succumb to the death that surrounded them. Visions of what may have happened bounced through my head. The cop took out the first rotter, didn't see the other one until it was too late and she had taken a chunk out of him somewhere. He wheeled, put a bullet through her brain, and slumped to the floor, blood pouring from a wound, his heart pounding, the truth running through his head. With tears in his eyes, he probably put the revolver to his head, said a quick prayer, and pulled the trigger. Maybe he had never been religious before and found it in that moment before taking his own life. I shook my head, took a deep breath, and moved down the hall.

The bathroom sat on the right, empty. A door separated the hall from the next room. I opened it slowly and peered in. Another desk sat near the center of the room, its chair pushed underneath it. Three jail cells lined the wall. The first two were empty. The third one held a man. He leaned against the bars, his back to me, shoulders slumped. I could see the body on the floor, pieces of meat still clinging to bone.

"Hey," I said, my voice barely a whisper. I coughed, repeated. The man pushed off the bars and turned. His head lulled on his shoulders. The front of his shirt was soaked in gore, his hands bony and bloody. He seemed to stare at me with his head down, as if he were looking through his forehead. A grunt escaped him. The skin on his face had sagged. I could see the bones of his eye sockets.

My heart sped up, my chest tightened. I lifted my pistol.

He grunted again, smashed his head against the cell door. He didn't lift his arms. Other than beating his head against the bars and grunting, he didn't do much at all. But there was desperation in those simple actions.

I swallowed. "Listen, buddy," I said, trying to reason with him if there was really any way to do that. "I know you're in a bad way, but I'm going to take care of you, okay?"

Another grunt was followed by another head butt to the cell bars. Skin split on his forehead. A thick, yellowish-red liquid seeped from the wound.

"Calm down, okay? I'm not going to let you stay that way. I promise. I'm going to set you free. Just give me a couple of minutes, okay?"

He stopped. For several long seconds, we stared at each other, he the rotting, reanimated corpse and me, well, I was as alone as they came, an old, western cowboy without the horse, boots, and spurs or the cowboy hat. In those Old West days, that would have been the stare down before the draw, before the six shooters came off the hips and gunpowder filled the air in a black heaviness that stung the nostrils. There would be no duel on this day, just me with my guns and him safely behind bars.

I broke eye contact and hurried back up the hall. I could have put a bullet in the man's head, but sound—any type, I learned—attracted the dead. No need firing the pistol before I gathered some valuable supplies.

I stopped in the main room. The gun case was held shut with a padlock. There were eight rifles and a couple of handguns as well as several boxes of ammo. I searched the desks for keys, found none. I turned to the cop, rolled him over, and searched his pockets.

"Jackpot," I whispered when I pulled out a ring with several keys attached. The fourth key produced an audible click that made me jump. With the gun case open, I unloaded the weapons, carrying as many as I could to the truck and going back for the rest. I wondered if the cop had thought about unlocking it before he died. If he had the foresight to think that, maybe he wouldn't have much time to open the case when the dead were closing in on his tiny town. *The case was still locked,* my mind said. *What do you think?*

After loading the last of the guns and ammunition in the truck, I went back inside and down the hall. The man had sagged against the cell door, his eyes facing the floor. That infected, yellowish-red blood seeped from the wound in his head and dribbled down the bars.

"Hey," I said from about ten feet away. "Are you still with me?"

He lifted his head slightly. His eyes were a filmed-over white. A fly landed on one of them, did a little dance, and took off again. My heart was like a tidal wave crashing along the shore, crushing blow after blow within my chest. He struck his head on the bars again, his mouth open. A low growl filled the room, like an angered whisper or a plea for help.

I lifted my gun, finger on the trigger. "If you're in there and can hear me, I hope you understand I'm not doing this because I'm mean or uncaring."

He stopped beating his head against the cell door. I saw nothing in his eyes, nothing in the way he stood, mouth ajar, arms dangling at his sides.

I wiped my mouth with one hand and swallowed hard. "If you can hear me and you don't want me to put a bullet in your brain, step backwards one step."

I waited, hands shaking, lips and mouth dry. He didn't move, not even a waver from side to side.

"Okay." I thought for a moment longer, daylight burning away outside, the hairs on my arms on end. "Okay. Listen up. If you can hear me, listen real carefully. I'm going to shoot you. I'm going to kill you…again. If you want me to do that, hit your head against that bar again."

It was a reach. But I had to know. I had to know if my experiment before was accurate, if there really were souls trapped inside those bodies.

Time stood still. We stared at each other, this stranger and I, until he lifted his head away from the cell door and brought it hard against one bar. There was the audible noise as his forehead cracked. Again, he hit his head against the door. Two more times followed.

"Okay, okay," I said. "You can stop now."

And he did.

I nodded. "Thank you."

His head snapped back with the sound of the gun. He fell backward, landing in a heap on the bones on the floor behind him.

Confirmation.

"They're in there," I said. "They're still in there."

I turned and walked toward the hall then stopped in the doorway. Standing between the door and me was another one. He shambled toward me, one arm held out, his jaw missing. I backed up and around the desk and waited for him to get inside the room. He was in bad shape, barely tottering and looking as if he could fall with his next step. He bumped the doorjamb, staggered sideways and through the opening.

I pulled the trigger while his face was turned from me. He struck the wall and fell. I stood, torn from the recent revelations. These were people with lives, hopes, and dreams. Someone gave birth to them; someone loved them at one point. They probably loved others and had dreams, and who knew, maybe the guy in the cell had kids or a wife. Either way, two experiments had led me to believe something that should be fundamentally impossible: the dead had souls, and those souls were trapped in the husks of what used to be.

I previously thought I would go to Hell for killing the dead. Maybe that's true. Or maybe I had to be the Grim Reaper and help these poor folks get to the afterlife…as painlessly as possible. Maybe surviving wasn't all that was left to do. Maybe finding other survivors wasn't all that was left to do. Maybe…maybe delivering the dead to…to where? Maybe ending their misery was the way to getting my soul back.

I stepped around the dead man and hurried down the hall, pistol in hand. I stopped at the cop. "Sorry, buddy, but I'm going to need that," I said and bent down. It took a little work, but I took his gun and slid it in my waistband and beneath my shirt. It was cool on my back.

Outside the police station, I glanced both ways, made my way toward the red car at the light further down. My memories raced, searching through thousands of files before finding the right cabinet, the right moment in time. I hurried toward the car—a Chevy much like the one Leland had bought a couple of years earlier. I couldn't see the tag from where I was nor if there was a bumper sticker on it that read, *Honk If I Made You Mad*, on the right-hand side.

From between two buildings, a woman stumbled, her hair matted to the side of her bloodied face. I turned the pistol on her, my mind firmly on auto-pilot as I approached the car. One shot, one kill.

A few feet from the car, Lee's voice echoed in my mind.

"How do you like her?" he asked as he ran a hand across the hood.

"It's alright if you like that sort of thing."

He shrugged. "I do."

Jessica had loved that car. She had screamed for joy when Lee showed it to her, a birthday present that kept on giving right until the end of the world.

I circled around the front of it, part of me terrified to see the tag, to see the bumper sticker Lee had put on as a joke—one Jessica wasn't too happy with, but she allowed it to stay to keep from scratching the paint while taking it off.

I thought of Lee as he and I and Davey Blaylock made our way from building to building, seeking supplies and survivors, putting bullets in anything that didn't answer our calls. I thought of how Lee rounded a corner and the hands

45

that grabbed his arm and the mouth that sank down on his bicep. I thought of the fear in his face as he pulled the trigger, taking off the top of the guy's head, how he laughed when he realized who it was.

"Son-of-a…" he said with tears in his eyes. The laugh was involuntary—shock, maybe—and he let it out, a high-pitched sound that could have been a whine or scream or a little bit of both. "Was that Paul Marcum?" he asked.

I glanced at the body. No doubt. "Yeah, it was."

"You've got to be kidding me," he yelled and kicked Paul in the side several times. He lowered his gun, squeezed off two shots, and screamed at Paul like it was his fault the world had died. After several minutes, he calmed and then laughed again. This time, it was an eerie realization that was carried in it. He shook his head. "Well, ain't this some crap?"

"We'll get help," I said. "We'll figure something out."

He shook his head again. "No, little bro, we won't. I'm a dead man, and I'm not going to be a burden on you guys." He pointed down at Paul Marcum. "And I ain't going to end up like that. Can you believe this, little bro?"

"No," I said. One brother was already dead, and Lee was going to join him. It was only a matter of time.

"Paul Marcum," he said. "Paul Marcum. I used to kick the crap out of him in school. You know, I hated him, man. Remember when he squealed on us after putting sugar in Mr. Robinson's gas tank?"

"Yeah, man. I remember."

He laughed again. "I can't believe it. I'm going to be taken out by a nerdy rotter. How ironic is that?"

I shook my head against the memories, looked through the dirty windshield. A man lay slumped in the front seat of the car, his brain spattered on the windshield and side glass. I could see flies buzzing about his body. I didn't recognize the face, and what little bit I could make out didn't look anything like I recalled of Mike Simmons' appearance.

Around the corner came three more rotters. I leveled my aim on one, pulled the trigger. Missed.

"Crap!"

There was no time for missing. Worse still, there weren't enough bullets to go wasting. I steadied my hand, squeezed off the next shot, and dropped one. Two more shots and the other two were down.

I rounded the passenger's side, glanced inside. No purse. No little kid toys.

More of the dead had come out into the street, probably to see what was going on. If they were lucky and me not so much, it would be dinner time.

Hurry, my mind screamed.

The one closest to me was a girl—a teenager who the boys probably liked a lot. Her light brown hair probably flowed with the breeze when she was alive. She might have been a cheerleader or danced in the school plays. At that moment, she was another one of the dead, her soul trapped in a body that only functioned to stumble about and seek out the living. I wondered if she were screaming inside as she approached me. The center of her head disappeared, and I made my way to the back of the car. I wanted to close my eyes but couldn't. I glanced down and saw...

...nothing on the bumper. No sticker, no scratches where Lee might have taken it off. The weight lifted, and I turned my attention away from the car, from what I had thought was Jessica's Chevy, and to the more pressing advancement of the dead. I counted six. Among them were two kids, both clearly under the age of ten.

I backpedaled toward my truck, slung the rifle off my shoulder, and aimed. One down. Two down. Backed up. Ran for the truck. I reached inside, grabbed another gun, checked the rounds, and fired off two shots. The children were last to go, slower moving than the rest and further off. I hated the feeling of nausea that swept over me, the way sweat spilled from my pores, the empty feeling in my chest as I first took down the little girl then the boy. They could have been siblings. Maybe even twins.

Urgency swept over me as another realization kicked in. No matter how much I viewed these rotters as once living, breathing, loving people, they were still dead, and they would just as soon kill me and tear me apart than let me walk out of there unscathed. It didn't matter that they were still inside those bodies. They weren't in control, or at least I didn't believe them to be. I turned in a circle, scanned the street, and saw no one else.

I got in the truck, backed it up to the car, and popped the release for the gas tank. As a kid, we learned the art of siphoning and even with the safety features on new cars, a hose could go down into a tank easily enough. Thankfully, a hand pump system made it easier. I grabbed the gas cans from the back of the truck, opened each one, and set them by the car. I opened the car door. The dead man slumped a little but didn't fall out. Bending down, I pulled the gas lever. At the back of the car, the small door popped open. The siphon hose went down into the car's tank easy enough. I squeezed the white rubber bulb several times until gas flowed through the hose and into the cans.

Another one of the dead came from behind one of the buildings. The front of her blouse was torn, exposing a ruined breast. I took a deep breath, let it out after putting her down.

With the cans full, I closed all but one of them and set them back in the truck bed. I poured the last one into the truck's tank.

I hopped into the truck, rolled the engine over, and pulled off. It was still early in the morning by the sun's dial. Noontime was a good two hours away. More supplies were needed, and a convenience store sat a few buildings away. I parked the truck, again pointing it toward the interstate. I slid from my seat.

"Hang tight, Humphrey," I said then added, "Don't leave without me."

The window to the store had been shattered. A brick lay on the floor a few feet away. I stepped through the opening, glanced around the dimly lit space. Glass crunched under my boots as I stepped slowly toward the first aisle. It still amazes me how ransacked some places were and how untouched others were. In this case, the place had been ransacked, but there were still plenty of canned goods on shelves.

At the checkout counter, I grabbed a handful of bags and stuffed them with as many cans as I could. Four bags went out to the truck, and then I was back in for more. From the corner of my eye, I saw the lurching man, his large stomach split open, a trail of intestines dangling between his legs, his mouth slack and bloodied. Even in death, carrying all that weight appeared difficult. I took a deep breath, aimed. A second later, he fell backward, his arms flailing forward as gravity pulled him down.

Back in the store, I stopped at an aisle holding chips and candies and other things that in another life weren't all that good for you. A man sat in the center of the aisle, his clothes dirty, hair disheveled. He was older, maybe pushing seventy. I took aim but lowered the pistol.

"Hey," I called. "Hey, you."

The man looked at me. There was color in his face, stubble on his chin. His brow was wet with sweat, and in his hands was a bag of chips. He shoveled a handful into his mouth and chewed quickly. He repeated this several times. I couldn't believe I stood twenty feet from another living person. He was as much skin and bones as many of the dead were, but he was alive, and alive was something I hadn't seen since...Davey's death.

I took a step forward. He cringed away from me, turning his shoulder as if he thought I would steal his chips. I stopped, not wanting to scare him.

"Hey...umm...it's not safe here. Not without a weapon at least."

He pushed onto his knees and then placed one foot on the floor. It took a few seconds, but he managed to stand though shakily at best. He stumbled away from me, grabbing another bag of chips as he did so.

"Wait a minute," I called after him.

He was faster than I thought and was through the EMPLOYEES ONLY door before I could reach him. I pushed it open, my pistol instinctively at the ready. Across the stock room was another door. He opened it and went outside.

"Not bright," I said and hurried after him.

Outside, I was met with the backs of the buildings, where trash and recyclables once went. A few cars sat where their owners had left them for the last time. And the dead were everywhere—maybe only ten or twelve of them but entirely too many to take on without any weapons.

The man hurried past the outstretched arms of a woman, her head sagging on her shoulders, a bone jutting through her neck. He weaved in and out as if he were afraid of nothing, as if the dead wouldn't turn on him. At that moment, I wished I could have been that fearless, but truth be told, every day I was scared, just like a child at night with the shadows playing across the wall. Only the boogeyman is real in this world.

Fearlessness like that could get someone killed. I knew this and took the cautious approach. I leveled my aim on the nearest of the dead, pulled the trigger. Three more shots and the path I needed to catch up to the old man was a little clearer. I passed near the woman with the bent neck, gave it little thought as I put her down. The skin of her throat tore with the broken neck she had suffered, and her head fell back on her shoulders before she hit the ground.

I saw the small house and made a run for it. The old man was almost to it when I reached him. He opened the door and looked back at me. His brow was creased, and I saw a hint of blue from behind slit eyelids. "Go away," he said. "Leave us be."

"Wait. What?" I said.

"Go away. We don't want you here."

He stepped inside the small house, made to close the door. I grabbed it with one hand and held it open. "The world is dead now. You can't stay here. They'll get to you eventually."

"We've made do so far. We'll be fine."

"Maybe so," I said, desperate all of a sudden for him not to close the door on me. "But you're the first living person I've seen in weeks and...and..." I was at a loss for words.

He grunted, then his eyes lit up slightly, the lids opening, showing some yellow in the whites. Red lines snaked through, like cracks on the yellow backdrop. He shook his head as if he were aggravated.

"Come on in. Besides, I need to get my Louisa something to eat. It's been a while since she's had any food."

I looked behind me. The dead made their way toward us, no longer a dozen but more like twenty or more. I stepped into a dimly lit room, candles flickered their shadow dancers along the walls. The old man slid a board over the door—a makeshift lock that hearkened back to the days of knights and Vikings.

There were guns lying about and bottles of water. The guy wasn't so helpless after all.

"Good to see you have some protection," I said.

"Give me your gun," he said.

I turned to him, saw the shotgun in his hands.

"Whoa, Mister," I said and put both hands in the air about face high. "I'm not here to hurt you or anything."

"I said give me your gun."

The first of many thumps struck the door from the outside. The dead had reached us.

"Give me your gun. I won't tell you again."

I nodded and lowered the hand with my pistol in it. He took it and tossed it on a dusty couch.

"Now the knife."

I slid the machete from my shoulder and dropped it to the floor. "Look, Mister, I don't know what the deal is, but—"

"I tried to warn you," he said. "But you wouldn't listen. Since you're here, my Louisa is hungry, and I'm all out of food for her."

"There's plenty of food back at that store."

He shook his head. "Not that Louisa will eat."

My stomach dropped. Even before he opened the only other door in the room, I knew what he meant. At that point, I prayed he didn't pat me down and find the cop's gun tucked in my waistband.

The man opened the door slightly and motioned with a jerk of his head. "Get on in there."

"You're making a mistake," I said.

"They all say that," he responded. He cradled the shotgun in the nook of one elbow and held the doorknob with his other hand. "Now get on in there. She'll take you dead or alive, and I have no problems putting you down before she gets hold of you. That'll keep the noise down since you won't be screaming."

I could take him. I knew I could, but I had to be careful. Reaching for the cop's gun was out of the question at that moment. I gave a nod and stepped forward, hands still in the air. As I approached the door, he opened it further.

"Louisa," he called. "Time to eat, Sweetie."

A groan echoed from the room. I peeked through the foot of space between the open door and the jamb. That room was darker than the one I stood in with no candles to keep it lit.

Three feet from the door, the man stepped to the side, pushed it all the way open. In the light of the dancing candles from the front room, I could see bones on the floor, skulls with hair still attached, faces that were half eaten. My stomach lurched as Louisa came into sight. She was a big woman with thick chords of gray hair hanging alongside her gore-stained face. Her housedress was bloodied and clung to her ample breasts that sagged to her belly. A meaty hand reached forward, and fear clutched me tight.

"Get," the man said and shoved the shotgun forward.

It was all reaction, maybe from having three brothers. I dropped my right arm quickly, the hand grabbing the barrel of the shotgun. The left hand came down across the bridge of the man's nose. It cracked, popped, and blood spilled down his face. He fell back against the door, stunned, the open hand reaching for his shattered nose. Louisa—his Louisa—grabbed his elbow, pulled him to her. His eyes widened, and he screamed as she bit down on his shoulder. The shotgun fell to the floor. I ducked. It didn't go off.

The man tried to shove her off of him, but her teeth were firmly at the base of his neck. His screams were loud and filled with terror. I could have helped him. I could have pulled out the gun from behind me and put a bullet in Louisa's head and pulled him free of her. But I didn't. In those seconds before Louisa had bit into him, I saw the remains on the floor, saw the crazed look in his eyes—he was going to feed me to her, his Louisa. That town had been through what every other town in the world had, but the survivors had faced something worse, being sacrificed to the very thing they were trying to escape.

Heat filled my face, and I finally moved. With my boot, I shoved the man and his Louisa back through the door and slammed it shut. His screams were muffled, but they were there. As I waited for them to die down, I stood listening, having exacted a measure of revenge for those he had killed. I heard, more than his screams, the sounds of the dead outside the door, their hands slapping at it, trying to get in.

I sat, my shoulders shaking with adrenaline. Long after the man had grown silent, I remained seated, my eyes on the door that hid Louisa from the world. What if I had been put in that situation? What if Jeanette or Bobby had been Louisa? Could I have put them down as easily as I did strangers or even those who were once friends? Or would I try to preserve them somehow like the old man did? Would I hunt for "food" for them? I didn't know and hoped I would never find out, but it made me think—something I had become good at since being alone in this world. You never know what you would do in any given situation. At any time, any place, with the right circumstances, anyone could lose their mind, and what once was wrong may not be so wrong after all.

I looked around the room as the dead continued to beat on the door, their moans muffled but there. A flashlight sat on a table. I tried it, smiled when it flickered before coming to life. At what I assumed was the bedroom door, I held my pistol, fully reloaded, and braced myself for Louisa. I shoved the door open, shone the light in the room.

Louisa sat hunched over, her arms moving stiffly from the floor to her face—she was still eating. I didn't bother getting her attention and stepped into the room, around the many bones—far too many to be just a couple of bodies—and placed my pistol inches from her head. She looked up from her meal and exited the world for the last time. She slumped over onto the old man. Her heavy body shook the floor.

I stepped from the room and closed the door behind me.

There were no windows, but they weren't needed to know the dead stood just beyond the door. They were louder now, like a rabid pack of dogs growling and howling as they chased another doomed animal. I picked the shotgun up off the floor, cracked it open. It was empty. I shook my head. How many people had he led to their deaths based on the fear of being shot?

I checked the other guns—all empty.

I reloaded my pistol, checked the cop's gun, and prayed it was enough to get me out of there in one piece. I had seen enough horror movies to know it wasn't going to end well— just keep them as far away as I could and hope not to run out of ammo. I picked up the machete and slipped the strap back over my neck.

My hands shook as I reached for the door. I was heading to my death. Though things had been lonely and I had little to hope for, I wasn't ready to die. The wooden bar removed, I opened the door. The first of the dead fell forward, and I started counting.

One shot. Two shots. Three. Four. Five. They fell as I emptied the cop's gun and stepped out into the bright sun. I tossed the gun aside and took aim with mine. There weren't as many as my mind made them out to be, but there were still enough of them that the only course of action I could take was to run straight forward, gun out in front of me, cutting a path in the dead.

A cold hand touched my arm, sending chills along my spine. I ran, still counting the bullets. Nine. Ten. Eleven. At the back of the convenience store, I looked back. Maybe half of them still stood and shuffled toward me. I pushed the back door open and slipped inside. I shoved several boxes in front of it, hoping to barricade the door.

Sweat spilled down my face, from my armpits, and around my groin. Breaths came in labored gasps. I ran one hand along my arm where the zombie had touched. I could still feel its fingers on my skin. There was no blood; I had escaped unscathed.

Hurrying to the front of the store, I reached the broken window and looked out. There were several more of the dead moving about, but none of them seemed to notice me. The truck awaited, and I ran, not worrying about grabbing any more food or water.

At the truck, I turned, emptied my gun on several of the dead, then got in, slammed the door shut, and locked it. The engine rolled over, and I shifted into drive. The tires barked as I mashed the gas and swerved into the center of the road. It was a mere minute before I reached the edge of town. From the rearview mirror, I could see the dead lurching about, the noise of my leaving attracting them toward me.

For the first time since the beginning of this whole mess, I left the dead standing. Part of me hated myself for not putting those souls to rest. The other part—the side that said I almost died—let out a long sigh of relief and mashed the gas harder.

Nine Weeks and One Day After It All Started...

I've never been good with directions. Jeanette always planned out our trips, routes, where we would stay, what we would do.

Turn left at the light. Hit the interstate. Just keep driving. Don't worry, I know where we're going.

Always in control, the true pilot of our vacations. I just navigated us where she said to go.

That's the way it was. The way it always was.

Now...it's not like that, is it?

Somewhere along the line, I got turned around. It didn't dawn on me until I fled Harkers, my skin still crawling with the thought of how close I came to being supper to an old man's dead wife. Part of me wanted to turn around, go back to that small town right out of Mayberry and put the dead out of their misery. That part of me believed that was the right thing to do, help them find rest—a final, permanent end. But it had been too close. I wanted to see another living person so bad my judgment had been clouded, and I put myself in danger.

It would be morning again before I thought much about the direction I had been going. The truth was I had been heading toward Charleston, the opposite direction of Table Rock. I wasn't even on the right interstate—26 not 385 like I should have been.

It dawned on me when I saw the sign for Summerville, a little town that claimed the Summerville Lights as one of its main attractions: a female ghost who was always searching, lantern held high, for her loved one. I pulled onto the shoulder, stared at the sign. Charleston was a few miles down the road—one of the bigger cities in South Carolina. There would be thousands of zombies swarming about that area.

I laughed, trying to keep from getting aggravated. I didn't succeed.

"Crap, Humphrey. We've been going the wrong way."

It reminded me of the time Jeanette and I had taken a wrong turn once before. Healing Springs had been the destination, a little elbow just outside of the small town of Blackville.

"None of this looks familiar," Jeanette said as she watched the world pass outside her window. It rained the night before, and the morning air was still cool. Gray clouds loomed in patches, surrounded by the clarity of blue skies.

"I thought you said take 321."

"I don't think that's right."

"You did say to go through Gaston, right?" I asked, pulled along the shoulder of the highway.

"Yeah, but we didn't pass the dump or the airport or—"

"The airport?"

She nodded. "Yeah, the airport. We should have gone by the airport."

"Babe, that's thirty minutes from the house—we've been driving for an hour. That didn't hit you until now."

She stared at me, blinked a couple of times, her eyes telling me she thought we were lost.

"That's Edmond Highway," I said. "It's the other way. I go that way to work every day, remember?"

We didn't make it to Healing Springs, which is kind of ironic now. Jeanette bought a GPS shortly after that trip and kept a notebook with traveling notes in it just in case the GPS died on the way. She became obsessive in her research of where and when. We never got lost again.

And there I was, on the side of the road, staring up at the big, green sign that said Summerville 1 Mile.

"We have to go back."

Humphrey said nothing.

I lowered my head to the steering wheel, my heart and hopes deflated. The longer it took me to get to Table Rock, the less chance I had of ever finding my family alive. I had taken too long already, spending way too much time in our hometown, wiping out as many of the dead as I could, burying them where I killed them. I lifted my head, punched the steering wheel. The horn had long since been dead and gave only a thump when I struck it.

Up ahead, I saw a handful of the dead coming toward me. Their bodies wavered from side to side as they lumbered my way. My face grew hot with anger, jaws clenched tight. "Stupid rotters," I said as I thought of my brother, Rick, how the doctors let him die after they realized what was going on. I thought of Davie Blaylock and how he died surrounded by a horde trying to draw them away so I could get away. I thought of Jeanette and Bobby, of how they begged me to go with them before I sent them away with my baby brother. I thought of Lee, the oldest of our group of four siblings and the rapid descent from healthy young man to the fragile, blood vomiting shell of himself and how his eyes held fear in them as he died while lying on the floor of a furniture warehouse.

"Little Bro, promise me you won't let me get like that. Promise me you'll put me down before I die."

I had promised, but in the end, I couldn't do it. I couldn't kill my own flesh and blood even as his eyes held hope and fear all at the same time. I had stared at his lifeless body, the warmth gone out of it, the stench of his bowels and bladder release hanging in the air. When his foot twitched—a slight movement I barely caught—I backed away, waited a moment for another body spasm that came in the form of that same foot moving, the knee bending enough to make it look like he would stand.

No gun has ever been heavier for me than my rifle as I stood above him, the barrel aimed for his forehead. When his eyelids fluttered then opened, I squeezed the trigger. Fear had swallowed me whole at that point. I couldn't let him get up. I might not have been able to put him down if I had waited any longer.

I thought of Pop, repressed the look in his eyes as he put the gun to his head with Lee and I standing there. His back had been mauled by several of them, and death was imminent. His body slumped to the floor, his life ended by his own hands rather than coming back—it was the only way for him to be sure he would remain dead.

"This is my burden," he said when we told him to let us take care of it. "Not yours."

All these thoughts raced through my head as the rotters lurched toward my truck, coming from the woods and the overpass and just down the interstate. I opened the truck door, grabbed my pistol and rifle, and slung the machete over my shoulder. The pistol went into my waistband.

What are you doing? I like to think that voice belonged to Humphrey, but the truth is it was probably just me in my state of grief and anger and the close call from days before and how fast the world went to hell and how I had gotten turned around and it was all rolled up into a package ripe for exploding.

"Hey," I yelled to the nearest one as I approached it. "You want some of this? You hungry?" I did what all stupid men do in times of extreme anger. I ripped my shirt off, slung it to the ground, and beat on my chest. A show of defiance to a world gone insane.

I no longer saw people trapped inside decomposing shells, their memories and feelings still intact, their souls still very much bound to their bodies. What I saw was death, a bunch of grisly grim reapers, their hands and mouths their scythes.

"Come on," I said to the woman with matted brown hair, her jaw slack, tongue lolling from between yellowed teeth.

The machete came from off my shoulder, and I dropped the sheath to the ground. I swung it in a high arc, the blade striking her just above the left ear and severing the top of her head. She shuddered before dropping.

"Who's next?" I yelled, turned to see an old man, his button-up, white shirt half open, a chunk of flesh missing from his chest. "Is it you? Are you ready for this?"

He groaned or growled. I'm not sure which. I swung the machete down as hard as I could, split his skull in half all the way to his upper lip.

There were others—more than I thought at first. But anger and hate combined is a powerful motivator...and an all too dangerous form of gasoline. Another woman was followed by a little girl, her skirt dirty, part of her leg missing. Two younger men came in quick, freshly dead or so they appeared. The pistol took them down. I focused on the singular zombies with distance between them and the nearest one.

A middle-aged man groaned as we neared each other. I screamed back at him before taking the top of his head off with the machete. The pistol took out several more, just click and boom and down they went.

I spun and saw another rotter moving toward me. His glasses were still on his face though hanging cock-eyed, just on the tip of his nose. His hair was short, a few cowlicks kicked off the edges. He was thin, and all I could think was Paul Marcum taking a bite out of Lee, essentially ending my oldest brother's existence. The man looked similar to him.

I backpedaled to the truck, climbed in the bed, and shoved aside part of the tin can alarm system. There were other guns back there, plenty of ammunition, but all I wanted was a vantage point.

The other dead approached, flies swarming around them, their stench filling the air, making my stomach churn. Even after these few months, that smell still makes me want to heave. I plucked them off one by one until only the Paul Marcum lookalike was standing at the tailgate. He was missing three fingers on one hand, and up close, he was a lot worse off than I originally thought. Skin had peeled away from his face, exposing facial muscles as tough as jerky.

"How you doin', Paul?"

He looked at me, gave a moan, and stretched out his arms.

"Okay, so you're not Paul—at least you weren't in another life. But today... Today, you're Paul Marcum, and you killed my brother."

I brought the heel of my boot down on the bridge of his nose. He stumbled backward, let out what sounded like a howl. He was in pain, and I was happy to put him through more of it. I jumped from the truck, landed a few feet from him. A quick whip of the machete on one arm and it separated from his body.

"You think that hurt?" I yelled as he groaned. "You haven't felt anything yet."

I circled around him, rage having consumed me entirely. The blade found the other arm. The snap of bone and the rush of fetid blood spilled from a new wound as the arm fell away. Another pain-filled howl left the Marcum lookalike. I pulled the pistol from my waistband and took two shots at his legs—two wasted bullets that I'll never get back, but at that time…at that time, wounding an innocent man who unfortunately looked like another one was all I cared about. The rotter fell to the ground, lay there with no hands to pull himself along, his legs useless.

With the toe of my boot, I rolled him onto his back. His teeth clattered together as he gnashed at me. His filmed-over eyes held anger in them.

"You're mad at me? Is that how it is, Paul? You kill my brother, and you're mad at me?" I laughed. Maybe the wheels had finally come off the car, and my mind had taken the short road to insanity. I don't know, but at that moment—that frozen, horrible moment in time—I didn't care about the pain the dead must have been in, the fear that must have been sitting in their undead veins. The only thing that mattered was revenge. Plain and simple. And revenge I would have.

I brought the blade down on the dead man's chest, yanked it out, and swung it down again. Over and over, I bashed the body of the poor man as black blood spilled from each wound, and dead tissues tore free, bones broke. After several minutes, I finally stopped, my arms aching, my breathing heavy and harsh in my ears. The zombie still stirred, his mouth still opening and closing, his eyes still focused on what could have been a meal.

And the anger was gone from me, all of it unleashed on that poor dead man. I shook from adrenaline and sudden guilt. A hand went to my mouth, and I dropped the machete to the ground. I took several steps back until my back hit the tailgate. The man still moved, still made little groans and moans, and his head turned from side to side like he was saying no no no no over and over again.

I pulled out my pistol, walked the short distance to the mutilated body, and pulled the trigger. The man's head ruptured, and he stilled. Hands shaking, I got into the truck, closed the door, and locked it. I could feel Humphrey's eyes on me, sense his disappointment.

"I'm sorry," I whispered as I stared out the windshield at the carnage around me. The dead were truly dead, their bodies lying where I felled them.

Feel better?

I looked down at Humphrey. He stared straight ahead.

"Not really," I answered.

You've blood on the side of your face.

I ran a finger along one cheek, wiped the black gunk from it, and stared at my finger for a while. Wiping the blood onto my pants, I cranked up the truck. "Reckon we should be going?"

Yes, we should.

I didn't bother looking down at the stuffed bear with its floppy bunny pajama ears. He wouldn't be looking at me—or at least not when I turned to him. With the truck in gear, I pulled onto the road, weaving in and out of the bodies. Up ahead about a mile, the Summerville exit would take me off the interstate. I could circle back and end up in the opposite direction, heading back toward home and, hopefully, Table Rock.

Nine Weeks, One Day, an Hour and a Half Later...

Adrenaline is sometimes painful.

The anger that coursed through my body as I mutilated —
and that's the right word for what I had done — the Paul
Marcum lookalike faded before I got back in the truck. My
hands and legs shook as the effects wore off. I guessed that's
what a junkie feels like after a high, after his head has been
totally messed up for a few hours or a day or whatever and
reality starts to come back. I was cold, and my joints were
stiff, and I shivered as if winter had arrived and brought with
it the northern winds.

I drove the mile to the exit ramp that led to Summerville
and pulled off the interstate. At the dead light, I turned and
crossed onto the overpass. There I stopped, got out of the
truck, and walked to the edge of the overpass. My legs still
shook a little, and I was tired and weak. I stared off toward
Charleston. In the distance, I could see a few of the dead
shambling about. How many? I couldn't say, but there was no
staying any length of time in Summerville. It could take them
a couple hours to get there. Or it could take them a couple
days. Honestly, it's not something I wanted to find out.

Back in the truck, I started the cross over and made my
way back toward the interstate. I passed a few bodies lying on
the ground and some burned out vehicles. One windshield
caught my attention. The blood had dried where the driver's
skull struck. The glass spider-webbed in all directions. The
front end of the car was crumpled in, the bumper slumped
toward the ground. The driver was wedged between the
steering wheel and the windshield. I couldn't help but

wonder about the events that led him to the point in time where his head became a ruptured melon. Was he fleeing for his life? Did he swerve to keep from hitting someone or something?

"An accident," I whispered.

More than likely. Humphrey sounded more and more intelligent with each passing day. The little girl's voice had been growing up as we went. I hadn't noticed it until then. I looked at him—at *her*—and I didn't see a stuffed teddy bear wearing a bunny costume. I saw a little girl who was no longer around four or five but closer to eight. Maybe nine. Her hair was long and brown, and there was a braid on one side. Freckles lined the bridge of her nose and spotted parts of her cheeks. The bunny ears were still there, still floppy and in need of cleaning, and the costume had stretched tight over the girl's body. The arms and legs ended at the armpits and mid thighs.

I couldn't pull my eyes from her. No matter how bad I wanted to, I couldn't turn away.

"Who are you?" I asked.

Humphrey, she said without moving her lips.

"No. Humphrey's a teddy bear. You're—"

Alive.

"What?"

I'm alive and—

At some point, I must have let my foot off the break. The truck rolled, but I didn't realize it. By the time I did, it had reached the exit ramp, crept off the edge of the road, and started down the grass and gravel embankment.

"Crap," I yelled and mashed the break as hard as I could. I leveled the steering wheel, trying to keep the truck straight as it skidded down the hill. The embankment didn't look that steep, but it seemed to go on for miles, all in a world of slow motion special effects that if this were a movie the viewer would have gotten to see the truck bounce and jostle and would have seen my face screwed up in determination, jaw clenched too tight as I held onto the steering wheel. The front passenger's side tire struck a large rock. The truck bounced up and over it, teetered to one side, then tipped over.

I don't know how many times I went head over heels. I do know the truck came to a stop at the bottom of the hill, upside down. I struck my head on the ceiling, and my left shoulder felt like someone had stabbed me with a hot poker. My left ankle hurt, as did both legs.

The world sat upside down, and the blood flowed to my head. Pressure filled my face, and there was a rush of water coming from somewhere in my skull, the flood echoing in my ears. I tried to move my left arm, felt a bolt of pain, and forced my hand across my lap. With the other hand, I pushed up on the ceiling, taking as much weight off the seatbelt as I could. I pressed the button, and the belt released. My head bumped the ceiling again, but I was free of the restraint. I rolled onto my right shoulder, grimaced as another pain tore through my left arm.

The pain was intense for a few minutes, but the danger I was in…that danger was far more real than the way my body felt. Laying on my side, the rushing waters in my ears subsided. A little relief but not much.

I pulled my feet free and got on my knees. My ankle barked once but nothing like my arm. I looked at my shoulder. I could see the swelling, the way it had pulled free from the socket.

The windshield was cracked. There were a few trees around us, and the grass was grown up considerably.

"You okay, Humphrey?"

She didn't respond. She just hung upside down in her car seat. I reached over, worked the clasp with one hand until it came free. Humphrey tumbled onto the ceiling, gave a sharp, *Ow.*

"Sorry, kiddo."

It's okay.

She sounded little again. I was okay with that.

"We need to get out of here, Humphrey."

Where are we going to go?

"I don't know. Maybe find somewhere to hole up for a day or two—my shoulder's killing me."

Outside, I could see only the grass and trees and the edge of the off ramp the truck had tumbled down. The engine hissed as fluid leaked from a busted hose. The door handle lifted easily enough, and I pushed the door open. It groaned as metal on metal tend to do. I grabbed the pistol and carefully poked my head out. I didn't know if any rotters heard the tumble, but I saw none of them either on the road just beyond us or on the hill at the top of the overpass.

A few minutes later, I had my pack over my good shoulder, Humphrey tucked in the top part, the zipper tight to keep him from falling out. The food and weapons were scattered about the ground. I grabbed as much ammo as I could fit in the pack and in my pockets and slung old Ox over my left shoulder and around my neck. The strap tugged on the wounded shoulder, and I grimaced as fresh pain raced down into my elbow and up into my neck. I made my way up

70

to the off ramp, each step I took sending hot bolts up into my left knee.

At the top of the hill, my worst fear had become a reality. Several of the dead had heard the truck crash and made their way toward me. One of them — a thin man with a chunk of hair missing on the side of his head — saw me. His upper lip twitched, and he groaned.

I reached for my machete. A panic came over me so suddenly it felt like electricity along my skin. The machete lay in the road a mile away where I had mutilated the Paul Marcum lookalike. I didn't want to fire the weapon. Not then. Not with only a handful of them nearby. The truck crash was one thing, but the gun would echo and carry further.

Limping along, I hurried away from the overpass and down a stretch of road that led away from the stores and restaurants the other direction promised. The center of the road provided distance between the buildings, and I moved as fast as I could, keeping eyes on the corners of the structures and the dead trailing behind me.

I don't know how far I walked. My ankle hurt, my shoulder pulsed, the skin felt tight, but stopping to check wasn't an option. Eventually, what seemed like a small shopping district gave way to an open road with a few cars along its side. Off in the distance and across what looked like a world of tall grass stood a house. No rotters came from that direction.

Behind me shambled a dozen or more of the soulful dead.

I started to cross the grass then thought better of it. What if there was a wayward rotter in there? Instead, I went to the end of the road that led to the house. It was more like a long, dirt driveway with gravel and rock lining both sides.

The house easily sat a hundred yards or so off the road, and though the dead were still a good distance behind me, walking didn't feel safe. I ran the best I could. At first, the pain in my ankle was like slivers of glass tearing at the muscle and bone, but after a dozen or so steps, it loosened up, and I ran with a slight limp. The pain in my knee did not ease up so easily. In my younger, less beat up days, I could have run that hundred yards in twelve or thirteen seconds. Not then.

At the house, I had my gun at the ready, arm extended, finger on the trigger. It was a two-story wooden structure with ornately carved rails trailing up the steps and frilly designs along the windows. The white paint flaked a little on the edges, and what probably was once red trim had faded to pink. A dozen or so steps led up to the landing where the door stood closed. The windows were boarded from the outside. Maybe someone still lived there. I could only hope.

I knocked, waited, looked out toward the road. The dead still lingered about. Some of them had shuffled back toward town. I knocked again. When no one answered, I tried the knob. It turned—it actually turned. I couldn't believe it. For a moment longer, I stared at the door then pushed it open.

Once inside, I closed the door, let it click shut. I set Ox on the floor and lowered the pack.

"Stay here, Humphrey."

Like he—*she*—was going anywhere. The kitchen was empty. The hall that led away from it had two rooms to the right, a bathroom to the left. No one occupied these rooms. Stairs led up to the bedrooms. I braced myself as I went up one step at a time. A few creaks sounded louder than they probably were. I cringed with each one and prayed the sounds didn't alarm anyone, living or otherwise, to my presence.

Four bedrooms and a full bath and not a soul to be found. Each of the bedrooms held their own particulars, their own characteristics, telling what type of people had lived there. The one at the end of the hall closest to the bathroom held my attention for a few minutes longer than I wanted it to. Posters of baseball players were tacked to the walls. Baseball bats sat in a rack bolted to the wall closest to the bed. A banner that said RED SOX 2004 WORLD SERIES CHAMPIONS—THE CURSE IS DEAD had been put up along the edge of the ceiling like a border. A ball sat in a glove on top of the dresser. It was definitely a boy's room. By the size of the bed, I would say a little boy.

Bobby played baseball. Second base. His old man played third, though I was a lousy hitter. Bobby swung a bat much better than I ever did. I closed my eyes and I saw him in uniform, taking cuts while standing in the on deck circle. At the plate was Charlie Rose's little boy, Chuck—yeah, he was a junior, but instead of calling him that, we all just called him Chuck. The pitcher was a kid I didn't know, his hair sandy blond and long with thick strands hanging out the back and sides of his cap. A large A in Old English font was plastered across the front of the opposing team's uniforms and hats. He threw the pitch, and Chuck singled into left field. The outfielder bobbled the ball, and Chuck, even at ten years old, knew to run to second base as quickly as he could.

Bobby came up to the plate, swung his bat a few times, then stepped into the batter's box. A first pitch strike was followed by a ball then another strike. The pitcher wound up and…

I don't know what brought me away from my thoughts. I was startled to see the sun was setting. How long had I been standing there?

I hurried out of the room and back down the stairs. With no one there, I thought it safe to lock the door. But with all the windows boarded up with plywood, I couldn't see outside. I opened the front door, looked out with the gun ready if needed. At the bottom of the steps, I saw what snapped me from my memories: one of the dead had made it from the road to the house. I reckon it tried to climb the steps but only managed to fall backward. It struggled to stand, but its legs were too rigid to bend.

I went back inside, very aware of the pain coursing through my shoulder. The arm had grown stiff. I grabbed Ox from the floor and went back outside. I made my way down the steps. White film covered the man's eyes, and his mouth snapped open and shut, open and shut. "End of the line," I said and brought the butt of the gun down on his head. It cracked, but he still squirmed. Again, I brought the butt of the gun down, this time much harder. His head split from forehead back.

A shiver traced up my spine, and I hurried back up the steps. That's something I never got used to: physically striking one of the dead. The thought of it made me nauseated. With the living, you could pull a punch and still do plenty of damage. With the dead, a pulled punch could be the end of your life. Still, my skin crawled, and I wanted nothing more than a shower that I wouldn't get.

With the door closed and locked, I went over to the couch in the front room. I was thankful there was no carpet on the floor. If there had been, I would never have been able to move that couch to stand in front of the door.

I walked the downstairs a second time. All the windows had been nailed shut from the inside; boards covered them from the outside. The backdoor window had also been covered with wood, but a hole had been drilled in it at about eye level. I wondered why the person who had taken all the precautions to board the house up didn't bother with drilling a hole in the wood in the front door as well.

Like a lot of houses, there were pictures on the walls, and these pictures showed a happy family. Two adults, a teenaged daughter, and a young boy, blond hair and shining blue eyes. He looked like a baseball player. Add a couple years to him, and he could have been that pitcher...

I grabbed my pack and Ox and headed up the stairs to the second floor. I was exhausted and wanted sleep, but there was the matter of my shoulder. In the bathroom mirror—one that was as tall as the door it hung on—I pulled my shirt off. The skin was tight and purple and red. The swelling covered the clavicle completely.

Dislocated.

I tried to lift my shoulder. Bright bolts of pain shot through my arm, and I let it drop. I spun in a slight circle, tears in my eyes.

"Come on," I said, looked at myself in the mirror. When did that beard grow in? When did those dark gray bags form under my eyes? When did I grow so old?

The pain was bad but would be worse if I didn't get the shoulder back in place.

I put my hand under the elbow and lifted my arm. The growl from my throat scared me. The pain of locked up muscles being forced to move brought fresh tears to my eyes. I pulled it as straight as I could and began applying pressure to it. With a quick shove upward, my shoulder moved with several pops.

I screamed. My vision filled with dots, and my stomach grew sour as the immensity of the pain threatened to swallow me. I yelled, long and loud, as I jammed the shoulder up a second time. My head swooned, and my vision wavered and grayed along the edges. I thought I would pass out from the pain, but then, just as suddenly as the lightheadedness had come on, it was gone. On the third try, there was an instant of relief as the shoulder went back into place. It was like an extracted tooth: It may be gone, but you still felt the phantom pain of it. My head grew light, and those spots in my vision became larger. I stumbled from the bathroom and into the room that belonged to the boy. I was breathing hard, and sweat poured over me. With the door closed, I slid the dresser in front of it.

To tell the truth, I don't remember crawling into the bed or setting my pistol on the nightstand beside it. I don't remember pulling Humphrey from the bag and setting him— her—on the pillow next to me.

What I remember is waking up with the sun shining through the slats in the blinds, my body aching and a tickle in my throat. I sniffled a snot runner and wiped my nose. A moment later, I sneezed. Then again. And again. And several more times after that just because my body wanted to.

My breathing came in phlegm-filled rasps. I sat up, fully alarmed at what appeared to be a cold setting in. My shoulder hurt but not like it had when it was out of socket. It was more of a dull throb that let me know it was still there and still hurt.

At any other time, a cold would be just that: a cold. But in these times, where a cold started this whole mess, my mind seized on the only truth it could: I was dying, and sooner or later, I would become one of *them.*

I sat up in the bed, holding my arm tight to my chest and hoping not to jostle the shoulder too much. I swung my feet to the floor. My boots scuffed against the hardwood floor, and I stood too quickly. The swooning in my head forced me to sit back down. I waited, eyes closed, head down, for the world to stop spinning. When it did, I stood slowly. My heart hammered my chest and the thoughts…the thoughts that traipsed across my mind…

What if I am dying? What if this is the Rotter Flu that took so many others? What do I do? There's no cure. Do I…

I shook my head to that thought. If push came to shove, I guess, then I would. That reminded me of what someone said when the rotters became a reality: Always keep a bullet for yourself just in case the worst happened. I checked my weapon. Plenty of bullets there. Which one had my name on it?

A tickle formed in the left nostril, provoking a sneeze that was followed by four more. I coughed, told myself that the scratch in my throat was nothing.

I limped my way to the door and eased the dresser from in front of it. From there, I made my way to the bathroom, opened the medicine cabinet. I don't know who owned the house before the end came, but they had medicine for both colds and pain. I took two of the cold pills dry and wished I had grabbed a couple bottles of water before I took off. But I hadn't.

Another cough.

Another sneeze.

Another snot runner sniffled back up into my nose.

"I can't be sick. There's been few people...barely enough to..."

The Paul Marcum lookalike came to mind. I bludgeoned him badly, and this was Karma biting me on the butt. Humphrey said something when I got back in the truck. He said I had blood on my face. I wiped it away—black gunk, thick like sludge. I had looked at it and then wiped it on my jeans without much thought.

I couldn't help but laugh. Like my brother, I had been done in by Paul Marcum—Lee by the real deal and me by the phony. How do you like those apples?

Down the hall in one of the other bedrooms, I found some clothes. They were a little big for me, but they were clean, and clean was good. I changed then dumped my old clothes into a trash bag that would probably never be moved outside that house. With my old boots on, I grabbed the pistol. The end of me may have come, but I wasn't going to go without a fight. And if I was going to fight, I needed my guns...

"Stay here," I told Humphrey after shoving the couch away from the door. She sat in the center of it, a loaded pistol on her lap. "I'll be back."

Are you sure?

I gave a nod. No, I wasn't sure. To be honest, I had no intentions of going back. Humphrey had been with me for a short while and he—*she*—had probably kept me sane through much of the Hell, and I didn't want to turn into a rotter with her there to see me. I wanted to leave and die somewhere else without Humphrey having to know. In a way, I guess I was sparing her the pain of watching me die. "You bet, buddy," I said.

The door closed with a click, and I lowered my head. She was just a stuffed toy. She wasn't real. All of the conversations we had were in my head. Right? Still, the guilt of lying swelled in my chest. I bit my bottom lip and shook my head. A deep breath and I headed down the steps, passed the dead person at the base of the stairs, and kept going.

I limped but barely. My ankle and knee were tight, but my shoulder hurt more. I sneezed and grimaced as something tore free in my chest. I spat a string of yellowish phlegm out.

Life is funny sometimes. Not that haha funny but more like a curve ball you just can't hit. There were no rotters walking around when I reached the road. I walked that same stretch back toward the shopping district, saw the overpass in the distance. The closer I got, the tighter my chest became. The anxiety of meeting death head on scared me as much as dying itself.

The first of the dead that appeared made my skin prickle. I moved between two cars, ducked down, and hurried around it. At the overpass, I looked down at my truck. Bottled water lay on the ground, and the dryness of my mouth begged me to run down and get some, but I didn't. Instead, I eyed a drug store about a block or so away. I hurried around the burned bodies and the car with the man's head splattered against the windshield.

After crossing the overpass, I realized that I had made a mistake. They were there, so many of them wandering aimlessly about. I didn't have near enough bullets to take them all out. I detoured into a parking lot where several cars sat and then hurried along the edge of a building, checking the corners when I had to step away and out into the open. At the drug store, I stepped over a body in the doorway. Flies hummed about it, no doubt getting their daily fill of rotting flesh and laying their billions of eggs.

I eased into the door, my heart hammering. A little girl leaned against the counter, her hair dirty and matted. I eased down a side aisle, almost frantic with panic. If I shot her, the others were sure to hear.

The pharmacy sat at the back of the store. Several corpses lay back there. I went through the half door, made sure it closed behind me. It would take a little work for the girl to get it open, and with the upper half clear, I could see her if she heard me and managed to make it back there.

In the pharmacy, I nudged the bodies. Someone had given them each a bullet to the head. I rummaged around in the semi-dark area. Though a lot of the drugs had been looted, there were still several bottles of good painkillers and cold medicines. Even better was the large bottle of 500 mg Amoxicillin in pill form. I set my pack on the floor, unzipped the front pouch. The Amoxicillin and painkillers went in along with the prescription cold syrups.

I realized as I stashed the drugs away that I wasn't ready to die. I was getting meds to try and fight off the sickness. I didn't think it would work, but I had to try, right? I needed to live. What if Bobby and Jeanette were still out there? What if they were looking for me? It had been extremely foolish of me to leave the safety of the house, but maybe…maybe if I could make it back with the meds, things might be okay. And even if I died, at least I would have Humphrey there to comfort me.

The sneeze was as sudden as the longing for my little stuffed traveling partner was. Snot and phlegm shot out of my mouth and nose. I inhaled deeply, and several more sneezes came. I tried to stifle them, but still, there was a noise with each sneeze. After the fit subsided, I heard the shuffling feet from outside the pharmacy door. I scanned the back part of the area for anything that could keep me from firing either of my guns. Sure, I could have used old Ox's butt again, but swinging the shotgun with the arm as stiff as it was didn't seem feasible.

What I found was a broom. That's all. It was an old wooden variety, the bristles well worn. I grabbed it and broke the broom head off on one of the counters. It made a loud crack that seemed to echo in the room. By the time I looked up, the little girl stood in front of the half door. She groaned or growled or mumbled. I don't know, but she sounded angry.

"Hey there, little girl," I said. She looked to be eight, maybe nine. I thought of Humphrey, of the voice I heard the day before. That girl had sounded about the same age as the one in front of me.

She growled and bumped against the door hard. She reached a stiff arm out that seemed to creak when she moved it.

Deep breaths wheezed in my chest, and that tickle came back in my nose. I stepped forward, the broom handle raised over my head. My scratchy throat only got worse as I swallowed hard.

The girl tried to break through the door, the one arm outstretched with blood crusted under the nails. Her eyes were cataract white and seemed to glow in the gray of the building.

"I'm sorry." I swung the handle down on her head as hard as I could. She stumbled back. If she had been alive, it would have dazed her and knocked her to the ground. She was far from alive, and though it seemed to daze her, she stumbled forward, a howl in her throat and black blood oozing down the center of her forehead. Again, I swung the handle, knocking her back. Then I opened the half door before she could step forward again.

I was vaguely aware of the pain in my shoulder but not enough to lessen the force of the blows. The next swing was like a baseball bat, coming across and catching her in the side of the head. She toppled to the floor. I brought a boot down on her throat. Still, her jaws chomped at me. A moment later, the jagged end of the broomstick jutted from one eye socket, and she moved no more.

"I'm so sorry," I repeated.

My breaths came in wheezing gasps, and my eyes itched. A sneeze came, and snot bubbled from my nose. I wiped it on the shirt, went back to the pharmacy, and grabbed my pack and old Ox. I scrounged about a little more back there, found a shoulder brace and arm sling among the braces and crutches. I pulled it from the packaging and tucked it in the center pouch of the bag.

Out in the store, I pilfered the few remaining water bottles. There were some chips and, holy cow, a can of Beanie Weenies. I drank down one full bottle of water, let the coolness of it relieve the scratch in my throat and quench my thirst.

I caught a glimpse of the dead girl, and my heart began to ache not only for her but for my little stuffed buddy and the girl in my head that owned her. That guilt resurfaced, and I thought of Bobby. Would I have left Bobby alone in an unfamiliar house with the dead walking around outside while I went off to die? No. Never. But I had left Humphrey, my traveling companion those few weeks. I hated myself. In my mind, I could hear her—because that's what she was, a girl—crying. I could feel her fear as the dead surrounded the house and threatened to bust down the door. And I hadn't bothered locking up, so getting in wouldn't be all that hard for a rotter that managed to make it up the steps.

Before leaving the pharmacy, I checked behind the counters. There had to be—and there was—a weapon. It was nothing more than a steel bar that someone had placed back there, something you would use for leverage on a lug wrench, but it was sturdy and hard and would probably only take one shot to take out any of the dead if they got too close.

As I had before, I hugged close to the buildings on the way out. In the parking lot, blocking my way to the road, stood an emaciated rotter. Skin hung off his body as if he had been a huge man at one time and had lost a full person's worth of weight. His head was bald, and he held that blue/gray tint of a person who had asphyxiated. His jaw hung slack, and the steps he took were nothing more than toe drags along the ground. There were deep grooves along his face where he had been scratched. I ran toward him, my knee and ankle no longer hurting like they did a day earlier, my pack heavy on my shoulders.

His skull ruptured with a loud *CRACK*, and he collapsed to the ground. Very little blood spilled from the gash in his head. Later on, I would think about that slight bit of sludge that leaked from the wound and wonder how long he had been dead. I would wonder about the longevity of the deads'

83

afterlife and if all the living had to do was wait them out until they finally rotted away.

That was a subject to think about for later, and if there was going to be a later, I had to hurry. The mass of dead seemed to have grown since going into the pharmacy. How many were there now? Forty? Fifty? A hundred? I always thought one was one too many. In this case, I faced a horde of shambling, stumbling zombies and if they... The good thing about being alive during this...this...apocalypse is you could run a lot faster than they could. Even on a bum leg. Many of them turned to me, their groans loud. I could hear the hunger in them. So many dead voices all at once. It was like cattle being led out to the pasture. It was as if they knew a meal stood before them, and they wanted it. And they were still pretty fast.

I ran, and I didn't break the one rule you always see getting broke in horror movies: looking back. No, I ran straight ahead, passed a car where a woman reached out for me. Her head cocked to one side when I hit her. She slumped against the car. I didn't wait to see if she fell or if she was dead. At the road, I darted across the overpass.

Being sick didn't help me though. My breaths came in sharp bursts and sounded like weak whistles in my chest. I reached the long, dirt drive and turned. That's when I looked back. I had thought there were maybe a hundred of the dead behind me. I thought wrong. They seemed to come from everywhere, as if someone rang the dinner bell and I was the main course. And unlike me, they weren't slowing down.

I ran up the road and wished I were young again. In the yard, I saw a rotter in all its glory come from around the corner of the house. She was an older lady, her hair somewhat blue and gray and matted, not one tooth in her mouth. Blood caked along her chin and the front of her moomoo. I didn't bother with the steel bar. The bullet split her skull, and she crumpled.

I took the steps two by two and reached the door. For a moment, I thought the handle wouldn't work, and at first, it didn't. Then I realized I turned it the wrong way. Looking back, I could see them on the road. Some of them had already reached the dirt driveway.

The door came open, and I hurried inside. I slammed it, locked the knob, and dropped my pack to the floor. I ran to the couch, pushed it in front of the door.

Then I grabbed Humphrey...

You came back, she said. Always a she. Never, ever a he.

"Yes, I came back. I told you I would."

I thought you were lying.

Tears touched the corners of my eyes, and I pulled the bear from my chest. "I was."

She said nothing.

"But I came back. And I promise, I'll never leave you behind again."

It was all in my head, but Humphrey felt warm. Or maybe it was me. A fever had taken hold by then, and the weakness of being sick settled into my muscles and bones, and I could feel the rattle of death in my chest.

The thump on the steps outside brought me from the embrace of a stuffed animal. I looked to the door and hoped it would hold against the horde outside. I grabbed the pack and the shotgun, and Humphrey and took them up the stairs. I ran back and moved the coffee table and a couple of nice chairs in front of the stairwell, even pulling them up the first couple of steps for good measure.

At the top of the steps, I looked around, saw nothing I could use to barricade that portion of the floor.

I'm scared, Humphrey said in her small voice.

"Me too."

In the boy's room, I closed the door and set Humphrey on the bed. The dresser went back in front of the door, and I moved the stuff from off the end table next to the bed. My guns—I only had three of them; the others lay near my truck off the ramp heading out of town—went onto it, loaded and ready. I cracked Ox open. Two shells. Maybe one of them would be for me.

We sat and waited. In the meantime, I took an antibiotic and a pain reliever and then pulled the sling and brace from my pack. I slid the shirt off and read the instructions on how to use the brace then slid it up my arm, put the flap over my shoulder, and put the Velcro ends together. The next part went around my chest, where I again connected two Velcro ends, holding my shoulder in place. The pressure of the brace relieved some of the pain and kept my arm from sagging.

With the shirt back on, one sleeve with no arm in it, I pulled a chair to the window. Part of the roof extended out from there. After a moment, I realized that it wasn't a roof but more of a patio area, a means of escape if I needed it. I longed for a rifle as I watched the dead approach the house.

I sat quietly, watching from that window, all the way up to when the sun began to go down. Some of the dead had turned course and went back up the road. Others stood idly, as if they slept on their feet. I went to the bed, lay down beside

Humphrey. My head was in a daze, and the room spun. I reached for a pistol and set it on my chest.

What's that for? Humphrey asked in her soft child's voice.

"Just in case," I said but didn't tell her in case of what.

I closed my eyes and prepared to die...

Ten Weeks (?) After It All Stared, Give or Take a Few Days

I never liked taking medicine. Waiting out a cold or sweating out a fever seemed natural to me. Drugs didn't. They were dangerous things, addictive things. That never stopped Jeanette from being on me to take my meds when I really needed to. It was just one of the many things she was good about.

As I lay dying in some kid's bed in some other family's house, I heard her talking to me, telling me, "Take your meds, Hank."

I sat up each time, even as the weight of the sickness pushed hard on my chest and the snot grew thicker in my nasal cavities, and even as I spat up chunky bits of yellow crap and the fever sent me to alternating hot flashes and cold spells. I took the meds. There always seemed to be water nearby, and I didn't seem to fumble with the caps to the pill bottles. It was like she was there with me in that house, trying to keep me alive.

My breath rattled in my chest and whistled from my mouth. The pain in my head kept me from moving too much. My eyes constantly watered, and I don't ever recall getting up to go to the bathroom.

"Take your medicine, Hank."

I opened my eyes, and there she stood, a picture of beauty, an air about her that glowed even in the darkness of the room. She held the pills out to me, the water bottle in the other hand. She smiled and leaned down, gave me a kiss with her angelic lips.

"You can't die, Hank," she said.

"Nothing I can do about it," I said—I think.

Her hands were warm on my face, soft and smooth, and I relished the way they felt. "You have to live, Sweetheart," she said. "Bobby needs you. He can't lose us both."

Those words woke me with a start but not before she started to change. My eyes snapped open, and I stared at the ceiling above me. The room was gray, not dark. The sun cast its rays through opened blinds. I turned my head to one side. The pill bottles sat on the end table, the water bottles nearly empty. Humphrey sat on the pillow next to me, her eyes glassy but somehow holding life in them.

The guns were not on the end table, and the one I had been holding was not on the bed. They all sat on the dresser across the room.

"Humphrey," I said, my voice scratchy and sounding nothing like it normally did.

She didn't respond, but I think I saw her pink, sewn-on mouth stretch into a wider smile.

"I'm still alive," I said. "I didn't die. I didn't become..."

And what were the words of my dream? Was that what it was? A dream? They came back to me. Jeanette holding my face in her soft, warm hands and telling me, *Bobby needs you. He can't lose us both.*

I sat up. Muscles and bones creaked and popped, and my entire body felt incredibly weak. How long had I been out of it? I didn't know, but the dream came back. Something was wrong with it. She spoke those words and then...then she changed. Her beautiful, blond hair became brittle; her skin went from white to gray, and her face—her always beautiful face—changed. Her lips cracked, her eyes faded to milky white orbs that sunk back into her skull, and there was blood on her face and she had…

A fear so sudden came over me, and I wanted to bolt from that house and run to Greenville if I had to. Strong and painful and real. I stood but fell down before I could gain my legs.

"No," I said over and over as I struggled to stand, made it up, and then paced the floor slowly, letting my legs adjust to moving again. With my body weak, I wouldn't be able to leave that day. I knew that, but I didn't care. I had to get out of there.

At the window, I looked down at the yard, the street beyond it. The beating of my heart stopped momentarily. What had been a couple dozen rotters when I first arrived at that house was now a swarm of them. They shuffled about aimlessly, but it was clear to me that they knew I was there.

"We're trapped," I said.

After watching them for several minutes, I turned back to Humphrey. My boots lay on the floor, my socks tucked into them. The guns lay on the dresser with nowhere near enough ammo to get me out of there in one piece.

"We're going to have to make a break for it, Humphrey."

She said nothing.

I sat down on the bed, slipped the socks and boots on, then grabbed one of the guns from the dresser—a nine millimeter with a full clip. I moved the dresser from in front of the door as quietly as possible, but it still sounded too loud in my ears as it scraped across the floor.

With the gun out in front of me, I opened the door. Nothing awaited me. Down the hall, I walked until I reached the bathroom. I relieved my bladder and turned to leave. The

90

bathtub was clean, and there was a bar of soap on a small dish in the corner of it.

There was a small closet next to the entrance. I opened it. Two shelves of neatly folded towels sat there. Above them was a shelf that held washcloths. I took a towel and washcloth and looked at the bathtub. Surely there would be little water, if any, still left in the pipes, but it was worth a try.

I turned one knob. There was a hollow clunk from deep in one of the pipes. A dribble of brownish water fell from the faucet just before it seemed to spit, cough, and clear its proverbial throat. Then a stream of wonderfully clear water spilled from it. It was cool, but I didn't care—it had been so long since I had a bath, since I smelled like something other than a sweating mass of flesh. I was quick about getting my clothes off, and then, just for peace of mind, I locked the bathroom door.

The soap was Irish Spring. I took in its heady aroma. I would love to say I took a long bath, that I leaned back and let the water fill the tub, that I closed my eyes and just enjoyed the moment. But I can't say that. No, there wouldn't be enough water for that, and I knew it. I was quick about washing, rinsing off the suds, and then getting out of the tub before the water completely ran out. I didn't imagine the water would last long, and I was right—just as I went to shut it off, the steady stream lessoned until it was nothing more than just drops dripping into the tub.

Being clean was one thing—if the dead managed to get me, at least their meal wouldn't taste so bad—but what I wanted was to get out of that bathroom, check the rest of the house for any means of escape.

I toweled off and got dressed, including putting the shoulder harness back in place. I went back to what was clearly the parents' room and pulled out another pair of jeans and a shirt and even a pair of underwear. Everything was loose, but I used a belt to hold the pants up and then dug around for some clean socks. Leaving the bedroom, I held the gun out in front of me, ready to take the head off of anyone, dead or alive, that could have been there. Down the hall, I stopped at the top of the steps. The door was closed; the couch still sat in front of it. The chairs and coffee table still lay cluttered at the bottom of the stairs.

Back up the hall and in the young boy's bedroom, I gathered what little gear I had left. There were still some pain meds and antibiotics. I took an Amoxicillin and followed it with two painkillers. My shoulder still hurt but nothing like before. The swelling had gone down, but still, I knew it had been hurt every time I moved.

I put as much in the pack as I could then went to the baseball bat rack on the wall. There were a few good, wooden Louisville Sluggers, but I opted for a thirty-eight-ounce aluminum bat, the barrel nothing more than a lean, straight pipe. I could swing a bat, I thought, better than I could swing old Ox. It dawned on me that an eight-year-old boy probably couldn't swing a bat that heavy all that well, but it had been in the rack with others, a collection maybe. I nodded. Definitely a boy's collection, and one day, if the world hadn't died, the kid would have been able to swing that bat and probably swing it well.

Before leaving the room, I placed Humphrey in the pack, this time shoving her a little further down and tucking her arms into the bag before zipping up.

Why so tight? she asked.

"I don't want you to fall out. I'm probably going to have to run, and I'm going to need my hands to shoot or..." I nodded to the bat on the bed. "Or play ball."

We're leaving?

"That's the plan."

I like it here.

I took a hard look at Humphrey. In another time, I might have liked it there as well. It was spacious. The yard was huge. I bet it even had a basement or an attached garage.

Garage?

I hadn't thought of that before.

If there was a garage, there might be a car, and if there was a car, I might have a better chance of getting out.

The backpack went over my shoulders. I winced a little when I first slid it on, especially as I pushed it over the bad arm. But the brace alleviated most of the pain even as it jostled about. There was no using Ox today and maybe not for a while. I still had never fired her but was certain if I had to right then, I would probably end up dying from getting knocked off balance by the recoil. I made sure the safety was on and slipped Pop's shotgun through the straps of the backpack. For the first time, I thought I needed a gun tote for Ox. Maybe one day, I would find one.

With one pistol in hand, one in the pack, one tucked into my waistband, and the bat in the other hand, I went back to the staircase and made my way down. I tried to be quiet as I moved one of the chairs and the coffee table, but I had placed them so precariously on the steps that moving one item caused the others to topple. The chair made a loud *CLACK* when it hit the hardwood floor.

"Crap."

I eased down the steps further and walked through the house, nerves on edge, eyes and mouth dry. If any of the rotters heard the chair fall, they would converge on the noise, and sticking around much longer wouldn't be an option. Other than the front door, there were no other doors in that direction. That left the kitchen area.

Past the front door, I stopped. Something thumped outside. Another thump followed. Then another and another.

They had heard the chair fall, and they knew where I was. I moved a little faster, trying to stay as quiet as I could. In the kitchen, I heard the moans of those just beyond the backdoor. It didn't look to be as sturdy as the front, and it was nearly ground level, but the windows were covered, and there were several two by fours nailed at the entrance so nothing could get in.

A second door sat off the kitchen where I walked in. It could have been a pantry, and if so, at least I would have a little food if I made it out of there. I opened it slowly, recalling what happened to Lee when he died. A careless moment where he hurried instead of took his time.

The door opened with a creak that may as well have been a scream. It wasn't a pantry at all but stairs that led down into the garage. I took a step down, then another, listening as I did so and wishing I had one of my lights from the truck. I heard only the beating of my heart heavy in my ears.

Another step down and my eyes began to adjust. Three more steps and the garage became less black and more gray. Objects took shape. To my right was a workbench and several tool boxes. Other tools hung on pegboards: shovels, rakes, hoes, hammers, saws. To my left were what looked like boxes and cans and other stuff—a storage area, I guessed. But what sat in front of me were the most beautiful things I had ever seen up to that point. Two vehicles: an SUV and a van.

"Yes."

I didn't go for the cars right away. There were tools to be taken, and if I could load them in one of the vehicles, I would. I hurried over to the workbench, rummaged around, letting my hands feel for objects that I could use. Near one of the toolboxes, I struck gold. My fingers came across the almost square object, found the handle. Near that handle was a button. My thumb did what it does naturally and pressed the little button.

The flashlight came to life.

"Yes."

That joy was short-lived. From up the steps, I heard the banging on the back door. A window broke, and glass hit the floor. Sure, there were boards in place, but that gave me no comfort at all. I went back up the seven steps and closed the garage door. Before doing so, I saw the glass on the floor and a hand sticking through the broken window. There was no lock, so the need to hurry became real.

I went back to the workbench, grabbed a screwdriver from one of the toolboxes and a hammer from one of the pegs. If I needed to break into one of the cars and hotwire it, I would need tools—at least the screwdriver.

The van looked newer than the SUV and probably got better gas mileage, but the other car looked more rugged, as if it could take running into something—like a walking corpse—and not get damaged too much. I went to the SUV, tried the driver's side door. It opened, and the body slumped from the seat.

"Crap!"

Startled, I almost shot the guy. There was no need to do that. There was already a bullet in his head. Blood and brains matted against the ceiling, and the gun sat on his lap where it fell after the deed was done. I shone the flashlight in the vehicle. My heart sank. There were five of them, all strapped in as if they were heading on a trip.

"Are we going to Disney World, Daddy?"

"Yes, Sweet Pea."

They were going somewhere, but Disney World wasn't it. The two older kids lay slumped in their seats. The woman in the passenger's side was leaning on the door, her window shattered. But it was the other child—the one strapped in the car seat between the older two—that hurt my heart the most. A baby—probably not even six months old.

I closed my eyes. The SUV was a mausoleum, their gravesite. I wouldn't be taking it. But I took the gun—every bullet mattered.

I shone the flashlight on the steering column, smiled when I saw the keys dangling there. Surely, there would be a key to the van on it.

I was right, but before I opened the van's door, I turned the flashlight on it. There were no dead bodies inside. I unlocked the front door and put the key in the ignition. After a moment of uncertainty and trying to get the motor to roll over, the engine purred.

Are we going to be safe? Humphrey asked.

"We're getting there, Sweetheart," I said and pulled Ox from its place. I set it between the two bucket seats up front. With Humphrey pulled free, the pack went to the floorboard in the driver's seat. Humphrey went into the passenger's seat.

96

"Stay here."

Okay.

I didn't know how much time I had; the dead outside continued to beat on the door, and I imagined the weight of their bodies forcing the nails in the two by fours to work out of the wall or door jamb. Eventually, they would get inside.

The back hatch of the van came up with ease. I searched the garage, grabbed the shovels off the pegs. A hoe as well. Some of the toolboxes were too big to carry, but others would fit in the back of the van nicely. I picked up what I could, and what I couldn't, I grabbed random tools out of. I took a plastic container that held a chainsaw in it. Who knew if I would ever need one of those?

Before getting in the van, I went back to the SUV. I hated doing it and still found it hard to believe that someone could kill their entire family, not give them a chance of surviving. I think they would have been okay for a while. At least until some stranger with a teddy bear ended up on their front porch bringing the dead along with him. I couldn't imagine doing the same to my boy and wife. It was hard enough putting Lee down after he rose again, but to actually kill them to keep them from turning into the dead? I couldn't fathom it.

I pulled the back latch, freeing the tailgate. It was as I hoped. Cases of water, dried foods, and blankets were all stashed back there. Several flashlights and boxes with who knew what in them. With no real time to sort it out, I transferred the contents from one vehicle to the next then closed the SUV's door.

From the upstairs came a loud *CRACK*. Not just one but several. Then came what I thought was the back door slamming against the wall. Another window broke, and more glass fell to the floor.

Hurry, Humphrey cried. I could almost see her glass eyes filling with tears.

"I'm coming."

I closed the back hatch of the van and got in the driver's seat. For good measure, I buckled Humphrey in and did the same for myself. I shifted the vehicle into drive and looked over at the little bear.

"Hang on, kiddo. This could be a little scary."

Easing off the brake, I let the car roll forward. There was no electricity, so we were going to have to go through the garage door but not like they did in the movies. No, we were going to go through slow, push the garage door out and up if we could.

The front of the van hit the door with a little more force than I wanted it to. The garage door lifted up a little. I bit down hard on my lip, my hands gripping tight to the steering wheel. A little gas and the van lurched forward. The door protested, but it went up.

Metal scraped on metal, and if I could hear it, so could they. By the time the front end of the van was free of the door, the dead were swarming. There were so many of them. Where did they all come from? Were they wandering from Charleston and Mt. Pleasant? If they were, then were they migrating in search of food? I didn't find that thought to be a good thing.

So many bodies crushed against the van, their hands beating on the sides of the vehicle, on the glass, reaching for door handles. Through all the noise, I could hear Humphrey whimpering like a sick puppy.

"Close your eyes," I said. "Close them, and keep them closed."

I mashed the gas harder, rolling over the ones in front of us. The van jostled from side to side as the bodies broke and crumbled beneath the tires. The driver's side mirror came off, and the antenna snapped free as the dead continued to grope for anything they could get hold of.

Again, I gave it some gas, this time smashing into more of the dead. They either bounced off the front of the van or disappeared beneath it. Sweat formed on my brow, and my knuckles must have been white. My muscles were tense, and the cacophony of sounds that came from outside the van was loud even with the windows all the way up.

Another rev of the engine and we lurched forward and out of the garage. I turned the van toward the road. I hadn't realized in either of my journeys to that house that the driveway wound around to the back and that if I were going to reach the road, I would have to plow through the horde before me.

There were souls in the dead, people jailed in the husks that were once their bodies. I hated hitting them, running them over. If I didn't kill them, then they would suffer the pain of broken bones and smashed insides, but I didn't have a choice. I had to get out of there, and there was no chance I could do so if I took the time to try and keep from running any of them over.

Body after body fell away as I pressed the gas harder, picking up speed and making my way up the dirt road toward the black top that would lead me out of there. We hit the street faster than I intended and almost tipped over in the process.

What took an eternity by foot took only half a minute by vehicle. Sometimes, we forget things like distances and traveling times and how walking and running were far different than speeding along in a car. As I raced up the road, leaving most of the dead behind me, I remembered the difference.

I hit the interstate entrance ramp and slowed before coming to a complete stop near my old pickup. I had little time. Surely, all the rotters weren't at that house. Some of them lingered. I had passed a few of them on the way.

What are you doing? Humphrey yelled—yes, she yelled at me.

"Guns and gas. I'll be right back."

In another time and another place, "I'll be right back," usually meant just that. But in this world, that same statement might be the last thing you hear from someone. Sure, we think we can make it to and from somewhere, but things aren't the same as they used to be. There's no store down on the corner where you know the owner and you can get a cold soda and a bag of chips and a tank of gas and be on your merry way. No, a simple ten-foot run from one place to another could get you killed.

I took a deep breath to calm my nerves, hopped out of the van, and ran the short distance to my truck. The guns were still there. So was the water and the gas tanks—thankfully, I had capped those. I grabbed as many of the weapons as I could, ran back, and slung open the side door. The gas came next. A couple of cans were lost causes, but I managed to secure six of them before the dead started down the hill.

Come on, Humphrey yelled.

I pulled out my pistol, took aim, and split the center of the first one's head. It collapsed, and the one behind it tripped over its body and fell as well. The water came next. By then, there were a handful of corpses stumbling down the hill and one coming from up the road. I took aim at an older woman with tangled, gray hair. She dropped to the ground.

Hurry!

I could hear the panic in Humphrey's voice. I could *feel* it in my chest. The food remained, and I had none in the van. I hurried to grab busted cartons from off the ground and ran back to the van. I didn't care if I dented the cans or damaged the inside of the vehicle. I tossed what food I could grab in and slid the door closed.

Rounding the van, I stopped. There were three of the dead near the driver's door. I put a bullet in the first one's head, took aim, and pulled the trigger only to hear *CLICK*. It wasn't my pistol. It was the one belonging to the man whose house I just came from.

There was no time to reach for the other pistol. I swung the gun down as hard as I could on the forehead of the corpse closest to me. Its skull gave a resounding pop, and he dropped.

It was the other one…the other one that almost got me. He was a thin, frail-looking person with drooping eyes, his mouth full of yellowed teeth and his bottom lip completely missing. His hands managed to reach my shirt, and his fingers tried to grip the cloth, to pull me toward him.

Fear—true, unadulterated fear—is like a jolt of electricity. There have been times since all this began that I have felt that fear, but on this day, at that moment, I had felt nothing like it. I saw my death in front of me again, this time not by a sickness but by the hands of a rotter. The world slowed again. It grayed, and the sounds of the dead moaning and my heartbeat and Humphrey's—yes, even when life was so precariously close to ending horribly, I heard a stuffed child's toy's voice—screams became muffled remnants. The adrenaline and drive to survive kicked in. I pushed him with both hands. It was all I could think to do. The gun came out from my waistband, and I put a bullet in his head.

The world came back in real speed, the colors no longer bled out. I turned, pulled the trigger twice, taking down the two women closest to me. I slammed the side door closed. Around the vehicle I went, squeezing off one more shot before getting in. I slammed the door, locked it, and shifted into drive. Dirt and pebbles from the side of the road shot up from the right back tire, and the vehicle swerved.

It was a few miles before I stopped again, not bothering to pull off the road. Something had been humming in my brain since rushing to get back into the van, a sound that seemed to follow us as we fled Summerville.

As I sat in the middle of I-26 heading away from Charleston, it dawned on me. The sound was someone crying. I looked at Humphrey, who just looked ahead, her eyes staring at the dashboard.

She wasn't crying. Not that I could hear.

No, it wasn't the stuffed teddy bear weeping at all. It was me…

Eleven Weeks After It All Started...

It was a sunny morning. The trees were a green so lush it looked like they could have been computer generated. But they weren't. They circled the open field I parked in the night before. I had made my way to the little field in Columbia the previous day.

I was still tired.

I still hurt. The pills only dulled the pain. Things were a little fuzzy in my head, as if everything was falling apart in my mind, just as it had in the world.

But I was alive, and the need to press on was stronger than ever before. I guess almost dying will do that to a person — give them a stronger resolve. In this world we live in now, almost dying could be considered an everyday occurrence. Searching for food, gas, a safe place to stay for a night or two — or a couple weeks — are now the ways of survival. Gone are the days of reaching into the refrigerator for a beer or going to McDonald's for one of their I-can't-believe-it's-not-soybean cheeseburgers or finding a hotel where they still leave a light on for you.

There are no luxuries. Only live or die, and if you die, you better hope it's because of a bullet to the head and not from being bitten by something resembling a person but not quite.

That field was a familiar place, and nothing feels more like home these days than a little familiarity.

It sat off Interstate 20. I had detoured from 26 just to find some rest. I crossed over I-20 in Columbia and headed there. It sat behind a huge church, and at the time the world died, it was being turned into a sports complex. The entrance was a dirt and rock path with a mobile home to the right and a playground and eating area to the left.

I thought about the mobile home, about possibly finding a bed to sleep in, but decided against it. If I wanted, I could sleep in the back of the snazzy new van I had. There was plenty of space to lie down once I moved the supplies around or took out that middle seat. Maybe one of these days, I'll find me a small mattress to put down in there—a luxury I longed for.

I drove down the dirt road and around the fence that separated it from the playground. The parking area was nothing more than dirt and grass, and there were a couple porta-potties sitting side by side. The field was lavishly green.

I parked in the center of it and got out. All around the field, the trees stood like ancient sentries over a holy land. They formed a U shape with the church directly behind the fields and an apartment complex in the opposite corner. The playground and exits sat up the hill I had come from. And along that hill just beyond the fields were steps that led up to the playground.

How many times had Bobby run up those steps after a game, whooping and hollering and having a blast?

I got out of the truck and took a deep breath. The world smelled clean. There was no smoke, no pollution, and nothing even close to the scent of decay. Just the crisp smell of nature. And maybe that's what this was. Nature doing what nature does and giving herself a bath to clean things up. Maybe she was spring-cleaning by getting rid of humans. I don't know, but I could have stood there the remainder of my life and been content if I didn't have a family to find.

There wasn't a rotter in sight.

Before the sunset, I had stood in the middle of Field 2. Bobby played flag football on that field when he was five. It was only a six-week season, but he disliked it from the first practice.

"I want to play baseball again, Daddy," he said before his second practice.

"Maybe in the spring, but for now, you said you wanted to play flag football, so you are."

"I don't like it."

"Too bad. If you start something, you finish it. You started this, so you're not quitting. Understand?"

He shook his head and cried all the way to practice that day.

I stood there, where he had played—begrudgingly—and I missed him terribly. My heart cracked, and my breath hitched. I thought about when I was sick, how I wanted to give up and put a bullet through the roof of my mouth and felt shame. What if he was still alive? What if he and his mom were in Table Rock waiting for me? My heart cracked a little more.

I could see him chasing the kid with the ball, trying to get that flag, his fingers extended but not quite able to reach it. And I think that's why he hated it so much. He wasn't quite able to run as fast as the other boys, or catch that football the way they could, or get that flag so easily. Unlike baseball, football didn't come easy to him. And he didn't like all the contact. More than a few times, he got knocked down, and he didn't care much for that. I reckon he got that from his mother.

That night, I dreamed of little dead boys chasing each other, but instead of flags, they were trying to grab the arm that one of the other dead boys carried. That boy was Bobby, and every few steps, he took another bite out of the flesh of what could only be another little boy's arm, never slowing so the other rotters could catch him.

And when morning came, I was tired.

I drove back up the small hill, stopped between the trailer and the playground. I don't know why I didn't look to the playground first, but I didn't. I went straight for the trailer. Grass was grown up around it, and there was a car parked on the side, an older model that had seen better days. Much like the rest of the world.

The steps were nothing more than a few cinderblocks stacked together. I tried the door. It was locked. I knocked softly and listened. I heard nothing, knocked again and waited. After hearing nothing again, I put my shoulder into the door. There was a jolt of pain in my arm, but it pushed in easy enough. I raised my pistol and stepped inside.

My heart hammered again, and my mouth became dry. My shoulder throbbed, and I thought of those pain pills sitting in the console of the van. I checked the first room. No rotters. Instead, there was a man sitting on the couch, one side of his head blown out and splattered against the wall beside him. I checked his gun — three bullets remained. I'm not ashamed to say I took it with me.

The kitchen held nothing other than a couple of butter knives and mostly spoiled food.

Down the hall were two bedrooms. The first one held two little girls lying in their beds, their heads covered by blankets, red patches bloomed like bloodied flowers. It became more and more clear to me that many parents couldn't handle the thought of one of their children turning into one of those monsters, and instead of trying to fight for their lives, they just ended them.

I looked around the room and found a box full of dolls. Next to the box was a basket of doll clothes. I think I smiled a little. I picked up the basket and made my way out of the room.

In the next room was a woman. Like the girls, there was a bloodied blanket covering her head. At that moment, I wondered just how hard it was for the man in that front room, or any of the fathers, to make a decision to kill instead of be killed. How bad did they feel before finally ending their own lives? They probably cried and maybe even had second thoughts about it but went through with it anyway. Why? In their eyes, there was no other way out.

I left the trailer with a box of baby doll clothes and one gun with three rounds in it. I closed the door behind me. I thought about all those houses in my hometown, the ones I had placed Xes on after searching them for any living people. There would be no X on this one.

I started for the van but stopped. The playground caught my eye. It wasn't the faded out slide or the rusted monkey bars and ladders. It was what sat beyond that: the eating area, completely covered. Several picnic tables sat beneath it. Sitting at one of those tables were two people.

I set the basket down and approached the play set. I crouched down and peeked over the side of the slide. I wiped my mouth with one hand and held my breath as I stood.

A boy and a girl, no older than their late teens, sat staring at one another. They were as dead as any other rotter I had encountered, but they didn't turn to look at me. They didn't get up and give chase. They didn't seem to smell me or hear me. They didn't seem to care. They only stared forward, like lovers do.

I cocked my gun, held my breath. If they stood to come after me, I would put them down.

I took one step forward then another.

The boy turned to me. His face was sunken in and gray/green. His hair was matted down as if he had crawled out of mud. But he didn't have any blood clinging to his face. As far as I could see, there was no blood on his clothes at all. The girl lifted her head. Her eyes were maybe green at one time, and her hair had been red. Now, it was a dirty rust color. Like the boy, there was no blood on her face or her blouse.

I took aim with the pistol.

One move.

One twitch to stand and I would drop them where they sat.

The boy turned back to the girl. The girl turned back to the boy. Here I stood, a potential fresh meal, and neither of them made to stand and come after me. They only stared at each other...like lovers.

I gave a nod, lowered the pistol, and took the few steps backward toward the basket of doll clothes. I picked it up, made my way to the van, and slid the side door open. I set the basket inside and went around to the driver's side.

Inside the van, I sat there and watched the two teens. They hadn't budged since I first saw them. Somehow, they controlled their hunger, their impulse for flesh, that carnal part of their mind that said humans were food, and it didn't matter that they were living creatures.

We pulled away and onto the dirt road, leaving the lovers behind. Maybe one day, they would lose the battle with their decaying minds, but not then. On that day, they were lovers who only had eyes for each other. And who was I to take that away from them?

"Hey Humphrey," I said.

Yes?

"I got you something."

What? She sounded excited—the first time I heard excitement in her voice since finding her.

"New clothes."

She didn't say anything, but I think she smiled.

Eleven Weeks and Three Days After It All Started...

I used to feel sorry for them. You know, the dead.
When the outbreaks started and people began to die and then get back up, everyone was scared. Panic filled the streets and hearts of most people.

Not Pop.

No, Pop told me the dead—whether they were truly dead or shambling around looking for someone to bite down on—deserved to be treated with respect once they were finally ushered from this world. It was Pop who told us that we should bury them. It was only right. And that's what we did until it was just me. Even then, I did it for a while longer.

Pop's gone.

Leland's gone.

Davey Blaylock's gone.

The four of us had set out to rid our little town of the undead. When all was said and done, there had been more dead than alive, and I was all that was left of our quartet.

And I had buried a whole town, my dad, and my oldest brother; and my best friend had sacrificed himself for me.

I felt bad for them. I felt sorry for them.

Until I reached Table Rock.

The family cabin sat just outside the state park—maybe a mile or so away—and I had to drive through a world gone to hell from my hometown to Summerville, to Columbia, and through Greenville. You never get used to seeing the carnage, the death everywhere.

So few people were left alive.

It was no different in Table Rock.

There's a stretch of road that leads to the cabin. Trees line either side of it. For a good portion of that road, there is a ditch along one side. Most folks never knew it was there. They just saw a grass-covered embankment and tried to keep themselves on the road.

When we were kids, Davey and Leland and I sometimes stole one of our mother's empty purses—always an empty purse, never one with anything in it. It would have been Hell to pay if our moms had caught us with one of their good ones. We'd head out along that stretch of road.

The good thing about living out in the country is there are all sorts of things to get into. Tree climbing, skinny-dipping, hunting for all sorts of animals. On those Saturday mornings when we had nothing better to do, we would hunt down black snakes—the longer, the better—and put them in the empty purse we had stolen out of one of our mom's closets. Then we'd set the purse along the side of the road—just enough on the shoulder to be off the grass but not in the road itself.

Then we'd hide, either in the ditch or just inside the trees, and we would watch. The anticipation was the worst, but it was always funny when a car slowed down and someone got out and grabbed the purse. They would run back to the car and drive off as if nothing ever happened. But then they would stop. The car door would open, and the purse would get thrown out, sometimes still open, and the snake would fly through the air.

We used to entertain ourselves for hours doing this.

As I made my way to the family cabin, I saw the dead lying in the ditch—the equivalent of those black snakes about to strike—or stumbling about trying to get up the embankment but not quite able to. Only one of them came close enough to my vehicle that I wished I still had my old, familiar truck. Swiping the dead would have done little damage to the front end of it. I can't say as much for the van.

I reached the dirt road that led up to the cabin a half mile away. It was bumpy, and a rooster tail of dirt kicked out behind the van.

Are we almost there? Humphrey asked.

"Yes."

Is this where your wife and child are?

"I hope so."

It was true. I hoped they were there and safe, but the road in gave me little hope. Nearing the cabin, I saw more and more of the dead. There had been a struggle here, and I didn't know how anyone could have survived with as many dead as there were lying about. I went around some of them that were in the road, ran over others.

My palms were sweaty, and there were a mess of butterflies in my stomach.

I'll say it now: That was the last time I was ever scared of anything.

I pulled the van up to the cabin, circled around the dirt drive that went in an oval in front of the place. The windows were boarded up, but the front door was open. Lying in the doorway was a body. Lying on the porch and all around the house were many more. A dozen? Twenty? I don't know, but my heart sank.

I didn't have to go inside to know that more of the people I loved had died. The view from the van told me. I reckon I already knew.

...

"Humphrey, stay here."

Okay.

I got out, grabbed several guns, and tucked a couple into my waistband. An extra pocket full of rounds and a flashlight and I started for the cabin.

I was a kid again, and it was summer time. Leland and Rick and I were walking up to the house, dirty from a long day of playing in the woods. Jake tottered along behind us, the youngest of the five brothers—well, four when you consider Charles died before I was born in an accident that was never talked about around Momma. I could smell Momma's cooking and hear Pop chopping wood, which was a good sign. Pop chopping wood meant we would be coming to the cabin on weekends and maybe even during Christmas vacation.

At the porch, which was nothing more than one step up, I was an adult again, and Rick and Leland and Pop and Momma were still dead, and I had no clue about Jake or Jeanette and Bobby. I held my gun out and checked the safety. It was off. I stepped around several corpses, nudging them to make sure they wouldn't be getting up.

In the doorway, I stepped over one more.

The inside of the cabin was shaded in gray, but I could still see enough to know that a fight had been had there. I flicked on the flashlight and let the beam fall across the room. There were a handful of dead rotters on the floor, all of which were missing some part of their scalp. Chairs were overturned, and the old card table we used to play poker at when Momma and Pop weren't around was crumpled beneath the body of a dead man.

I didn't need to go any further inside to know no one was there, but I went anyway. What if they were in the back room and they didn't know help had arrived? Worse still, what if they were like every other dead person in the world right then? I hated the possibility of that, but I had to face the truth, the reality of the world, and the time I lived in.

Quietly, slowly, I made my way across the room, light in one hand, the other carrying one of my guns. There was no real hallway in the cabin, only a square area that branched off into a bathroom and three bedrooms. There was a back door off the last bedroom at the very back of the cabin.

The bathroom was empty.

The first bedroom—the one Leland and Rick slept in when we were kids—was empty. There were several splotches of blood on the wooden floor. A bad feeling crawled up beside me. In the bedroom across from the first one—where Jake and I slept—the linens on the bed were stained. My stomach flip-flopped, and my breath felt like it died in my chest.

The last bedroom held nothing but the furniture. If the sheets wouldn't have been ruffled, it would have looked like no one had been there in years.

I didn't try the back door.

Back the way I came, I stopped halfway across the front room. The front door had been open when I came in, but I hadn't realized how much so. It was shoved all the way against the wall. The door wasn't what stopped me. The white paper taped to it was.

I walked over, pulled the paper free of the door—there were four pieces in all, and the same hand didn't write them.

114

Back outside, I went to the van; any reading could be distracting, and I had figured out those four sheets of paper were important.

Everything okay? Humphrey asked.

"I don't know, little buddy."

The first letter was unmistakably Jeanette's handwriting. Part of me let out a relieved breath. They made it to Table Rock—at least I knew they had gotten that far. That relieved breath was gone entirely too fast.

Dear Hank,

Please take care of Bobby. You're all he has left. If you find this, please know I love you—I've always loved you. Be strong, Hank. Be strong for me. Be strong for Bobby. I'm so sorry I won't be here when you get here. Please, just know I love you.

Love,

Jeanette

Her writing had been shaky, and there were splotches of dried moisture where I believe her tears had fallen. The dream back in Summerville came back to me hard, like a punch to the face.

You can't die, Walker. Bobby needs you. He can't lose us both.

It hadn't been a dream after all. She had been there. Jeanette had found me and sent warning that I wouldn't find things the way I wanted to when I arrived there. Things were bad—real bad—and she had to tell me, had to help me get better one last time so I could carry on and find my son.

The tears tugged at my eyes, a couple of them spilling down my face as a pain so strong in my chest formed that I thought I would die right there in the van.

Humphrey asked her question again, *Is everything okay?*
I shook my head.
She said nothing else.
Jake wrote the second letter. His hand was unsteady as well.

Hey Brother,

I smiled. That's what he always called me. Brother. Jake never called me by my name. Most folks didn't. I was simply Walker to everyone except for my wife and Bobby.

If you're reading this, then you made it to the cabin. I'm sorry, Brother. Things got a little crazy, and there were too many of them.
We held them off as best we could, but a few of them got in. I guess you've done figured that part out, haven't you?
Only me and Bobby made it out without any marks. He's a brave boy, that son of yours. I don't know where he learned how to shoot, but if you taught him, you did a good job. Bobby did everything he could to protect Jeanette. I did too. But, Brother, there were so many of them, and when they got inside, I could only do so much.
I'm sorry. I'm really sorry.
Jeanette got bit by one of them, and Bobby unloaded his entire gun into it. She didn't cry. She refused to. She didn't want Bobby to see her all sad, and crying would have been the last thing he needed.
I just want you to know she didn't suffer. She went pretty quickly after being bit — less than a full day.
And she didn't turn either. I promised her I wouldn't let her, and I know you wouldn't have wanted her to be like that.
Bobby and me, we've moved on, heading toward Saluda — remember the old Armory out that way? A few soldiers came by,

and we're about to leave with them now. They said there's a safe haven in Saluda.

If you get this note, then please, come and find us in Saluda. Bobby needs you. I need you, Brother. I'm scared, and I ain't as tough and sure about things as you are.

I hope Leland and Davey and Pop are okay, and if they are with you, then thank the Lord for big favors.

I gotta go, Brother, but one more thing before I do. I buried Leland's family and Jeanette around the back of the Cabin. Jeanette wanted me to leave you something on her marker. I hope you get it.

I pray we meet again.

Jake.

Emotions are a horrible thing. A wide range of them struggled for dominance in my head and heart. Sadness. Anger. Pity. Fury. Rage. Urgency. But no fear.

I set the letter on the dash and got out of the van. The sun was still high at that moment, but it wouldn't be for much longer. If I was going to get out of there while it was still daylight, I needed to do so soon. But I needed to do something first.

My body shook as I walked back to the cabin. My eyes were blurred by tears. At that moment, a rotter could have come out of the woods, and I probably would have been a dead man. I gathered myself when the thought hit me, wiped my eyes, and pulled the gun from my waistband.

"No need getting killed now."

My voice startled me.

I looked around, saw no one, and then rounded the side of the house. Trees were only about twenty feet away—how could that have been safe? How could an area where the dead can't be seen long before they arrive be safe? I wanted to punch myself. I wanted to scream. I sent them there.

It'll be safer there, I had said.

I was wrong—there's no place safe in this world. What I had done was isolated my family from the rest of the world and sent them to their graves. The weight of that decision—a split-second thought that seemed rational at the time—bore down on my shoulders, threatening to crush me.

At the backside of the cabin were eight graves, dug by my baby brother. Each one held a handmade cross of tree branches held together by twine and nails. Jake had carved the names of each person onto their respective cross. I had done something similar for Leland and Pop. But this was Jake, this was the little kid I had been charged with to protect when we were kids.

And I had let him down.

I had let them all down.

I didn't need to see her name to know which grave belonged to Jeanette. The gold necklace I had given her on our first wedding anniversary had been hung on it, her wedding band with it.

My legs gave out, and I dropped to my knees. Everything I lived for was gone. My family. Jeanette. Probably Jake and Bobby as well. There's no way they made it out of there without something happening. Maybe their vehicle was along the side of the road on the way out and I had missed it. I made a mental note to go slow and see if I came across Jake's beat up pick-up.

I wept.

I don't know how long I sat there, face to the ground, tears flowing, snot bursting from my nose, my heart broken in a million tiny pieces. There would be no putting it back together.

Unless I made it to Saluda and Jake and Bobby were there and alive and...

The sound off to my right caught my attention. I whipped around and stood in one motion. My gun was up and pointing toward where the dead man stood. It could have been anyone's father or son...or brother. His salt and pepper hair was matted to his skull, and he looked like he had fallen down at some point, dirtying himself in the mud. One eye was missing, and the other one drooped. His mouth was slightly open. The few teeth in his mouth were gray and jagged. He shuffled from between the trees and out into the open before his foot caught on a root and sent him to the ground. I heard the sound of bone breaking, and he let out a noise that sounded like a muffled scream.

That muffled scream...I don't know what it was about it, but I felt my jaws clench, and everything I had ever felt came rushing back, just like with the Paul Marcum lookalike just outside Summerville. But, unlike then, I didn't lose my mind or get angry. My emotions were already spent.

I walked toward him. He struggled to move, to crawl toward me, but both of his arms were broken and bent at awkward angles. I pulled the pistol from my waistband and aimed then stopped. He was harmless at that point, but he could still move. I gave him a wide berth and came up behind him. With the heel of one boot, I brought my foot down on the back of one knee. There was another one of those loud cracks and that same muffled scream from the dead man. I did the same to the other leg, but it took three stomps before the leg snapped.

He groaned.

I just shook my head and left him there.

Back at the crosses, I was careful not to walk over the graves. At Jeanette's, I lifted up her necklace and ring. It was cold in my hand, and then it was cold against the back of my neck and on my chest after I put it on and slid it in my shirt. I touched the cross and let new tears come.

I cried again.

And I cried for a long while, my hand on her cross, my forehead on the hand. No rotters came around. No birds sang. The day started to wane, the sun fading and bringing with it night.

There were clouds coming in, gray and black and dreary, much like the way I felt inside. I sniffled several times, wiped my eyes with the backs of my hands. By the trees lay the dead man, groaning as if in the worst pain of his undead life. Maybe he was. I didn't care.

I bent down, kissed the cross, and whispered, "I'm sorry, Baby. I'm sorry I wasn't here to protect you. I'm sorry I let you down." A sob tore free, and I cried again, but after only a minute, I composed myself. "I love you, Jeanette. I hope you knew that. I'll always love you."

With that, I stood and walked by the dead man. He snapped his teeth at me, and I wheeled on him, bringing the toe of my boot across his jaw. It broke, the skin ripped, and the jaw hung off the side of his face. I kicked him again as if kicking a football. His jaw tore free and bounced along the ground. I knelt down, stared into its dead eyes.

"You're going to die here. You're going to wilt away until there's nothing left of you." I stood, teeth clenched. "I hope you suffer."

I left him there, went back to the front of the house, and flipped on the flashlight. I didn't think there would be supplies there, but I looked anyway. I was wrong. In the basement were plenty of supplies — things I thought Jake would take with him but had left behind. Water and canned goods and a lantern with oil. I hauled them up the steps and to the van, setting them on the ground and going back for more.

Before I left, I went through to the back bedroom. The beds were singles. I pulled the mattress off of one and carried it out the cabin and to the van. I thought pulling the back seats out would be hard. I was wrong. The back seats didn't even need to come out. They folded down and made a somewhat level back area. I slid the mattress in, shoved it as far to one side as it would go, leaving just a little room on the edge where the door was. I went back, grabbed a pillow and some sheets from the closet. The van wasn't huge, but it was big enough for the little mattress to be in the center of the van and then a space in the very back where the hatch was for supplies.

I loaded up, strapped the supplies in place, and got in the van.

Before leaving, I looked back. The place my family spent many summers in my childhood was no longer ours. It now belonged to the dead. I doubted I would ever be back.

I also doubted I would ever care if one of the dead hurt inside or not. They were the enemy, and as far as I was concerned, every one of them had killed my Jeanette.

Are you okay? Humphrey asked as we pulled away.

"No."
I don't think I ever will be again.

Eleven Weeks, Four Days, and Fourteen Hours After It All Started...

Silence.

The new world—or maybe it's still the old world—is all about silence. The quieter you are, the less chance you have of attracting attention from the dead.

"Let's play the quiet game," I said.

What's that? Humphrey asked.

"It's where we see how long we can go without talking. Whoever talks first loses. My brothers and I use to play it when we were kids. The loser got a punch in the arm from all of us."

Humphrey didn't respond. I guess she went ahead and started.

We drove along in silence, me with my memories and Humphrey with, I reckon, her thoughts. Images danced through my head, each one crying out, "remember me," or, "remember this," or "remember when."

Most of them centered on Jeanette.

I met her by accident. Literally. She bumped into my car in the parking lot when she was backing out of her spot. Instead of driving off like most people would have, she sat and waited for me to get back. When I arrived at my car, she got out of hers and approached me. She was a pretty girl with that blond hair, white skin, and blue eyes. My heart sped up. I didn't know what she was up to, but I thought it might be my lucky day.

"Hi," she said nervously. "I kind of bumped your car earlier." She pointed. I looked. "I'll be more than happy to exchange insurance with you and—"

"I don't see anything," I said.

"Right there." She touched a spot just over the top of my bumper. Maybe she had dinged it a little.

"That's nothing. Don't worry about it."

"Really, let me at least get it fixed. I'd feel better about it if—"

Again, I cut her off—not to be mean but because I was suddenly afraid she would walk away when the conversation was over and I would never see her again.

"I tell you what. I'm heading over to The Dairy Barn for a bite to eat. If you want, you can come with me, and we can talk about it."

"I'm really not hungry," she said, still nervous.

"I'm not either."

"Then why go eat lunch?"

"I thought it would be a good way to spend some time with you."

We didn't end up at The Dairy Barn but at a local ice cream shop. We had milkshakes and talked like we had known each other our entire lives. We were rarely apart after that. I was twenty-two; she was nineteen. The next time I saw my brothers, I told them I had found the woman I was going to marry. They thought I was nuts.

Maybe I was.

. . .

. . .

The only time we weren't together was when the world went to Hell. I sent her off with other people. And she died.

...

I failed her.

...

...

...

It was dark by the time I realized I was lost again. This time, it was okay. I was in no hurry, and if the dead tried to get me, well, I thought I might let them. The chances of my baby brother and son making it to Saluda were as slim as they could get. The desire to live was all but gone.

I pulled into a parking lot in some small town that I don't recall the name of. There wasn't much to see there, a bunch of brick buildings and run-down shacks, a few houses that looked like they could have been built before the Civil War, but other than that, there wasn't much of anything there. I shut the van off and killed the lights but left the key in the ignition.

The world was black. It was as if I never noticed it before. The clouds overhead blocked out the moon and stars, and whatever posed as streetlights in that town were long dead.

My shoulder throbbed. A few swallows of bottled water washed down two pain pills. I sat there, staring out the windshield, my thoughts on hold. My head grew heavy, and I started to doze. I crawled to the back of the van, set my gun by the edge of the mattress. Somewhere between lying down and my head hitting the pillow, I was out. There were no dreams.

A thump brought me from sleep. Another thump and my eyes opened. There was a haze in my head, a cloud that threatened a storm all its own. The third and fourth thumps brought me fully awake, the clouds dissipating and my head clearing. I reached for one of the guns, flipped the safety off, and crawled toward the front of the van.

Humphrey sat completely still in her seat, but she looked terrified with her glass eyes wide and shimmering as if on the verge of tears. I reached forward, unsnapped her seatbelt, and pulled her free. I placed her on the mattress.

The thump came again, and the van rocked slightly.

"Are you okay?" I asked.

Rotters, she said.

"I see."

Rotters. The obvious answer. For all I knew, it could have been a living person trying to get in the van, but the doors were locked. That wouldn't have stopped the living. No, they would have found a stone or a pipe, something to smash one of the windows in, and then they would have been able to unlock the door. Easy as pie.

Don't go, Humphrey said.

A finger to my lips, I shushed her politely. I eased into the driver's seat, pistol still in hand. There were a couple of guns on the floorboard on the passenger's side. Another thump came right next to my door. I flipped the headlights on.

A heavy fog hung low to the ground, thick and a smoky white. In that fog, I saw the legs of a dozen or more of the dead trundling about. Another thump came against my window, heavy and loud. The face of an old man was plastered against the glass, his jaw moving up and down, his teeth scraping against the window. He could have been anyone's grandpa.

They closed in on all sides, shuffling and stumbling. I couldn't hear them with the windows up, but they had to be groaning and growling and hungry.

"Looks like a party," I said.

Are we leaving? Humphrey asked.

I didn't answer right away. My thoughts went back to Jake and Bobby and Jeanette. I wondered if that was how it looked when the dead closed in on our little cabin. Did it start as one or two coming out of the trees or shambling down the dirt road? Did they try to hole themselves in, or was it a big horde to start with, and those filthy creatures forced their way in? How long did they fight? Who was the first of the living to die?

Part of Jake's letter came back to me. Bobby unloaded his gun into the zombie that bit Jeanette. What was he thinking when he did that? What was he thinking when the dead man got to his mother? Was he around when...

Sometimes, thinking is a bad thing.

Did he get to say goodbye to her before she passed away?

The more I thought, the more my mind conjured up images of a horrific battle between the living and the dead. And the angrier I got. I had started losing sight of what Pop had told us at the beginning of this whole mess. They were once people. I had done a few experiments along the way, getting a few results here and there and proving to myself there were still souls inside those rotting bodies. But I didn't care anymore. A bunch of those former people were responsible for my entire family being wiped out, and as far as I was concerned, they all had a hand in it.

Back in "the Before"—when the world was still living and daily life consisted of wake up, grab a coffee, go to work, come home, eat several times a day, playing, a little fun with the wife after the kid was in bed, and then sleeping just to wake up and do it all over again—anger was something most people felt over stupid things. "He took my parking spot." "She cut in line." "She's prettier than me." "He gave me a dirty look." People got mad about things like that. That anger was hot. It made your face flush, your blood boil, and in many cases, it caused arguments, fights, and sometimes death.

As I sat in a van I stole from a dead family who opted out instead of facing the swarms of dead, my anger wasn't hot. My face never grew flush, my blood never boiled. My jaws clenched, and my eyes might have narrowed a little. There was none of the spur of the moment "I'll teach you a lesson" mentality. No, the anger I felt was calculated, like a woman in a bad relationship, one where the man just beats the crap out of her for nothing. Eventually, they break down, break out, or break free. If they break down, their spirits are broken. If they break out, they are like a convict that escaped from prison, always on the run and looking over their shoulders, afraid of being caught. But if they break free, the man paid a price — and deservedly so.

I was that woman sitting in the corner of her bedroom, her nose broken and bleeding, her eye swollen, blood seeping from between her legs where her man was brutally rough with her. When he was done, he might have said, "When you get cleaned up, get my supper and a beer for me." I don't know. Something like that.

I was that woman who waited for him to fall asleep, who calculated every minute, trying to figure out the right time to strike. And when the time came, there was a gun or a knife or maybe someone conveniently broke into the house and did the job for me after his palm was greased with a few dollars, or maybe a little bit of rat poison went in his coffee each morning until he was too weak from the consumption that a baseball bat or a pillow over the face would do the trick nicely.

That woman…that woman doesn't act on anger. She acts on revenge, on hate. She might even go to jail when all is said and done, but she would be free. Free. And there would be relief—a big weight off the shoulders that led to tears of both sadness and joy and fear.

I was that woman as the old man zombie thumped his rotting head against the window of the van, his teeth scraping glass, leaving streaks of brown muck behind. And in that moment, I felt nothing. No pain. No hurt. No anger. Nothing.

I left my seat, went to the back of the van. It was dark back there, and I could have easily flipped on my flashlight, but no need to draw any more attention than I already had. Sure, taking out Grandpa would be easy, but that fog was like a cloak, and I had no clue how many others were out there waiting for a meal.

What are you doing? Humphrey asked, her voice shaking.

"Preparing."

For what?

"Revenge."

I checked my guns, made sure they were fully loaded. I took the baseball bat and suddenly wished I had a helmet with a facemask on it and maybe some long sleeves. I also wished for the machete I threw away, but wishful thinking never got anyone anywhere. I placed several pistols in Humphrey's seat, the baseball bat leaning against the passenger door. A box of Cheez-its and a bottle of water later, I was back in the driver's seat, eating the breakfast of champions and watching Grandpa chew on the window.

"Don't you go anywhere," I said and took a swallow of water. "You've had your last meal."

And like the husband with the wife beater shirt and bitter snarl on his face, Grandpa kept at it, trying to break through, trying to get me to break down.

The sun finally burned off the fog, revealing the parking lot for what it was—a department store. There were two other cars there, but they were unoccupied, and their owners could have been any of the dead shambling around. I counted twelve, most of them with sagging bodies and drooping shoulders. None of them looked fresh, which meant they probably all died in the beginning.

Grandpa was worse off than I thought he was. The skin on his head had split, exposing a portion of white skull. He had both eyes, but they were a thick white. His teeth were brown and yellow, and he was missing his bottom lip. Somewhere along the line, a chunk of flesh was torn from his left cheek, and his nose had been ripped off.

I reached for the ignition to start the van and then stopped. Sure, I could roll the window down and put a bullet in his head, but then what about being quiet?

"Twelve rotters. Small town. Open parking lot."

Walker?

"It's okay, Humphrey," I said. "Just planning my moves."

To Grandpa, I gave a wink. "I think I'll save you for last."

I turned the ignition. The van started, and I put it in gear and pulled away from Grandpa. The sound attracted the others, but that was okay. I pressed a button on the door, and the window rolled down.

Who would be first?

The woman by the entrance to the department store looked like a good candidate. She also seemed to move faster than the others. With the window down, I could hear her grumbling moans. With the van in gear, I let it roll toward her, nice and slow. As we grew closer to each other, I put my arm out the window, pulled the trigger. Her face vanished, and she fell backwards, her hands lifting in the air as if she were part of a Hallelujah Chorus group. I parked the van and got out.

That woman in the corner who had the crap kicked out of her one too many times was loose. There was no poison in the coffee, no pillow over the face, no knife to the throat. There were guns loaded with bullets and the messy leftovers of a killing rampage soon to follow. I let them get close, ten or fifteen feet, before taking them down. I wanted to see their faces, their eyes, feel their hunger and desperation. I wanted them to feel the same fear every living person has felt before they were killed by one of *THEM*. I wanted them to feel my fury.

In the Before, I would have been called a ruthless murderer, killing for the heck of it, maybe pissed off and on a shooting spree. In the Now, I was a beaten down survivor who had had enough.

The bodies formed an odd circle around me. The smell of decay and gunpowder hung heavy in the air. Flies buzzed about madly. Sweat spilled down my face, and that adrenaline rush that comes with the change in emotions humans often experience coursed through my body. I pulled the trigger on a little boy, not caring whose son he had been at one time, not caring if he played baseball like my Bobby had, not caring if there was a soul in there crying and afraid. I didn't care at all. The dead had taken everything from me. They were the enemy. They no longer deserved my pity or respect after their second deaths.

Grandpa staggered toward me, one arm raised, a single crooked finger extended as if pointing at me and telling me to stop. Whatever, Grandpa. I walked back to the van, letting the old man follow me. Here's the bait. Come and get it.

I opened Humphrey's door, grabbed the bat. It felt right, like it belonged in my hands. I think I smiled as I turned around.

Two steps forward, arms back, shoulder up, elbow even with my chin, I swung for the fences and connected. There was a loud pop, and Grandpa's head snapped to the side. He spun on his heels and fell to the ground.

I almost threw my hands up in the air and tossed the bat aside like a baseball player who had just hit a game-winning homerun. Instead, I looked around the parking lot, saw no more rotters, and calmly walked back to the van. Once inside, I locked the door and pulled Humphrey from the back and set her back in her seat.

We were silent for several minutes.

Are they all gone?

"Yup."

Dead?

"As a doorknob."

Are we leaving?

"Probably—I want to have a look around first."

Okay.

Again, we were quiet. Again, she broke the silence.

You spoke first.

"What?"

We were playing the quiet game. You spoke first.

"What? When. I don't remember speaking first. You did."

You asked if I was okay — you lose.

I laughed long and hard. When I was done, there were tears in my eyes and a cramp in my stomach, and my jaw muscles hurt. I settled down, chuckled once or twice, then stopped laughing altogether.

"I guess you're right. You want to hit me?"

No, she responded. *I'll save it for later.*

I gave her a sly look then put the van in gear. "You do that."

Eleven Weeks, Four Days, and Seventeen Hours After It All Started...

The town was smaller than I originally thought. A couple of stores lined the streets, and a police station that could have been mistaken for an outhouse seemed to divide them. There were no street lights and no meters along the curbs in front of the few businesses along Main Street. There was an ice cream parlor—yes, parlor, not shop—that proudly proclaimed, "The best root beer floats in town." I couldn't help but think, *Not anymore.* The biggest building was the department store I had just left. There wasn't a whole lot in the store itself, mostly empty shelves and bare display mannequins.

We drove along, Humphrey and I, my head like a swivel and on the lookout for anything on two legs. The small town was as dead as any other we had come across. There was no need to forage from the other buildings. If the department store was any indication, then the rest of the town had been picked over.

A little further down the road, Main Street gave way to a dirt road. In the rearview mirror, I saw a rotter shamble from behind a building. I started to park the truck, maybe hop out for a moment and bash its skull in, maybe take some more batting practice. My shoulder would be mad at me when I was done, but at least I could exact another measure of revenge for all I had lost. I shrugged—I would be coming back that way, and I would make sure and get him. I didn't think it would be too hard to recognize him. His light blue shirt was stained in the front, his jeans muddied, and he was missing one arm.

Then I saw the church. It stood another two hundred or so yards away. It looked small, maybe large enough to house fifty people on a good day. It was brick with several windows. There were cars in front of it, as if the entire town was meeting for Sunday services. I doubted that was the case, but the cars would have gas in them and maybe some other supplies as well.

I drove to the front of the church, circled around it, looking for a place close enough to park. Most of the vehicles were placed near enough to the building that someone could run between them and the church with little room to spare. This struck me as odd, as if they thought this out before parking, as if maybe the whole town really was inside. There was a tree not too far from the church, a tall oak, its leaves rustling softly with the breeze blowing in from wherever. Summer was fading, and fall was on its heels. Soon, winter would set in, and heat would be another necessity. Food. Water. Shelter. Weapons. Heat. It would be nice to find some people, but that wasn't really a necessity.

I parked beneath the tree, the front facing back the way I came. In the distance, I saw a handful of rotters. I wasn't sure if any of them was the one-armed dead man I saw a few minutes earlier, but I was positive getting out of the van without a weapon wasn't a good idea. I checked a couple of pistols, emptied a half a box of bullets into one pocket and then got out of the van.

Walker?

"I won't be long, Humphrey. I'm just going to check some of the cars, maybe look around inside the church. No need to waste an opportunity to search for supplies."

But the rotters.

I glanced down the dirt road. There were at least six of them now, and they were still a good two hundred yards away, about the same distance I was when I saw the church. Enough time, I thought, to do a quick search, maybe siphon some gas.

Up close, the church was bigger than I thought. Instead of fifty people, it probably could have held twice that number and still have room to spare. The brick structure was solid, and the windows had been boarded up. Halfway across the lawn, I stopped and cocked my head to one side.

"Impossible."

A few more steps and what I thought was just in my head turned out to be real. I heard a voice, loud enough to be shouting but not screaming. I followed the sound, hoping… You understand that, right? Hope, hoping, hopeful—that maybe that voice was real and not imagined, that maybe I had finally found other survivors. My skin prickled in excitement.

I stopped at the front stoop, which was nothing more than a slight step up onto a wooden platform. That voice was so much louder now. I could only imagine what it would sound like if there were nothing between it and me. The double doors awaited me. I didn't think they would open, but I turned the knob—a once painted black, now peeling piece of round metal—and heard it click. I pushed the door open and waited.

The voice was a baritone. Its owner must have had strong lungs to bellow the way he did.

There was another set of double doors, no knobs attached, just the swinging type. I stepped into the church, onto its plush, red carpet. There were tables to either side of the door with pamphlets and circulars and bulletins on them. I picked

up one of the programs and read the date. September 5 —
Sunday. The message was to be given by the Reverend
William White. The title? *And Judgment Shall Be Upon Us.*

My brothers and I were raised in the church, raised to
believe in God and Heaven and Hell and to do the right thing.
We were raised that sin was bad, but we were boys, and well,
boys will be boys. My life was never sin-free before the dead
got up. And I can't say I have sinned less since. Sin is sin no
matter whether it's telling a little white lie to your momma
when you took a dollar from her change purse or killing a
man trying to eat you.

I stood inside that church, itching to go further in, but I
wasn't too sure I wanted to hear the message being preached.
What I did want — what I needed more than anything at that
moment — was to see other people. Living people. Without a
doubt, I knew they would be in that sanctuary.

From beyond the double doors, the voice began praying. I
could hear him giving praise and thanks and asking for the
deliverance from their sins.

"Oh touch their souls, touch their hearts. Forgive us all for
the sins we've committed." The words came out, *Oh-wa, touch
they-ah souls, touch they-ah hearts-ah. Forgive-ah us all for-ah the-
ah sins we've-ah committed.* He was a typical back woods
preacher-man.

There was a small chorus of amens and a pause — in the
movies, it would have been great for effect. It worked well
then also. The preacher — the Reverend William White — began
his message softly, or I imagine it was soft for him since his
voice came loud and clear through the door, his southern
drawl accentuating each word.

"Today, we read from the book of Ezekiel, chapter five, verse nine. And the good book says: 'Therefore in your midst, fathers will eat their children, and children will eat their fathers. I will inflict punishment on you and will scatter all your survivors to the winds.'

"And from verse twelve of the same chapter: 'A third of your people will die of the plague or perish by famine; a third will fall by the sword outside your walls; and a third I will scatter to the winds and pursue with drawn sword.' Can I get an amen?"

That small chorus of amens came again, a couple of males, a couple of females—probably not more than fifteen people in all if that.

"People, I say we are in the midst of the Great Cleansing. Children devour their fathers. Fathers devour their children. The great prophet, Ezekiel, spoke of these things thousands of years ago, and now, his visions have come to pass. The world and all of its evildoers have suffered the wrath of —"

I pushed the door open and stepped into the sanctuary. Pews sat to either side of a center aisle, the carpet as red as the one in the foyer. The windows that were boarded on the outside held brilliant stained glass images on the inside: angels and crosses, the mother Mary. Candles sat in sconces along the walls, and candelabras sat near the pulpit and alter.

The Reverend William White was a short man with flaming red hair threatening to turn gray in the near future. He held a Bible above his head, his arm seemingly frozen in air. His mouth hung open, and his head was tilted to one side. The parishioners turned and faced me. There weren't fifteen or so like I thought. There were only eight of them, and they were all adults, most of them pushing fifty with only one younger man that looked like he was on the downhill side of life. His face was the color of gray ash, and his eyes were set in rimmed-red sockets. I knew the condition. The guy had a fever and was dying. If they didn't know how a bite from one of the dead led to the infected becoming one also, they were going to find out soon enough.

At that moment, we all stared at each other: me in disbelief at seeing nine living, breathing people and them probably a little in shock as well. I had survived this long with little human contact, but right then, I felt the cogs of my brain reverse a little. I had been slowly losing my sanity, each minute ticking away and bringing me that much closer to the brink of madness. But seeing people—*people!*—pulled me from that edge just a little.

White broke the stalemate. "Well, what do we have here? A visitor to our humble church?" He lowered his arm, the Bible still clutched in his hand.

"Hello," I said. It sounded lame, but it was all I could think to say. I took a step forward.

"Nope, son. You stay right there."

I listened but kept my hands to my sides and out of my pockets. There was a sudden change in the atmosphere, a tension. I wasn't welcome there, and the joy of seeing people quickly vanished and was replaced by an apprehension that I could be in more danger in there with the living than I ever was outside with the dead.

William White walked toward me with a limp. As he approached, I could see his face was damp with sweat and that there was a splotch of red on his pants just below his right knee.

"I didn't mean to interrupt the service—I heard your voice, and it's been so long since I've seen any survivors and—"

White stopped about twenty feet away from me and shoved his hands into the front pockets of his gray slacks.

"Survivors?" he asked. "Is that what you think we are?" He laughed, turned to his congregation of eight. "He thinks we're survivors. Are we survivors?"

His flock shook their collective heads. A few of them murmured "no" and "nope" and "we're the Chosen."

"The Chosen?" I asked, suddenly wishing I had never drove away from the highway. What was I thinking? That I would find friendly people? That I would find a place to lay my head without the worries of a rotting corpse attacking me in the middle of the night? Maybe so. What did I get? The Jim Jones Chosen Ones Convention.

"Ah, yes, the Chosen," White said with a crooked smile. "It's the end times, son. The end times. And Israel has the face of the prophets set against it and—"

"This isn't Israel."

White's mouth hung open again, then it snapped shut. He took a deep breath, and that smile reappeared. "It's a metaphor. You see, Ezekiel was told to set his face against Israel and that they would not be spared the wrath of—"

"I know the story, Reverend. I was raised in the church."

"Ah, so you're one of the Chosen as well, then?"

I shrugged at that. "I don't know about being chosen for anything. I think I've been a little lucky. That's about it."

"There is no such thing as luck, only fate."

"Fate?" I nodded, pursed my lips. "So all them dead people out there walking around, that was their fate? What about all the people the dead killed? Was it their fate to be eaten alive? Is that what that is? Fate?"

White's eyes narrowed. His jaw clenched. "If you read your Bible, son, then you would understand that this was prophesied. Children will eat their fathers, and fathers will eat their children. It's right here in the good book." He waved the Bible at me.

"The dead—those people who died of the sickness—came down with the plague just as it was promised, and they died from it. Those who were devoured by the dead were killed by the sword that is vengeance. And those of us who were scattered to the ends of the Earth are the Chosen."

"Where does it say anything about the Chosen in the Bible?"

"In Revelations, it states that 144,000 will be sealed, will be chosen."

I shook my head. I had found living people, and they were all nuts. I looked past White to the few people behind him, most of which had stood up and began to make their way toward us. They didn't hold the same conviction in their faces as White did. I wasn't too sure they all believed they were chosen for anything except maybe to die and rise again but not in rapture.

"You know, I think me coming here was a mistake. I think I'll just…ummm…show myself to the door."

"You will do no such thing—you are here, which means you've been sent to us. You are ours now."

Ours now? What type of church was this?

"With all due respect, preacher-man, I don't belong to anyone, least of all you."

He slid his hand behind his back and then pulled it back out. In it was a knife. The blade looked sharp, as if it had never been used.

"You stand where you are, and don't you dare try to leave."

"You're going to lose this fight, Reverend," I said and drew one of my guns from the back of my pants. "Now, I'm walking out this door, and I'm just going to pretend I never came across you folks. Got it?"

White took a step forward, his teeth exposed, his brows pushed down over his eyelids.

I lifted the gun, the safety off, and placed a finger on the trigger. "If you are one of the Chosen, then you might want to go ahead and back away. I'm trying to end this peacefully, but if you come at me, I will put a bullet right between your eyes. And believe me, over the last few months, I've had a lot of target practice."

The preacher didn't take another step forward. Instead, he took a few backward. A couple of moments later, the young man collapsed to the ground near the pulpit. His body shook, and his feet and head crashed against the thick carpet. His glasses shot off his face and landed in the center aisle. One older woman with bluing hair screamed while two of the men tried to hold him down.

White ran to them, put his hand on the young man's head, and then pulled it away. He lifted both hands in the air and began to pray for the boy's deliverance from evil, that the devil had him and that Satan had no hold there.

Then the young man stilled as if by some miracle.

It was no miracle.

I've been through this before. I've seen the dead rise up, and it doesn't take long. I started toward the front of the church where the kid lay dead. That close to him, I saw he really was a kid, maybe twenty if that.

"Get away from him," I yelled.

One of the men stood and placed himself between me and the corpse. "You don't be tellin' us what to do, stranger."

"He's going to turn into one of those corpses that eat people. You need to kill him."

"He's already dead," Blue-haired Woman said.

"Get out the way," I said and aimed my pistol toward the kid.

"No," the woman yelled and lowered herself over his body, her arms on either side of his head, her face an expression of grief, tears spilling from her eyes.

"Ma'am, you need to move." Always ma'am, even in these times where manners and respect have been thrown to the wind. Pop might have been proud of me if he were still alive. That's the thing. He was gone, and these people were too stupid to realize that the dead were among them and one of them would be directly in their mist.

I saw the kid's foot jerk. It was just a twitch, barely noticeable. Someone was yelling something about "put the gun away." Someone else babbled on about letting them be for crying out loud. And Reverend William White prayed his prayers. Somewhere in all of the noise, I heard him say I was the devil, that I was the reason for the calamity brought upon the world.

I was in danger but not because of the dead. The Reverend had stood. The scene playing out before me held my interest long enough for him to get in close enough to drive his knife into my skull if he wanted to.

Blue-haired Woman began to scream, drawing everyone's attention away from me. The boy had awakened, and both of his hands held her throat firm to his mouth, silencing her. Blood splashed over his face and clothes and the plush, red carpet of the church as the color drained from Blue-haired Woman's face. She tried to push up but couldn't. Her arms gave way, and she collapsed onto the boy, but he didn't seem to notice. No, she was nothing more than a meal at that point, something to bite down on until he was able to stand and go after someone else.

"Get her off of him," I heard someone yell, and two of the men, probably well into their sixties, bent down and grabbed the woman by the arms. One of them, a man with more hair in his ears than on his head, slipped in the woman's blood, dropping to his knees. The boy released the woman and grabbed the man's leg. He shifted enough to bite down into the thin khakis the man wore. The man gave a loud shriek and dropped the woman's arm, knocking himself off balance.

Rotters aren't all that fast after they've been dead a few days, but fresh ones still had the limberness of a living body, having only passed minutes earlier. Rigor mortis hadn't set in yet. The boy moved quickly, grabbing the man's wrist and biting off one of his fingers. The man howled as he dropped to his butt and held the mangled hand up with the other one.

There was little time to waste. I took aim at the kid, pulled the trigger. His body went limp. The old man scuttled away until he bumped into the altar behind him. He whimpered in shock as he stared at the bloody stump where his finger used to be.

144

"You should have listened to me," I growled.

No one said anything. With the exception of the old man's crying, there was no noise in the church at all. Two of their nine were dead. I suspected a third would be joining him soon enough, but I had no plans to stick around and find out.

White finally turned to me, his face dabbed in sweat, his eyes wide. He still held the knife, but I don't think he realized it. "Look what you've done."

"What I've done? What I did was save your lives; that boy could have killed you all."

"You brought Hell with you. We were fine until you showed up."

"That kid was dying before I got here. It was only a matter of time before he was one of them."

"One of them?" White snarled. "Do you even know what you're talking about? One of them? Ezekiel was commanded to tell the dry bones to rise. He was told to command the breath from the four corners to enter into those bones. He did as he was told, and the dead rose up from the grave, and a vast army stood around him, their once dead bodies alive again. The dead of this land are that army, and there is no escaping them for someone like you. The devil resides in your heart, and you will perish by the sword, and the dead will devour your flesh."

"I came here hoping to find refuge, a place to rest, but this is just a madhouse—and an unsecured one at that. You go right on and pray, Mr. Chosen One. I'm leaving."

I headed back up the aisle to the doors leading to the foyer. I pushed through them, took the several steps to the door, and opened it.

"Oh crap," I said.

The dead had been so far away when I walked in. How long had it been? Five minutes? Ten? Had the events lasted longer than I thought? Had I stood inside the foyer longer than I could recall? It was only a minute or two. Not more. It couldn't have been. But there they were, the dead, weaving in and out of the cars and trucks, bumping into them and keeping on. A dozen—no, two or three dozen—and they were close enough that going out the front door wasn't possible.

I turned around. The Chosen Ones were still stunned by the recent deaths of two of their own. They were probably questioning themselves, their preacher, their own religion for that matter. I could almost hear their thoughts.

How could this have happened to us? We're the Chosen. This was not supposed to happen. Have we been forsaken? Are we the sinners?

That last thought probably hung in their minds like a heavy mist on a cool October morning in the mountains. If they were the sinners, then they were as good as dead—at least in the good Reverend William White's eyes.

Back up the aisle I went. "Is there a back door?" I asked. "We need to get out of here."

One of the men weakly raised a hand, his thumb extended. He jabbed it toward a door just beyond the pulpit. It was smaller than a normal door, maybe something that belonged on a bathroom closet and not as a church exit. What if there had been a fire or some other catastrophe? What if Hell was released right outside their door and they all had to flee out one way or get caught in the wrath they believed so dearly in?

The only woman left in the place, a gray-haired lady with wide-rimmed glasses, looked at me with confusion in her eyes. "Why do we need to leave?"

"The valley of dry bones is knocking at the front door," I said and bent down to help her stand. She pulled her arms away from me and shook her head.

"My sister and nephew are dead."

"And you will be too if you don't get up from there."

"What are you talking about?" White interjected, his face flushed red.

"The dead are coming, preacher-man. They're right outside the door."

White motioned to one of the men. "Johnny, go take a look."

Johnny was probably a bigger guy in his younger days, but age and life, and probably hunger, had withered him down to half the size I thought he had been. Skin drooped from his neck and jaws and arms. He shook his head.

"I...I don't want to go look," he said, a quiver in his voice.

"You do what I told you to do, or so help me..."

Johnny's eyes grew wide, his bushy white brows lifted. He stood from the pew he sat on and made his way slowly toward the front of the church.

"There's no need for that," I said.

Johnny stopped.

"Do as I said, Johnny."

Authority. White held authority over them all. I could see it in their faces. They didn't believe they were chosen for anything but to eventually die in the mess that the world had become, but White wouldn't let them speak otherwise. He thought himself a god, and the few people left in that little town were his worshipers.

"Johnny, stay away from the door. There's no need to look. Trust me on that."

White came forward, his lips like a line across his face. "Johnny, you will listen to me. You will do as I say. Remember who saved your behind when you needed it most. That was me. I saved your soul, Johnny. You *owe* me."

I *was* right. He did think himself a god. Johnny went to the door, faster than before. He reached the foyer doors and went to open them. I was yelling no, but it was too late. I saw the foyer doors swing inward, the one on the right clipping Johnny in the nose. He fell backward and landed hard on the carpet. His head struck the back of a pew, and the dead were on him.

I lifted my pistol. One shot, two shots. The first of the rotters were down, but there were so many more. They tore into Johnny, one ripping his shirt at his belly and sinking its teeth in the exposed, white flesh. Others collapsed on him. I heard bones crack and break, but they weren't Johnny's. Those noises belonged to the dead. Some of them tipped over as their knees ruptured, but they didn't cease trying to get a piece of the old man.

There were more—so many more, where did they all come from?—and they just pushed by the dead on the floor. Some fell and burst open. But not enough of them to slow the horde down. I shot several more of them as I backpedaled, leaving a litter of bodies strewn across the floor.

I shoved past William White, and he grabbed my shirt.

"You're not going anywhere. The devil is here for you, and I'm going to make sure he gets you." His southern drawl was looser, making his preaching seem like more of a show. He tried to hold me with both hands, but he was older than me and heavier, making him slower. I shoved him then put my knee into his stomach. He doubled over, reached for me again.

I'd like to say I'm innocent of murder even if the dead had souls still trapped inside rotting bodies, many of which I had put down over the previous few months. But was that the same? I don't think so. My hands were no longer clean after he tried to grab me that second time. I brought the butt of my gun down on his forehead. The Reverend William White fell to the floor.

As I said, I'd like to say I'm innocent of murder, but things have a way of not working out the way you think they should. Two of White's congregation ran past me and tried to help him. Loyal to the end, they gave up their lives in a futile attempt to save his. The rotters clamored over them. One of the men tried to get away, but they reached him easy enough, pulled him to the floor, and swarmed him.

In the chaos, several of the candles were knocked from the walls, their flames catching the carpet on fire. The church wasn't a house of kindling, but the blaze spread quickly along the floor, igniting the pews with their lush cushions.

I tried to get the woman to her feet. She sat there, cradling herself and rocking back and forth.

"Come on," I yelled.

Again, she pulled free. She wasn't leaving. She was ready to die, and I guess I understood that. There were only two members of White's congregation left to save at that point, and one of them walked with such a severe limp that he could have been one of the dead. The woman who had died minutes earlier (at the hands of her now dead son) snagged the cuff of his pants and bit into his ankle. The man went sprawling, his hands out in front of him.

I could have helped him. I could have shot Blue-haired Woman before she grabbed him, but I didn't. I only watched as she bit into his ankle, and he screamed and fell, and then she crawled up his body, trying to get at something a little tenderer. I could have helped that lady refusing to get up. I could have picked her up and slung her over my shoulder, but what good would that have done? She would have been like dead weight, and that was something I didn't need or want.

Instead, I ran through the narrow doorway that led down an even thinner hall. At the end of it was a door that stood open. I didn't think much about why it was open. I hurried through, my gun raised and ready. The dead hadn't reached the back of the church yet. I rounded the corner. I could see the van easily enough. It was a straight line forward. It would take less than thirty seconds to reach it. The keys were in the ignition, and the door was unlocked. Safety was half a minute away.

"Help me."

It was the old man with the hairy ears. He was huddled along the wall, not far from the door. He still held his hand tight and in the air, the blood seeping from the wounded finger and down his arm. His face was pained, lips pulled back and exposing his teeth.

"Please, help me."

I went to him, knelt down. His eyes were fading, he had lost so much blood. I shook my head. "I can't help you. I'm sorry."

"Help me. Don't leave me here like this."

I stood, took a few steps away from him, and then stopped. I looked back. I could smell smoke, and I could hear the dead inside the church, moaning and groaning, maybe in pain from the flames that engulfed them. I felt no pity for them or for White, who, if his body and head didn't burn completely, would become one of them. It dawned on me then that maybe he was right. Maybe he was one of the Chosen but not in the way he thought. Maybe he was one of the skeletons in that desert valley that Ezekiel spoke to. Maybe he was sent to devour.

"Please," the old man said again.

"You know how this is going to end, don't you?" I asked.

He nodded.

I pulled the trigger.

Then I ran.

The gunshot attracted attention, but I had more than enough space to reach the van before they could get to me. I didn't waste any of it. I was in the van with the doors locked, the windows up, and the engine rolled over. I put the van in gear and then shoved it back into park.

Shuffling along was that first rotter I had seen on my way up to the church. I remembered the light blue shirt, the missing arm. He hobbled toward the van. I floored it. The front tires spun at first then found traction. I yelled as I ran into him. He bounced off the van, his head striking the windshield and cracking the glass near the hood. A smear of blood was left behind where he had struck. He landed several feet away. I mashed the gas, circled around and back toward him, this time making sure to steer the van over his body. There was a slight bump then a second one as the front wheels then the back ones went over the corpse. I looked in the rearview mirror to see the crumpled remains of the armless corpse.

I drove back down the hill and along Main Street. If the dead had come from there, they were gone for the time being. I could see the black, billowing smoke from the church in my rearview mirror. We were almost through the town and hopefully heading back toward the highway when Humphrey spoke. I wasn't sure I heard correctly, and I asked her to repeat herself.

What were they like?

"You mean the people back there?"

Yes.

I wasn't sure how to answer the question. They were loons, and that was putting it nicely. Instead, I said, "They were searching souls misled by a deceptive voice."

We reached the highway sooner than I expected. Turns out we weren't so lost after all.

I thought about it as we drove along. What if they were right? I didn't believe they were. I think they didn't believe either. More than that, I thought of the four people that I had a hand in killing and knew that Hell awaited just as it had since I put the first rotter down.

Eleven Weeks, Four Days, and Nineteen Hours After It All Started...

Life is all about choices. Every choice you make, every decision, alters the direction of life. It changes which road you follow. If a person makes one decision, it takes him this way. If he makes a different decision, it takes him a different way. Growing up, that was one of the things Pop drilled into our heads.

If you make the wrong decisions in life, it will lead you down a dark and difficult path.

There were times when we boys thought Pop was blowing smoke, just talking to hear himself talk. We never said as much—we just thought it. The thing is, he was right.

I sat at the edge of the highway at the top of the hill overlooking the small town we had left behind. Humphrey was safely strapped into her car seat, the windows cracked enough to let the cool air in, and the doors were locked. I could see the smoke coming from the old church. I thought about the Chosen ones that died there minutes earlier, the old man with the hair in his ears and missing two fingers thanks to one of their own rising up from the dead and biting them off. His eyes held that haunted look in them that so many people have when close to death. There was fear there—real fear. Not that contrived fear that our minds conjure up when we think things are worse than they really are.

I had a boss, a cool guy named Kyle, who said "they're killing me" a lot. He was taking over for my old boss, who had a run-in with colon cancer and called it quits before his surgery. I was apprehensive about things. He was making

153

changes—too many of them as far as all the workers were concerned.

"Hank, what are you afraid of?" he asked me one day, just out of the blue.

At first, I said nothing. Then I responded as honestly as I knew how. "Losing my job."

"You're not going to lose your job. None of you are. I'm not here to kick you out. I'm here to make you better."

"I hear what you're saying, but that really doesn't change the uneasiness everyone is feeling right now."

He nodded, pursed his lips, and then smiled. "Do you know what that is?"

"What?"

"That's fear: False Evidence Appearing Real."

I repeated the words back to him. "How do you figure?"

"Simple. You think you're going to lose your job. Has anyone told you that was going to happen?"

"No."

"Then why would you think it?"

"I don't know—it's just the way things feel right now."

"So your perception is that you and your co-workers are going to lose your jobs. It's not true. I'd be a fool to get rid of you guys—I don't know anything about the system here. I'd be cutting my own throat if I got rid of any of you. Your perception is false evidence appearing real."

I never forgot that conversation. I wonder what happened to him—if he made it out of the city or if they really did kill him.

I shook my head. Everyone I knew and loved were gone: family, friends, acquaintances. It was now only me and a stuffed female bear who bore a male's name.

As I sat there, the van's engine idling and the fresh memory of that old man's eyes pleading with me, saying what his brain wanted but what his mouth couldn't vocalize.

Kill me, please.

He knew what he would become if he died. He knew the dead were in and around the church and that it was only a matter of time before they caught up to him. He slumped against the church wall when I shot him, his bloodied hand dropping into his lap, his mouth popping open. His head hit brick and bounced forward before settling on one shoulder.

All of that could have been avoided. If I had stayed away from that church. If I had just made my way out of the town instead of playing "in search of," then the dead wouldn't have followed me to the dinner table. Maybe they would still be alive. Maybe not. The young man died while I was there, and those people seemed oblivious to the truth. Surely some of them would have died if not all of them, all while Reverend William White prayed his prayers and refused to believe that deliverance was in the shape of a door that led to the back of the church.

Still, my decision brought the dead to their front step. My decisions cost White and at least three of his congregation their lives. My decision ended old Hairy Ears' days on this Earth.

Decisions. I thought of all of those as I sat in that van watching the smoke rise higher into the sky.

Then I thought of other choices I had made. One stood out among them all: telling Jeanette to take Bobby and go to the cabin, go to safety. The more I thought about it, the more I realized we would have been safer if we had just stayed put. We could have boarded up the house, fortified it enough to wait it out. There were windows on all four sides of the upstairs. It would have been easy enough for me to pick them off as they neared the house. We had a basement straight out of the eighteen hundreds with a door in the floor that I don't think any walking corpse would have been able to lift even if they tried.

We would have been safe.

I knew that. In hindsight, I knew it when everything was going down, but the natural reaction was to flee, find higher ground, and wait it out as if we were caught in a flood. It was a decision born of panic. It was the wrong decision.

And my family died because of it.

I put the van in gear, pulled all the way onto the highway. *Where are we going?* Humphrey asked.

"Home."

Home?

"Yeah. We should have never left there."

It was a long drive, one that was spent in reflection, like so many other times. Every once in a while, I would see some of the dead shambling along, mostly one or two at a time, but there was an occasion where there were four in an old wheat field off 385. I stopped each time. The single ones, I took out with a bat. The group of four was three bullets then the bat — no use wasting ammo on a one-on-one situation.

I could have kept on, not stopped, let the dead continue on, but I didn't. I chose to stop, to end their existence. No need for them to catch sight or sound of the van and then turn to follow. I had made that mistake in that small town earlier. It wasn't happening again. If I saw a rotter and I could safely take it down, I did so.

156

My world had suddenly become a game of "what if?" What if I didn't stop? Could those rotters find another survivor and kill them? What if there were kids involved? Though I would have never known, in the back of my mind, I would have been wondering, "what if?" There was no time for "what if." "What if" could get other people killed.

I saw the sign for *Sipping Creek, South Carolina, POPULATION: 700+ AND GROWING.*

My mind fixed on the sign, whispered in my ear, *Time to change that number.*

I passed through that great, invisible border that separates one town from another and continued on. The small neighborhoods took shape, most of them the way the living left them when they fled that proverbial flood. There was *some change* by way of my gun and shovel and the graves where the dead had been buried after being put down.

I slowed as I approached the street my family had lived on in better times. My stomach was all nerves and my palms sweaty. I wasn't so sure I was ready to face the reality of living in that house without my family. A left turn followed, and I crept along the road. It was quiet, almost peaceful. The doors still held the red, spray-painted Xes on them. I backed into my yard, pulled the van right up to the porch steps, and turned it off.

Where are we? Humphrey asked.

"We're home."

My home?

It hadn't occurred to me that Humphrey had once lived with another family. Sure, I remembered where I had gotten her, but the thought that she wasn't home didn't cross my mind. She had a girl who probably loved her at one time. That

157

girl lived in a different house, a different *home*. For a moment, I thought to crank the van up and make my way back to that house. I remembered it well enough: a U-shaped cul-de-sac, the picture of the little girl and her parents, Humphrey held in her arms. There had been no fences around the yards in that area. I shook my head—a little harder to fortify, I thought.

"No, not your home, Humphrey. Mine—or at least what used to be mine."

Humphrey didn't move, didn't make a small grunting sound when I picked her up and slipped her in the pack, zipping it up around her. She didn't say anything when I put the pack on my shoulders. The pain in the one arm stretched down into my shoulder blade, making me aware it was still injured even though it was back in place. I reached into the console, grabbed a couple of pain pills, and popped them in my mouth, chewing them instead of swallowing them whole. They left behind a nasty, chalky residue in my teeth and tongue.

"Come on," I said and grabbed a pistol.

The front door greeted me with thousands of memories. My knees grew weak, and I almost fell to the ground at the base of the porch.

Walker, are you okay?

"Yes," I lied.

To lie is to make a decision not to tell the truth. It was often a bad decision, a habit I seemed to have gotten good at. Not lying but bad choices. I would make a few more of those in the coming weeks and months of trying to survive in the dead world, not the least of which was turning the knob to open the door and finding it locked.

Then I remembered. I had locked the door the last time I left just before placing the big, red X on it. I thought I would never go back, but there I stood on the same familiar porch in that same familiar town. A knot formed in my stomach. Reaching in my pocket, I pulled out a set of keys. They weren't mine. No, they had never belonged to me, not even then—they belonged to a family who killed themselves about a hundred miles from Sipping Creek. My keys were still in the ignition of my overturned truck. I was in too much of a hurry to grab them when I wrecked and then again when I went back to retrieve my guns and some supplies with the dead closing in on me.

"This isn't a good idea," I said.

Then we should leave, Humphrey whispered.

I had a chance to turn around, to get out of there. I had a chance to make a decision to escape the demons that were inside that house. What did I do? Yeah, I went down the steps, rounded the side yard, and went into the back yard and right to my shop. I tried not to pay attention to the toys on the ground or the parts to the old car I had been working on or the playhouse I had built when Bobby was still barely crawling.

The door was closed but not locked. I pushed it open, not taking for granted the shop would be empty. The sun flushed part of the darkness inside away. Dust mites danced in its rays. There were cobwebs hanging from the ceiling, the worktables, and shelves. It looked like spiders had taken up residency. I pushed away some of the webs and stepped inside. Humphrey let out an unhappy squelch.

"You okay back there?"

I hate spiders.

159

"Yeah, me too."

Really?

"Yeah." Another lie. "They're good at hiding, and you run into their webs and do that weird 'oh crap, I just ran into a spider web' dance."

Humphrey giggled.

A coffee can sat on the third shelf of a tin unit near the door. I grabbed it. It wasn't as dusty as I thought it would be, and the top came off easy enough. The key sat in the bottom of it. I looked at it for a long while, plucked it from the can, and turned it over in my fingers.

Then I was standing at the front door, the key in the hole, the tumbler clicking loudly, the front door open. Those same rays that shone in the shop now shone into my house, making it look older than it was. I stepped inside, closed the door behind me.

Back in the old world, that would have been a great feeling. Coming home after a hard day of work, kicking off the boots just inside the door, letting my feet air out. A cold beer and maybe a football game—yeah, being that it was early September, football season would have just started.

I slid the pack off, set it on the light blue recliner that I used to sit in every night. I used to read Bobby stories right there, his little body tucked under my arm. He loved *The Monster at the End of This Book,* and I did a great Grover impression and pretended to try to keep him from turning the pages. He would laugh until there were tears in his eyes and he could barely breathe.

Yeah, it was a bad idea returning home.

I stumbled over to the couch. I plopped down and sat back, my hands went between my knees. I don't know if I cried or if

I just sat there staring into the bleakness of nothing, but eventually, I snapped out of it, and the sun was coming up. Yes, coming up. But somewhere in between, I believe the sun had set and risen a time or two more.

"We need to leave," I said and stood. My legs were tired. Maybe I had slept instead of just sitting there, letting time pass me by. I took the few steps to the recliner, grabbed the pack, and opened the front door.

Outside, the air was crisp. There was a slight breeze, and the sky was still somewhat gray as the sun continued its ascent. Before I reached the van, I saw her. She was one of Jeanette's best friends. Her hair was brown and brittle. Once upon a time, she had beautiful hazel eyes the shapes of almonds. From the looks of the wounds on her arms, neck, and the gaping hole in her shirt, I gathered she had survived the sickness only to succumb to the dead and then become one herself. She stumbled along the road, looking like she was sleep walking. Maybe she was.

I set Humphrey in the van, checked my gun. A full clip.

Slowly, I walked toward her, keeping plenty of distance between us.

"Sherri," I whispered.

She continued to trundle along.

I followed behind her. How did I miss her? Was she alive when I went inside her house but hiding somewhere I didn't look? Did she think I was one of the dead that managed to get inside and was looking for a fresh meal? Was that why she didn't come out when I was there?

"Sherri," I said a little louder.

How many times had she and her family eaten dinner with us? How many times had Jeanette confided in her about life's little problems? How many times had we laughed together? She was the maid of honor in our wedding, the godmother to Bobby. She was everything to Jeanette.

"Sherri," I yelled.

She stopped. Her head lifted slightly as if she were listening for something.

"Sherri, it's Hank."

She groaned. I imagine she was trying to say my name.

"Sherri, turn around."

And she did so. My stomach flipped, and the skin on my arms and neck bubbled with cold chills. I should have just put a bullet in her brain and not said anything, but I didn't do that. When she turned to me, I saw the torn lip, the caked white eyes, the sallow skin. My breath hitched, and I stared hard at her.

"Sherri, are you in there?"

Another groan, then a step. She lifted a hand toward me. Her fingernails were long—they hadn't stopped growing.

"Sherri, stop right there."

Sherri took another step. Her other arm extended out. She was missing her thumb.

Jeanette had known her since third grade. They graduated from high school together. They both went to the university over in Columbia. They had been inseparable even after they both got married.

A growl tore from her throat, and she stumbled along a little faster, her arms outstretched, something akin to brown sludge coming from her mouth—the drool of the dead, I reckon.

"Sherri…" I shook my head, my breath held tight in my lungs. "I'm sorry."

The pistol recoiled. The boom somehow silenced in my ears. Sherri fell backwards, landed on the ground with a soft thud. Her head hit the blacktop, and reddish/black blood made a crown beneath it.

I stood staring at the body of my wife's oldest friend for several minutes before making my way back to the shop around back of the house. There was a shovel hanging on its peg on the wall. It had been a while since I had dug any graves, but I spent the next couple of hours doing just that. I couldn't leave her on the street to rot. When I was done, I drove the shovel into the soft mound of dirt to mark her grave just in case…just in case I came back. I didn't think I would, but I had thought that before, and look where I ended up.

"Time to go," I said as I slid behind the wheel.

Where to now? There was a hint of frustration in her voice.

"Saluda maybe?"

Where's that?

"Sixty miles along 378, just before you get to Newberry. It's pretty country. Not so close to the city. Lake Murray is out that way. We could find one of the houses out there and make it our own if nobody is in it. And we can start over."

What about your son?

It took a while for me to answer, but when I finally did, I realized why I had chosen Saluda. "The Batesburg armory is out there, about twenty minutes or so from the County Line Store. I figure we could check it out first. Maybe Bobby and Jake will be there."

And if they aren't?

I took a deep breath. "Then my search is over."

Twelve Weeks After It All Started...

In the old world, there were crazies everywhere. Corrupt officials. Corrupt cops. Corrupt teachers. Corrupt sports figures. Kids killing kids. The world was on the verge of killing itself when the dead began to rise. The difference between then and now? The crazies aren't arrested for the things they do now, and there is no media circus to follow them around, reporting on their every move.

It took longer than I thought it would to get from my home down I-20 toward Saluda. Roads had been blocked by accidents or stalled out cars or bodies, so many bodies. I moved what vehicles I could and detoured where I couldn't. I ended up on Old Batesburg Road where the houses looked worn and the yards were mostly unkempt. Occasionally, I would stop and take out a couple of the dead, but for the most part, Old Batesburg Road was abandoned, much like I guessed most of the world was.

That two-lane blacktop would lead me close to the Batesburg Armory. I hoped to find my baby brother and my son there. If not...

If not wasn't something I wanted to think about.

I slowed down when I saw the vehicle up ahead—a truck that was bigger than mine—sitting in the middle of the road. I saw people, but I couldn't make out if they were living or dead. One of them had to be alive. It looked like a struggle taking place, and someone needed help.

What's wrong? Humphrey asked.

"I'm not sure, but there's something going on up there."

Are we going to check it out?

"That's the plan."

We drove forward until we were about thirty yards from the other truck. It was high off the ground, the wheels lifting it up taller than the top of the van. It was a rust bucket color, and it definitely belonged to a couple of country boys. I put my window down enough so I could hear the commotion at the front of the vehicle.

Someone was laughing—it was a taunt if I've ever heard one. Someone else was speaking, his voice deep.

"You want some of this?" he said. "I know you do."

The alarms went off in my head. They had a woman, and they were going to rape her. That's the only thing I could think. I couldn't quite see them, but hearing was enough.

I grabbed my pistol, checked to make sure it was fully loaded, and then stood from the truck.

Hank?

"Stay here, Humphrey. This could be bad."

She let out a low whine as I closed the door gently.

With their truck being high off the ground, I thought they would have seen me or at least the van. But they were too preoccupied with their taunting and teasing, and I could only imagine the poor woman they were terrorizing. I rounded the front end of the truck, pistol drawn. I aimed before I saw.

There were two men, one scrawny and dirty, his hair greasy and his clothes just as filthy. He held a rope in one hand and a knife in the other. The other end of his rope led to a woman's neck. The second guy was bigger and taller. It looked like all the meals Scrawny missed, Fat Boy made up for. He held a rope as well, and like his buddy, the other end of it ran to the woman, this one at her waist. Her top was ripped, and she only had panties covering her privates.

The woman was dead. She had probably been very attractive when she was alive. A brunette, tall and petite. She had been someone's wife—the ring on her left hand told me as much.

I stood, watching in disbelief as they tugged on their ropes each time she got close to one of them. If she grew close enough to bite Fat Boy, Scrawny yanked his end of the rope. If she were too close to Scrawny, Fat Boy gave a hearty tug on his end. They bounced her around as they reached for clothing. Fat Boy held a torn cloth in his hand. It was her skirt.

I couldn't move. I couldn't lower my pistol or pull the trigger. I was in disbelief of what I was seeing. They were going to rape a dead woman.

Scrawny reached for her shirt, grabbed the front of it, and pulled hard. The cloth stretched then ripped part of the way down, exposing a yellow bra.

Fat Boy cheered and gave a yank of his end of the rope, knocking the woman off balance and teetering backward.

I stepped from around the edge of the truck.

"What are you doing?" I asked, my voice surprisingly calm.

Both men looked at me then back at each other. Fat Boy spoke up first. "None of your business, boy." He held that pissed off, "go away" look I had seen before on other men's faces when they were caught doing something they shouldn't and didn't think the person catching them was worth their time.

He was wrong. It was every bit my business. The woman inside of the body was probably scared enough with the monster she had become. She was probably wishing herself

166

dead again, this time for good, even before she had her little run-in with those two punks. My mind whispered Jeanette's name, and it posted pictures on the bulletin board of my psyche, images of Jeanette terrified of two rednecks about to rape her, but not after she was dead, but while she was still alive. I could see the fear on her face, feel her heart's steady thumping, and hear her voice as she screamed for them to stop.

It was my business. It always had been, hadn't it?

"Again, what are you doing?"

Fat Boy rubbed his scraggly beard. His eyes narrowed.

"I said, none of your business."

In the Before, I had run into several people like those two guys. There was no reasoning with them. They were going to do what they wanted, and no one was going to stop them.

"Let her go," I said.

They both laughed at me.

"Or what?" Scrawny asked. "You gonna shoot us if we don't?"

"Yes."

They both grew quiet, exchanged looks again. Fat Boy tugged the woman back toward him when she got a little too close to his buddy. She stumbled and almost fell to the ground.

Jeanette entered my thoughts again. My jaw clenched. I felt my muscles flex several times.

"You ain't gonna shoot no one," Scrawny said. "You ain't noth—"

The bullet went through his forehead, blowing out the back of his skull. He fell, pulling the rope and the girl in his direction. Fat Boy jerked forward, stunned from what had just happened. He let go of the rope and put his hands in the air.

"Look, mister, we was just having some fun. That's all."

"You call that fun?"

"Where's the harm in playing around with her? She's dead."

"The body might be dead, but there's a person still trapped inside of it."

"That's crap. There ain't nothing in there. That's a monster and—"

I pulled the trigger again. His right knee disappeared, and he collapsed to the ground, releasing the rope and clutching his leg. He screamed much like I thought the woman rotter had been doing inside. Blood spilled onto the road.

"What's wrong with you?" he yelled.

The female turned toward Fat Boy.

"Nothing," I said and turned to leave.

"Wait. Wait. What are you doing? You can't just leave me here like this."

He was right.

I turned around, took several steps toward him. The female was drawing closer, her lips pulled back and a growl in her throat. She looked angry. I took aim at her head but didn't pull the trigger.

Again, my thoughts turned back to Jeanette. What if that woman had been my wife? What if she had been alive and these men had done that? They would have taken great joy with what they did to her. Who knows; they might have killed her when they were done. Probably just like they were going to do to the dead woman. Have some sick, disgusting fun and then crush her skull. All the while, that woman would be inside screaming and begging for them to stop.

I stepped on the rope, and the woman stopped. Her hands stretched out, but she couldn't quite reach him.

I pulled the trigger.

Fat Boy's left shoulder exploded and dropped him onto his back. He screamed again.

"You better pray you're right," I said. "You better hope that when the dead come back, there's nothing inside, that the body is just a husk."

His eyes grew wide with recognition.

"Please," he said. "Please, don't do this."

"I'm sure you've heard those words before, haven't you?"

"No, no, no—I've never—"

"Don't lie; you've done a lot worse. You don't think I know what you and your buddy were going to do here?"

His jaw went slack. Understanding covered his face, the truth of what he meant to do and what he would have done if I hadn't come upon them.

"You're a sick person," I said. "You deserve what you get."

I lifted my foot off the rope. The woman fell forward, her arms still outstretched.

Fat Boy screamed as she sank her teeth into the gap where his knee used to be. She pulled her head from side to side, ripping off a piece of meat. Fat Boy punched the back of her head. When he did this, I stepped forward, shot him in the other arm. Again, he howled.

The woman worked her way up, found his stomach with her scabrous hands.

I turned away, walked back to my truck as Fat Boy screamed and cried and the woman ate. I crawled in, closed

169

the door, and put the window up. I don't know how long I sat there. Two minutes or two hours. I don't know.

Hank, what happened?

"Nothing good, Humphrey. Nothing good."

Are there any survivors?

I thought on this a moment. There had been two. One of them was dead. The other one would be soon enough if he wasn't already.

"No."

Are we going soon?

"In a little bit."

What are we waiting for?

"I need to check out the truck."

Oh.

Another few minutes passed. I stood from the van and closed the door quietly. From the back of it, I pulled out a baseball bat and made my way back around Fat Boy's vehicle. Flies buzzed around Scrawny's head, landed for a taste of blood, and then flew away.

The woman sat on the ground. She was no longer eating Fat Boy's insides. She stared blankly at him.

"Miss," I said.

She turned her head, but there was no hunger in those filmy eyes. There was shame.

"It's over," I said and shot her. She slumped to the ground, hopefully at peace.

Fat Boy was dead. He was missing a couple of fingers on his right hand. I guess he tried to push her away and she bit them off. She had taken more than a couple of bites at his stomach and chest and throat. Too bad she missed one vital area. He stared an empty stare at the sky, his eyes seeing nothing, his chest not moving.

It was an hour later when his hand twitched, then his bottom lip. His head moved, and he lifted it off the ground with a groan that I like to believe was full with pain.

"Hey there, Fat Boy," I said and knelt down a few feet from him, placing the bat's head on the ground in front of me. "Are you in there?"

He tried to reach for me, but his arms wouldn't lift high enough.

"Come on, Fat Boy. I asked you a question. Are you in there?"

He grunted and growled, and his teeth gnashed at me, but he couldn't get up. I had made sure of that earlier. Now, it was time to see if he was right. I knew the answer, but Fat Boy didn't.

I stood, nudged one of his shoes with one of my own. He didn't seem to notice.

"Did you feel that?"

Nothing.

"No? Okay."

A little closer and I straddled his legs. I lifted the bat over my head and brought it down as hard as I could on the kneecap that I hadn't shot out. It cracked and popped, and Fat Boy groaned. It wasn't as loud as his screams had been, but it was long.

"Hey, Fat Boy. Still think there's nothing inside? Still think they are just monsters?"

He snapped his mouth at me.

"You do? Okay."

I smashed the leg again and then stepped up to his side and brought the bat down on one of his hips. Like before, there was a sickening thud and crack, and this time, Fat Boy's groans were more like his screams from earlier.

"Did you feel that in there? Does it hurt?"

I brought the bat across his outstretched hand, striking it hard enough to slam it into his bloodied midsection. And Fat Boy moaned, his mouth open in a wide grimace. He wasn't hungry, and if he was, there was no meal for him there. No, he was in pain. Pure pain. And somewhere in that newly rotting corpse was his soul, all black and stinking of the foulest crap.

"You need to answer me, Fat Boy. If you don't, I'm going to keep hitting you. Does this hurt?" The bat struck his elbow. It popped and bent awkwardly in the wrong direction.

There was another scream.

I bent down, pulled the gun from my waistband, and shoved the barrel in his mouth as far back as it would go, pinning his head to the ground.

"You have one chance to answer me. If you're in there, I want you to try and lift your pointer finger on your left hand. If you don't move that finger, I'm going to continue to beat you until I feel better about the last several months."

I moved the gun, stood straight, and backed away.

"Does this hurt?" I brought my boot down on his ankle. Another crack rang loud, but Fat Boy didn't groan or growl or scream. A moment passed, and I saw it. His pointer finger on his left hand moved. It wasn't much, but it was enough.

"So you're in there, right?"

This time, the movement of the finger was more defined.

I nodded.

"Good."

The gun went back into my waistband, and I picked my bat up from the ground. Then I turned and walked away. I climbed up into his truck. There were guns in the cab and all sorts of stuff in the bed. Water and cans of gas and canned foods and a couple of lanterns and knives and alcohol. There were other items, things I was certain they had stolen off the dead or maybe even the living before Fat Boy and Scrawny came across them. Things like watches and shoes and more than a dozen pair of women's panties and a box filled with jewelry. I thought of the brunette's wedding band. When they were done, it would have been taken and added to their box of trophies.

I shook my head and glanced in the direction of Fat Boy. Part of me wished I hadn't shot Scrawny in the head. He needed to suffer just the way Fat Boy was, but I reacted, and he was as dead as dead could get.

I did my best to unload as much of their supplies into the van as I could. A lot of it went onto my mattress, but I didn't care. Supplies were more important than the comforts of a pseudo-bed.

The sun was setting as I piled the last of the supplies into the van except for a bottle of Jack Daniels.

But I wasn't done. I grabbed the shovel from the van and went to the side of the road, opposite of where Fat Boy struggled to move. The grave wasn't as deep as I would have liked it to be, but it would do the trick. I lay the pretty woman in the hole and found her skirt on the ground not far from where she had killed Fat Boy. I set it over her hips, and then I buried her.

The sun was gone by then. I went to the van, got in, cranked it up, and put it into gear.

Are we leaving now? Humphrey asked. She sounded different. Scared, maybe.

"Yeah."

Good.

I said nothing as I uncorked the whiskey and took a big swallow. It was liquid fire going down my throat and settling in my stomach. It set my ears to buzzing.

I let off the brake and eased by Fat Boy's truck and then by Fat Boy himself. He writhed on the ground, one leg and arm moving, his head jerking from side to side.

In the old world, the crazies were everywhere. As we drove down Old Batesburg Road, I began to think maybe, just maybe, I had become one of the crazies of the new world.

Twelve Weeks and One Day After It All Started...

The Batesburg armory was a lost cause. I found that out after a fitful night of sleep on a hill behind a house in Leeseville. There had been a battle there (if that's really what it could be called. It was more like an attack and an attempt at defense). The dead lay scattered along the lawn but also in piles closer to the building as if the soldiers just shot and shot and shot until the dead stumbled over each other and got stuck outside. I pulled the van up close to the lot but parked in the road. I mashed the horn as hard as I could. It was a manly sound, not one of those friendly little beep beeps that was more apologetic than warning.

What are you doing? Humphrey asked.

"A test."

For what?

I looked at Humphrey. Her eyes were shiny glass that looked real at that moment. She looked like she had been crying or was about to.

"To see if any of them get up."

She didn't respond.

Nothing moved beyond our windows. I pressed the horn again, held it for several seconds. Still, nothing happened. I pulled the van into the parking lot, mindful of the bodies, though I guess I didn't need to be. They were all dead, and if they weren't, then they needed to be.

I mashed the horn one last time as hard as I could with both hands. I held it down for a good ten seconds. Like I thought, a couple of rotters came around the corner, but they moved so slowly. They were more skin and bones than anything else. The one moving the fastest was tall and missing patches of black hair, and his arms hung down at his sides. His head lulled on his shoulders as if his neck had been broken. The other one was shorter, but one of his legs had been wounded, and he seemed to drag it behind him as he hobbled along. I thought he would fall over, but somehow, he kept his balance.

I took a long swallow off that bottle of Jack Daniels I had pilfered from Fat Boy's truck. I wiped my mouth and got out of the van, gun ready, flashlight in my back pocket, a knife, also taken from Fat Boy's truck, in its sheath on my belt. I tucked the gun back in my waistband and reached into the van for the bat.

"Hi guys. My name is Hank Walker, and you killed my wife. Prepare to die." I think a smile crossed my face as I thought of *The Princess Bride*, a movie from back in the eighties. Inigo Montoya had said something similar about his father. I didn't have a sword like Montoya did, but I did have a baseball bat, and I planned on putting it to good use. I swung at Patchy Hair. His head spun on his shoulder, a burst of blood spraying out. His neck was broken. Patchy Hair tilted to one side, spinning on his heel, and then fell forward, right into the shorter one. They both fell to the ground. I brought the bat down on the shorter one's head. And just like that, they were both down for good.

I looked around, waiting for more of them, but none came. I took a deep breath and a closer look at the carnage. It told me they had been overrun a while back. The bodies had already taken on a parchment look, and the stench wasn't as bad as I thought it would be. It was pungent but fading. There were plenty of flies and rats and a few snakes, but they scattered as I walked through the corpses.

Bodies blocked the front of the armory, making that door impossible to enter. I made my way to the back. The gate had been knocked down. There were no military vehicles behind the building, and the back entrance was propped open by a couple of bodies. I entered the darkness, flicked on the light. My boots weren't as quiet as I hoped, giving off hollow clops that echoed throughout the building with each step.

There wasn't much to the place. A few rooms along the back and what looked like a warzone in the front. There were as many dead inside as there were outside. The floor was sticky with dried blood. The clopping of my boots gave way to a sickening *shwisk* sound.

To my right, someone moved. I caught the turning of his head on the outskirts of the light's beam. I turned to see a soldier who was little more than bones with chunks of flesh still on them. One side of his face was missing, as if he had shot himself but missed his brain. I unsheathed the knife and walked over. His teeth clattered together as he snapped at me.

"I'm sorry," I said and drove the blade into his temple. I took the gun lying beside him, shoved it in my waistband.

There were other weapons, most of which still had bullets in them. I did what I had done for what felt like my entire life at that point: I pilfered the weapons, making trips back and forth. The van was getting full, and there was no real way of sorting things out. Not there at least. The mattress was completely covered before I arrived, and I had taken to sleeping behind the wheel again. The weapons went into a helter skelter pile near the back.

Searching for my baby brother and son was a slow process. Gathering supplies in the process took even longer. Still, I had to get everything I could use. *Leave nothing behind*, I told myself.

I was worried that at any point, I could turn over a body or lift one off of another and find Bobby or Jake. I wasn't sure what I would do if they were there and one of the dead, especially if they hadn't already been put down.

I found some clothes—army fatigues and boots and shirts—folded in footlockers. Not that I wanted clothes, but winter was coming, and there was no need to freeze when I could try on a few things and take them with me.

Hours passed, and when I was done, Bobby and Jake were nowhere to be found.

I let go of a heavy breath and made my way back to the van.

Did you find them? Humphrey asked in her sweet, childish voice.

"No."

What now?

"We ride."

I drove away, the half empty bottle of Jack between my legs and a hole in my chest. It was then that I realized I would never see Jake or Bobby again. I took a long swallow of the whiskey, wiped my lips with the back of one arm. The beginnings of a good buzz began to kick in.

I meant to head for the lake, for the seclusion of a body of water. Maybe I could find a boat and just float out there until I died. At that moment, dying didn't seem such a terrible idea as long as it was permanent.

There were turns made, straightaways taken, more turns. I think I was trying to get lost in a world that had been that way for several months. Why not? Everything else was gone.

…

Everything.

…

…

As daylight began to die out, I found myself along Highway 321. I was nowhere near the lake. In fact, it was just the opposite direction. Another turn and I was on Highway 78.

I had succeeded in getting lost.

Further down the road, I saw the sign for Blackville. A mound of charred bodies lay by the road.

"Someone's been here."

Who? Humphrey asked. There was a quiver in her voice. One I understood quite well. So far, all the living people we came across were on the wrong side of losing their minds, a byproduct of the fall of civilization as we once knew it.

"I don't know, but…"

Can we leave?

"What?"

Can we leave? People scare me now.

I nodded. "They scare me too."

I pulled onto Road 3 and stopped.

After not seeing people for months, I had managed to run into an overzealous preacher and the remains of his congregation and two good old boys with a hankering for dead women. Now, I came across some others, this time Native Americans.

179

They were surrounded by a horde of dead, fighting them off as well as they could.

Let's go, Hank. Please, let's just leave. A whine was in her voice.

"We can't leave them like this," I said. "We can't leave any of them like this."

They didn't have guns. That was the first thing I noticed. They did have knives and sticks, but that meant close quarters combat. From the looks of it, they were losing.

I grabbed several guns, left the van, and slammed the door shut. Before it closed, I heard Humphrey crying.

I ran, getting close enough to take aim and hit the dead and not the living. One shot, two, three, four, all true. Five and six and seven. More dead fell away. Some of them turned to me. Several more shots and I could see the Native Americans. Some were soaked in blood. There were a few on the ground, dead or dying, chunks of flesh ripped free from throats and stomachs and arms and faces.

I dropped an empty gun, pulled another one from my waistband.

It took only minutes, but it seemed to last much longer. Finally, the last of the dead dropped to the ground. He was an older man. His hair had been gray when he was alive but had become a nasty yellow in death. He had been kneeling over a body, his jaws snapping and ripping at the flesh of the dead woman lying there. The top of his head disappeared, and he slumped forward over the woman's body.

In the aftermath, I heard crying. I turned back to the truck, thinking I had left the door open and that I was hearing Humphrey. The door was closed. The crying came from a little girl lying on the ground. There were teeth marks on her right bicep, and blood washed her skin and clothes in red. A woman knelt beside her and pulled the little girl's face into her breasts. She was crying also.

"Thank you," one of the men said. He was older, his hair gray and pulled back into a ponytail that ran down to the small of his back. His jeans were dirty, and his shirt was blood-soaked. There were splashes of blood on his skin. He held a wooden spear with a stone head. On his back was a book bag.

"Did they bite you?" I asked.

"No, not me but others." He looked around. Three of his people were dead, and the little girl would be soon. He drove his spear into the skull of the woman the elderly dead man had been eating. Then he turned his attention to two men, both older, maybe even close to his age. He stabbed first one then the other in the skull and then went to the woman and little girl.

Blood dripped from his spear as he stood over them. I was looking at a man who knew what he had to do but who was too attached to do it. I wondered if that was his granddaughter. I wondered, not for the first time, if it were Bobby, could I put him down?

"We must hurry," he said and took the girl in his arms.

"What are you doing?" I called after him. "She's going to turn. You can't save her."

"There is still time."

"Time? She's been bitten. Time is not on her side, and if she turns, it might not be on yours either."

"Thank you for your help, for saving us. But we have to go now."

"Where are you going?" I asked.

181

"To the Healing Springs."

I had heard of the place before. Jeanette and I had once tried to find it but never made it there. Images flashed in my mind of that day, little snapshots that cut deep into my heart. I always thought the stories told about it were all a bunch of hogwash parents told their kids. It was nothing but a hoax, a place where the sick went to drink from the fountain of healing. Whatever.

But what if it were true? What if there was a fountain or lake that could heal wounds and save those who were infected? I heard myself speak softly. "Where?"

"No time to talk. She is dying, and we must get her to the Healing Springs."

"Where is it?"

They turned to me—six adults with sad eyes. The older man spoke up. "Down the road a way."

"A way? As in miles?"

He nodded. "We don't have time to talk. We need to get Alaya there soon, or she will die."

I'm not entirely too sure I believed him, but his belief in the ability of this water, this Healing Springs, gave me hope. And she was just a little girl. How can you not help a child?

"I'll take you," I said. "I can't get you all in the van—it's kind of full, but I can take you and the girl."

He looked at me then to the crying woman beside him. She nodded. So did he.

"Thank you."

Before leaving the five adults behind, I gave them weapons and hoped there was enough ammunition to get them to the Healing Springs safely.

"I hate to do this, Humphrey, but you have to move for now." I took Humphrey out of the car seat and then unstrapped it. The man got in, the girl cradled gently in his arms.

She glanced at me and then at the stuffed bear. "Would you like to hold her?" I asked. "Her name is Humphrey."

The girl reached out, her hand trembling, and took the bear.

Humphrey didn't make a sound. She just went into the child's arm and lay still as the child took comfort in her.

We drove.

By foot, it would have taken a couple of hours to get to Healing Springs. By vehicle, it took only a few minutes—ten at the most. I learned the old man's name was Imeko, and he was almost eighty. The girl was Alaya, and she was almost seven.

Imeko directed me around a turn and into a neighborhood. "Just down that way," he said.

I rounded another curve and followed a straightaway until it turned into a wooded area. The trees made a cul-de-sac. There was a stream that widened, then narrowed as it went back into the trees. There were several wooden squares on the ground made of landscaping boards. In the middle of each square was a set of PVC water spigots—four spouts on each one. There was a stone picnic table that looked as if it had been there since the beginning of time.

A blue sign with white lettering sat on wooden posts. It read:

GOD'S ACRE
HEALING SPRINGS

ACCORDING TO TRADITION, THE INDIANS REVERENCED THE WATER FOR ITS HEALING PROPERTIES AS A GIFT FROM THE GREAT SPIRIT. THEY LED THE BRITISH WOUNDED TO THEIR SECRET WATERS DURING THE AMERICAN REVOLUTION, AND THE WOUNDED WERE HEALED. THIS HISTORICAL PROPERTY HAS BEEN DEEDED TO GOD FOR PUBLIC USE. PLEASE REVERE GOD BY KEEPING IT CLEAN.

The closer we got to it, the more the Healing Springs looked like nothing more than a swamp area. The plant life had grown wild along the edges of the trees. There was high grass in spots. The water looked like it wound its way as far to the west and east as it could go.

I parked near the picnic table. Imeko stood from the van, Alaya in his arms and still clutching Humphrey tight. There was blood on the bear's pajamas.

Alaya didn't look well. She was sweating, and the whites of her eyes were a deep pink verging on red. Her mouth hung open. A moment later, she threw up blood over Imeko's shoulder.

"Help me," Imeko said when he reached the stone table. I held her head as he laid her down. Her skin was hot. Her body jerked, and I thought she was going to go into convulsions. I was more than concerned—I had never seen the infection take hold that quickly. It had been less than twenty minutes since she was bitten, and her body was already giving up.

"She's not going to make it."

Imeko paid me no attention. Instead, he went to one of the squared in spigots, turned the handle.

The clearest water I have ever seen came out of that spigot. No rust. No sediment. Just water.

Imeko slipped the book bag off his shoulders, unzipped it, and rummaged around. He pulled small things from the bag —mostly kid's toys—and set them on the ground. Then he found what he was looking for: a child's plastic cup. He filled it, stood, though it looked difficult for him to do so, and went to Alaya.

"Lift her head."

I did as he said, lifting not only her head but also her upper body. I sat down on the table and held her against me to keep her from falling over. It reminded me of Bobby, of the time he was sick with pneumonia. Jeanette and I took turns cradling him at night. It was eleven days of trying to sleep sitting up in a kid's bed. It was three months of constant worry. Every time he coughed, we stopped what we were doing to check on him. "Are you okay, Bobby?" "Are you sure, Bobby?" "Do you need your inhaler, Bobby?" "Don't overdo it, Bobby."

I'm sure that got old.

It made me wonder, is Bobby okay? If he is, is he safe? Where is he? Is he still among the few living? Or is he one of *them*?

A hint of panic rose in my chest, and my breath caught in my throat. I had to fight the urge to drop Alaya to the table and run, to get back in the van and high tail it out of there. Bobby had to be out there somewhere. He had to still be alive.

It was the slight burning sensation in my left hand and right side of my body that brought me back and settled me down. Alaya's fever had grown worse. Sweat spilled from her body, and she was unresponsive.

Imeko worked quickly, first splashing water onto the wound—a space of only about three inches in diameter. He hurried to the spigot, filled the cup, and came back to the table.

"Alaya, you must drink."

Her head moved but not much. We were losing her.

"Here," I said and took the cup. I tilted Alaya's head back then tipped the cup to her lips, letting a little of the water spill into her mouth. She licked her lips, and her eyes came open a little.

"Drink, Alaya," I said.

Her small hands went to the cup. They were weak, and she could barely hold them up. But she drank it all.

"More, please."

Imeko retrieved another cupful. She drank all of it as well, and then she settled into a deep sleep.

Then we waited.

It was a little over six hours before the others arrived at the Healing Springs, but they *did* arrive. It was dark, and at first, I thought they were some of the dead. I raised one of my guns and took aim.

"No," Imeko said. "They are alive."

I lowered the gun, thankful to not have to shoot anymore that day.

Alaya's mother took over holding her. My back and legs popped when I stood. It was sweet relief.

The hours went by slowly. A couple of the Native Americans slept while the others stood watch around Imeko, Alaya, and her mother.

None of them talked to me. Instead, they gave me leery stares, as if they were suspicious of me. Maybe they were.

The sun came up, banishing the night's darkness. Everyone looked weary. Alaya still lay across her mother's lap on the picnic table. I wanted to relieve her, to at least give her a moment to stretch and walk around. When I offered, she shook her head and snapped out a quick, "No."

Sometime in the night, the wound had been bandaged with a torn shirt. After the sun came up, Imeko took it off. The bite mark had been an angry red the day before, and I expected it to be gray, verging on black then. Instead, the skin around the wound was light pink, and the wound itself looked as if it were healing. What should have been dead tissue was still living, still holding true to its color...

...and healing.

"How's her fever?" Imeko asked.

"She has none," Alaya's mother responded.

In the daylight, I took the time to walk around. The names of hundreds of people had been written or carved on boards and parts of trees where the bark had shed. There was a sign nailed to a piece of wood quoting Revelations. But what struck me most was the small figurine of the crucifixion attached to one of the trees with a U-nail. The figure's head was bowed down in death. Chills ran the length of my body and...

Imeko came up behind me.

"I want to say thank you again, Mr. Walker," he said. "My granddaughter will live now. If not for your arrival, I fear we all would have died yesterday."

I heard his words but really only caught what he said about Alaya. I had seen little response from her. Though her wound was better and her fever gone, I couldn't believe she would live.

"Why do you think she will live?" I asked.

"The water will heal her."

"How do you know?"

"Because it will."

"What makes this water so special?"

He didn't answer for a long while. I feared—and I still believe—I had offended him. When he finally answered, his tone was polite if not measured.

"My ancestors lived on this land many years in the past. They were here when the soldiers came. They were told to bury the soldiers when they died. There were two others, neither of them injured in any way. They stayed here as my ancestors bathed the wounded in the water. They watched men who should have died live.

"This land—this water—was touched by God. It has healing powers that no other spring has. No medicine can do what the Springs can."

"Why didn't you put Alaya in the water? Just bypass the need for a cup."

"The infection. I didn't want it in the water."

"But if the water is touched by…"

"Man has contaminated this world enough already. We are being punished for our transgressions, Mr. Walker. This is God's Acre. This is a holy land. We will not sully it with the dead."

"The dead? You don't believe this…this healing springs can save your granddaughter?"

"I believe what will be done, will be done, and if God so wills it to be, then it shall be. I only provided her the chance."

188

I was starting to think I had run into another bunch of overly religious quacks. Unlike Pastor White and his flock, this man's belief was sincere and passionate. He believed the will of God, and he hoped that will involved his granddaughter's survival.

I can't say I shared the same belief. I had lost enough to question my own beliefs. I had seen enough of the new world and what the dead could do. I had witnessed answers to questions and had those answers confirmed.

"Fair enough," I replied.

I thought of leaving, of getting Humphrey and taking off the first chance I got. Then I would swear off all survivors and find somewhere to be, somewhere to live out my last days. Maybe I would find my way back to Lake Murray and...and...and I didn't know. I didn't know what I would do. What I was certain of was I was tired of roaming, of running from the dead, and searching for them as well.

Then it happened.

Alaya woke.

She opened her eyes and sat up in her mother's lap. She didn't look sick. She didn't look like she was dying or even close to it.

Her mother cried. So did the other adults.

Imeko went to her, took the bandage off of Alaya's arm. He touched her face and checked her eyes. He pushed on her stomach.

"It's a miracle," he said and lifted his hands to the sky. "Thank you, thank you."

Tears spilled from his eyes, and he hugged Alaya tight.

I walked over, the world passing far too slow for me to be moving. I saw her, saw the life in her face and movements, saw the wound on her arm. It wasn't an infected hole, and the flesh wasn't gray or black or green. The wound itself was pink. The flesh around it was the same as the rest of her skin. The whites of her eyes were no longer red but white.

She was smiling.

And she held Humphrey close. Humphrey seemed to be smiling as well. Her glass eyes appeared to sparkle, as if there were tears in them. If I didn't know better, her short arms were hugging Alaya.

I knew then...

"You see," Imeko said to me, his face radiant with joy, "the water is blessed."

I nodded. It was all I could do. What if I had known about this before Pop had been bitten? Or before Davey Blaylock or Lee had been bitten? Maybe they would still be alive. Maybe...

Maybes are for people who live their lives as dreams rather than reality, and my life was no dream. It was all nightmares.

I stayed with them another night, each one of us keeping watch. The following morning, Alaya was better still. She showed no signs of regression. She was as healthy as a little girl could be.

"You need to move on, Mr. Walker," Imeko said to me that morning. "You have helped us, helped Alaya, but you must move on. There is nothing here for you."

"What about you? What about your people? What are you going to do?"

He nodded toward the entrance to the Healing Springs, to God's Acre. "We will take one of the houses as our own. We will survive."

"Sounds like you have a plan."

A nod. His eyes held the steely gaze of a man who had made up his mind. I wasn't wanted there. I didn't belong with them.

"Can I take a jug of that water with me?"

"It is not mine to give but yours to take if you so choose."

I chose.

I drank the last of the water I had in a gallon jug. Then I filled it with the water God had touched. It was my shot at redemption if I ever got bit. I took a clump of clay from close to the water and marked the jug with a brown HS.

It neared noon and the time to leave. I went to Alaya and held my hand out to her. "I need to go now. Can I have the bear back?"

She looked from me to Humphrey and back to me. With her lip poked out, she pulled Humphrey away from her chest and lifted the stuffed bear up. I took Humphrey in both hands. Her white bunny pajamas were stained red and were rough where Alaya's blood had dried. If I would have looked beneath the clothes, I'm sure Humphrey's fur would have been crusted red as well.

"Are you ready to go, Humphrey?"

No, she whispered.

"What?"

I don't want to go.

"But we have to. Imeko said we have to leave."

Then leave.

"Humphrey…"

I'm not leaving.

"What are you…what are you saying, Humphrey?"

I want to stay with her. She needs me.

"But…"

191

I need her.

I could say nothing. For a few minutes, I didn't move. If there had ever been life in that little bear, it was at that moment. There was a fierceness in her eyes, much like Imeko's had been. I squatted to eye level with young Alaya, six years old and almost seven and who will see another day as a living person thanks to what I always thought had been a myth. I placed Humphrey in her hands.

"You take good care of her, okay?" I was talking more to Humphrey than Alaya, but it was the girl who answered.

"Yes, sir. Thank you."

I turned and went to the van. I didn't look back to see if Humphrey was watching me leave. Part of me was afraid she wouldn't be.

Twelve Weeks, Three Days, and a Few Hours After It All Started...

Rain. It was appropriate.

There were no real clouds in the sky when I left Healing Springs. But an hour away, my life changed yet again. Clouds appeared off in the distance. Fat, nasty, gray clouds with black ones lurking behind them.

I pulled off the road at a gas station that I'm certain had little gas to give. I still had plenty of full tanks in the back of the van, but it wasn't gas I was after. I needed a map.

A rumble of thunder came from overhead. In the far away clouds, I could see the strobe effect of lightning. Then came thunder again.

The glass door of the gas station had been busted out. I stepped through, pistol ready. I surveyed the gray-tinted store. Near the counter was what I needed. I walked over, reached for the South Carolina Roadside Map. I took it and didn't bother looking around the store after that.

Still, I saw the dead man in the aisle. He was probably the store clerk. From the looks of him, he had been dinner to several of the dead.

"I'm sorry," I said and put the bullet through the center of his head.

Outside, there were a couple more rotters making their way toward me. Even as members of the dead race, they had seen better days. I could have probably let them rot away, but there were souls trapped inside. I knew this sure as the day was long. I should have saved the bullets, but the bat was cruel, and they had suffered enough. Besides, I had no desires to exert any more effort than I had to at that time. Two shots, one to each head, and they were finally at rest.

In the van, I looked at the map.

"We're on 321, Humphrey," I said. "If we take it out, we can pick up Number 1 here, and that will take us back toward Batesburg and—"

And Humphrey wasn't there. I looked at the empty seat where she had sat for so long with me, where she had been my constant companion. I wiped my mouth. My breaths were deep. I fought back the tears that threatened to fall.

...

I missed her terribly.

...

...

I wanted to whip the van around and go back for her, take her from that little girl. What good would that have done? She didn't want to leave her. I can't blame her—Alaya would probably play with her, would probably love her the way any child would love their stuffed animal.

What had I done to show that I loved Humphrey?

...

Nothing.

...

I had abandoned her once. She had been scared in some of the places we went, by some of the things we saw, probably even by me. I had changed. I was no longer the crumbling man who found her in an abandoned house. I'm not really sure what I was, but I wasn't the same.

And I was alone again.

I followed 321 and then hit Number 1 just as the map showed. Eventually, I was back on Old Batesburg Road. Not too far down the road would be the turn for the armory. From there, I would proceed to 378.

But first...

Fat Boy's truck appeared down the road. By then, it was raining, and I had finished off the bottle of Jack Daniels I had pulled from that truck. I pulled up beside the vehicle and got out. Scrawny lay dead in the middle of the road. The woman's grave was on the opposite side, the dirt like puddled mud now.

Not too far away, maybe a hundred yards or so from where I left him, was Fat Boy. He had managed to somewhat crawl away, mostly on his belly. His intestines trailed behind him.

"Hey there, Fat Boy," I said. "Remember me?"

He stopped, craned his neck toward me, and let out a growl.

"How you feeling in there? I reckon it sucks, doesn't it?"

Another groan, and then he turned back to his crawling away. He remembered me. He remembered what I did to him.

"It's the end of the line, Fat Boy. Say hey to Scrawny when you get where you're going."

I pulled out my knife and shoved it into the base of his neck and drove it upward. He collapsed. I didn't bury him or Scrawny.

I got back in the van and followed the road past the armory and further on down until I reached 378.

A left would have taken me to Newberry and Prosperity and Clinton. But straight took me to Lake Murray. I kept thinking about that boat and drifting my days away. I could do some fishing, catch my own food, clean it, and cook it.

195

Surely, the lake would be teeming with fish by then. I doubted anyone had been fishing there for a while.

I crossed over 378 and followed the road until it forked to the left. I stayed straight and passed a church on the right. The windows had been broken out. I thought of Pastor White and his congregation. I wondered if anyone went there seeking refuge but instead found an overzealous, end-of-the-world, come-follow-me-to-your-death type. Or if they found salvation on their knees with hands and voices lifted high. I hoped, if there had been any seeking shelter from the dead, they found what they wanted and made their peace. I hoped they survived. Though more and more, it seemed like very few lived, and those that did had lost their minds.

I turned left on a street that seemed to lead further toward the lake. I passed a dirt road on the right, stopped and backed up, then turned onto it. I could see the water from the entrance, maybe a hundred yards away. Probably less.

The dirt road circled around in a U until it came out on the road I had been on to start with. There were a handful of houses, a couple of trailers, and several boats that sat near piers. Circling back, I stopped at the first place to the right. It was a trailer and kind of ramshackled at that. A brick house sat in what looked like the trailer's yard. Behind them both was a fence where it looked like animals had been kept. Off to the left was another trailer. This one looked sturdier, but it was lower to the ground. I pulled onto the easement to the right and to the side of the first trailer. There was a tractor beneath a wooden canopy and another smaller building beside it. I found out later it was a tool shed.

It wasn't the perfect place, and there was plenty of work that needed to be done to make it safe. The stairs leading to the back door were high off the ground, and the ones in the front could easily be removed, making it harder for the dead to get inside. I would have to board up a set of glass patio doors, but for the time being, it would do for shelter.

"Come on," I said, reaching for Humphrey. Again, I had forgotten she was gone. My hand hung in the air for several seconds before pulling it away.

Before heading to the trailer, I downed the last of a bottle of water. Some of it spilled down the side of my mouth. The whiskey had been gone for about an hour, and the water would have to do. I can't really say if I was a little drunk. If not, I missed a good chance to be. My ears hummed, and the world felt a little off kilter.

I peered in through the patio doors. The place was dark, but the sun shone through enough to see a dining room table, a couch, coffee table, and a door off to the right with what looked like the entrance to a kitchen to the left. I saw no bodies of any kind. The patio door, like so many others after people abandoned their homes, was unlocked. It slid open with ease.

The place was cooler than I expected. And clean. No one had ransacked it searching for supplies. I went around the dinner table and stood in the living room. A useless big screen television sat across from me along with a recliner, a rocker, and a piano. A small hallway led to the back door. Across the hall was another room. There were pictures of children and adults, a family portrait full of smiling people.

The door to the right led to a bedroom and a bathroom. I left that room, crossed the living room, and stepped into what amounted to a small hall that really wasn't a hall at all but more like a two-foot-wide divider between the two rooms.

There was a table in the room in front of me and several full bookcases, a computer desk, and another piano. They must have liked pianos. Across the room and to the left was another bathroom and bedroom.

The bathroom was white tiled with a forest green toilet and bathtub. The sink was the same green, but there were no toiletries on the counter that surrounded it. Instead, there was a five-gallon jug, like one that belonged at a water cooler. The water in the jug was clear, probably cleaner than any water from a faucet but not as clean as the water from Healing Springs. A hose ran from a fitted cap to another jug, this one more like a pot with a lid. The pot sat on a homemade oil burner. On the floor next to the counter were items I didn't expect to see in a bathroom. Cornmeal, sugar, malt, and yeast, all of them opened at one time but now held shut with clothespins.

A homemade still. I couldn't help but smile. If I hadn't been already well lit, I probably would have tried the shine. But, at that time, I didn't.

The house was empty. No living. No dead.

I left the bathroom and walked back out into what I could only think of as a den. On the wall was a picture of a woman in her wedding gown. Her hair and eyes were brown, and she had a great smile, a genuine smile. Her face was radiant. She was a pretty woman.

"You made someone very happy, didn't you?"

Thankfully, the picture didn't answer.

Evening would be coming soon, and the sun would lay itself to sleep. I had work to do, but I was tired. So tired. My head was heavy and swimming. My body told me to lie down and rest before I passed out. The world was out of focus. It had been a long time since I drank anything besides beer. The whiskey had gotten to me.

Standing in that room, staring at the picture of the beautiful woman on the wall, I imagined life in that house. Did she live there? What was her name? Did she have kids?

The sounds of children, a boy and a girl, came from behind me. I spun on my heel, pistol drawn, surprised by their voices. Giggles filled the room, and footsteps ran away from me.

I crossed the room in four long strides, searched the next room, then the kitchen and the back bedroom.

Nothing.

But I heard it.

What's wrong, Walker?

"Did you hear that?"

Hear what?

"The children. They were laughing. They ran off. I heard them. I heard their footsteps."

There are no children. There is only you.

I turned, searched the room. Humphrey's voice was so loud, so real, so much older than I had recalled. But there was no Humphrey.

The laughter came again. I circled the kitchen and went to the front door. I found no one.

"Who's there?"

Footsteps followed, the heavy thumps of kids who still hadn't learned to run soft.

No running through the house.

I turned, gun out in front of me, finger on the trigger. The voice had a melody to it, a sing-song tone. It was beautiful.

But there was no one there. My head spun, and I wavered a little on my feet.

The back bedroom was still empty except for a dresser and two beds—probably where the children slept. There were no toys, no clothes in the dresser and only a handful in the closet—none of them belonging to children. There was no one in the closet or in the bathroom. I pulled the shower curtain back to see a green tub and several full jugs, much like the one on the counter.

Laughter again, this time more than the happy giggles of children. There were adults, both young and old, and they were in the living room. And I ran back in there and…

Nothing.

The laughter filled my ears. Bits and pieces of conversations filtered in. I turned, my pistol out at arm's length, looking for ghosts that weren't there. A whisper on my neck and I whirled, pulled the trigger. A hole appeared in the piano, but there wasn't a person lying dead on the floor.

I shoved the gun into my waistband, slid the pack from my shoulders.

I remember doing that.

Then everything went hazy and gray around the edges. White dots filled my vision, and it was tough to breathe.

Then I was falling…falling…

Twelve Weeks and...Almost Four Days After It All Started...

The world is a dark place. Has been since the beginning of time. The darkness in our hearts goes right along with the darkness of the things that lurk in shadows.

I heard her calling me long before I woke to the darkness of that house. It was faint at first.

Walker. Walker, wake up.

As I lay unconscious, the voice speaking to me, I could see Jeanette kneeling beside me. Her hand was stroking my hair, my cheek. There was a tapping coming from somewhere in the house.

Walker, please get up.

Her eyes sparkled even in the blackness that surrounded us. She continued to stroke my face as she begged me to stand, but her lips never moved.

The tapping was like rain on glass or maybe small hailstones.

Walker, if you don't get up, you're going to die here.

Jeanette's features washed away, and she was gone. The tapping continued, but it was less like rain and more like thumping. I tried to wake up. I could feel myself on the edge of consciousness but too paralyzed to wake fully. My body felt heavy, my eyes glued shut.

Wake up, Walker!

And her voice grew more and more frantic.

The world swam back, and my eyes snapped open. I lay on my stomach, one side of my face smooshed into the plush carpeting.

Walker, hurry!

It was Humphrey, and she was on the verge of panicking. And then I was as well. My heart hammered, and I was disoriented for a few seconds before realizing where I was.

Pushing myself to my knees, I shook my head. I was fully awake, but for some reason, the thumping was still there.

Walker!

I looked toward the kitchen, to where the dining room table was and the sliding glass door just beyond it. One of the dead stood on the other side, her hand steadily beating on the glass. I wasn't sure, but it sounded like she had something in her hand and was trying to break the glass out.

I stood on legs of lead, my head like a ten-pound weight on my shoulders. I went to the patio door. I didn't remember locking it, but I must have. Or maybe it had been the ghost of the giggling children or the pretty, brown-haired bride. The dead struck the glass harder when I stopped. She smashed her face against the door, sludge spilling from her mouth like drool.

The gun came from my waistband, and I took aim. She stopped beating on the glass as if she recognized what a gun was and what it could do to her. She took a step back like she was afraid of me. Another step and another, her hands down at her sides. The woman toppled off the edge of the patio deck.

I slid the gun back in my pants and looked around the kitchen. A knife with a thick blade sat in a cutting block. I took it and went outside.

The rain had stopped. The moon was high and bright, casting a blue light on the world. It wasn't quite full, and it seemed a lot closer than it should be, but it provided enough light for me to see the woman on the ground by the patio, her legs buckled in odd directions, one arm broken and lying beside her. Something like blood oozed around her head, soaking into the ground. Her eyes stared up, looking at the sky in sightless wonder.

The moon's light shimmered off of something near the woman. The ring glimmered on her hand, and I knew that was where the glassy, thumping sound had come from—her wedding band. For several minutes, I looked at her, hoping it wasn't the brown-haired beauty in the picture. I knelt beside her, turned her head to look at her face. It wasn't the picture woman but someone else. I let out a long sigh before walking back inside and closing the door behind me.

I flicked on a flashlight and glanced around, hoping to see Humphrey in the backpack I carried when we left the van, hoping leaving her with Alaya at Healing Springs was just a dream.

It wasn't. Humphrey really was gone.

I made my way to the first bedroom on the right. Closing the door behind me, I locked it. The pack went on the floor.

I stood in the middle of the dark room for a long while, my head still in a slight fog, my limbs aching. I should have just laid down and went to sleep.

Instead, I left the room, crossed the house, and entered the back bathroom. I scanned the jugs in the bathtub, my light shining over each one. The liquids were mostly clear except for a dark red one that seemed thick. It reminded me of blood, something I had seen too much of over the past months. There were wine bottles interspersed among the jugs. I picked several up, scanned their handwritten labels. Apple

203

Cinnamon Cider. Strawberry Rush. Blackberry Crush. Lemon Tongue Curler.

Lemon Tongue Curler? The name alone made the decision for me. I left the bathroom with the bottle and went back to the bedroom. I closed the door, locked it, and then pushed the small dresser by the wall to in front of it.

I pulled the cork free. A hot smell like kerosene rose from the bottle and burned my nose. I tipped it to my lips, took a sip. Liquid fire ran down my throat, searing my insides and warming my stomach. My eyes snapped completely open and filled with tears in the process. My head was suddenly clear, and I think I spun around in a circle and then braced myself with a hand against the wall.

What's wrong? Humphrey was still in my head. I wonder now if she always was.

"Strong."

Strong? Strong what?

"Alcohol. I haven't tasted anything this potent in years."

Should you be drinking?

"Probably not."

Are you going to drink more?

"Probably so."

The conversation ended. It was the last one I ever had with Humphrey.

I drank.

I drank too much.

At some point in the night—or was it early morning?—I stood at the window of the bedroom, a big double glass version that slid left and right instead of up and down. From where I stood, I could see the water shimmering off the lake. I could see the other homes, most of them actual houses and not trailers like the one I was in. I wondered if I shouldn't take one of them as shelter instead.

It doesn't matter, little bro.

Lee stood beside me, staring out at the tranquil scene in front of us. He had a beer in his hand, and he wore the flannel shirt and jeans he had on when he died. His head wasn't an exploded mess, and there was no bite mark on his arm.

"Why's that?"

You can't defeat them. They'll keep coming and coming until they get you.

I held my tongue. The moonshine left a buzzing in my ears. My face was hot.

They got us all, Hank, he continued. *Me, Pop, Davey Blaylock. Wilson and Nancy and Rick. Michael and his son. Mike Simmons. My Jessica and the kids too. Paul Marcum. Mrs. Crenshaw. Jeanette. Jake and Bobby.*

I turned and looked at Lee. He stared back at me, his eyes sad almonds on his face. There were whiskers on his chin.

There's nowhere to go, little brother. Nothing you can do. You can fight and fight, but sooner or later...

"I can't give up, Lee."

He laughed, hardy and loud, a sound that startled me.

Hank, you already have.

"No, I haven't."

You can't BS me, little bro. You gave up the moment you found out Jeanette was dead.

"I went to the armory, where Jake said they were going. It was overrun."

Lee tipped his beer up, took a long swallow. It was as if the old days were back, but Rick wasn't there, and neither was Davey or Jake. It was just the two of us.

Do you remember Roscoe?

"Roscoe Harris?"

That'd be the one.

"Yeah. What about him?"

Remember when he killed his brother out in the woods that day. Calvin was there. So was Joe and Shawn, I think.

"I remember."

He killed Rhonda too, you know?

"No, I didn't. I thought she just disappeared—left him after he was arrested." I continued to stare out the window, not flinching at the revelation offered up by my older brother.

Nope. He killed her.

"How do you know?"

I was there.

"Really?"

Yeah. He took another swallow of his beer. It was the action of a man deep in thought, of someone pondering life things. *She was such a whore. She cheated on Roscoe a lot. But he let it go. Then he just flipped out, put three bullets in Robert's chest and drank a couple more beers before heading home.*

"I'm drunk," I said.

That you are, little bro.

I humored myself—I was the only one there. Lee wasn't real. He couldn't be—and asked, "You were there when he killed her?"

Yeah. We thought he was on the run, you know, fled town for the mountains. We were wrong. He came in while she and I were...you know...

I looked at him again, this time acknowledging that this bit of weirdness was taking place.

He killed her, threatened to do the same thing to me if I didn't help him hide the body.

Disbelief. That's what I felt.

"I don't believe you."

You don't have to; you're drunk, and you're talking to dead people, Hank. But that's not the point. Roscoe gave up on life when he killed his brother. Just like you have.

I should have stopped then, stopped drinking and gone to bed and slept it off.

I didn't. I took another long swallow, sucked in a breath of air as the fire raced down my throat and the buzz became more of a full throttle beehive between my ears.

Pop was sitting on the bed, his hands in his lap. I never realized how old he looked. He lifted his head to me.

You still have my shotgun, Hank?

"Yes sir."

You ever gonna fire it?

"I don't know."

Don't let it break your collarbone. It's got a heck of a kick.

"I won't."

The dead. They're going to get you, Hank.

It wasn't Pop this time but Mrs. Crenshaw. Her hair was some shade of blue or purple and up in rollers. She stood by the dresser, a ruler in hand, much like when she was a teacher.

Do you hear me, Hank Walker? I ain't going to keep spoon-feeding you. The dead will get you.

I looked at the bottle, shook my head. It was half empty.

"Not if I drink myself to death first."

And it was out. My intentions weren't to drown my sorrows but to drown myself. Lee was right. I had given up already. I was tired of running, tired of fighting. Tired of being alone. Maybe I would get drunk enough to go down to the lake and take a swim to the bottom.

You can't give up, Hank.

Jeanette was there beside me, her hand on my shoulder. She was as beautiful as ever, but her eyes held all the sadness and pain in them that they could possibly hold.

"Too late," I said.

It's never too late.

"Oh, it's too late, Jeanette. It's way too late." Tears spilled down my face, and I turned to look at her.

She was gone.

At some point, I ended up on the floor in the bathroom just off the bedroom I had barricaded myself in. My gun was still in the waistband, the butt jammed into my stomach. The tile was cold on my face, and when I lifted my head, it felt like it would explode. I stood, and my head swooned. My stomach lurched. Vomit spilled into the toilet as I heaved several times. When I was done, I reached up and pressed the lever. To my surprise, the toilet flushed.

Stumbling across the floor, I kicked the bottle. It clattered away, spilling the remaining Lemon Tongue Curler.

I lay down on the bed. Humphrey was there but didn't speak. I guess she was mad at me. I gave her a look, and she didn't seem right. Her fur was missing, and she was a deep gray color. Her eyes were gone, and there were wisps of blond hairs on her head. I turned away from just another hallucination and focused on the ceiling.

The world was out of control, both outside and in there with me. I thought of my family. My brothers were all dead. Pop and Davie Blaylock. Jeanette…

Bobby.

With tears streaming down the sides of my face, I slid the gun from my waistband and fingered the safety off…

Twelve Weeks and Some Days (?) After It All Started…

I don't know how many people died between the outbreak and the time I laid in an unfamiliar bed in an unfamiliar house. Thousands? Millions? Billions? I didn't know if the entire world was infected with people dying and getting back up, the dead killing and eating, a relentless army of rotting flesh, never stopping, never resting, always hungry.

How many people did the dead kill? How many of them were screaming and crying and begging for someone to help them, begging for their lives against creatures too unfathomable to believe were real, though they were?

I thought of Max Baxter. He had killed his boys while they were asleep in the bed. He did the same to his wife before turning the gun on himself. He opted out. He didn't give his family a chance to survive. He was a coward. Or maybe he knew something the rest of us didn't.

I thought of Jake, not more than a young man when I sent him off with the rest of my family, forcing him into a leadership role he probably wasn't ready for. He tried so hard to take care of the group. He tried so hard to protect Jeanette and Bobby. The last I heard, it was just Jake and my son. I didn't know if they were dead or alive, but the odds weren't too good for them to still be among the living. But he had tried.

…

…

My baby brother had tried.

…

I thought of Jeanette dying. I hadn't been there, but I had seen Lee die and turn, and I had a real good image of what it may have been like for her.

What would she think about me after this? Would she think me a coward like Max Baxter and all those others who opted out?

...

Probably.

...

Lee's figmented ghost came to mind. He still held a beer in his hand, and he was looking down on me.

See? I knew you had already given up.

Given up? Is that what it was? Giving up?

...

I thought of Davey Blaylock.

...

...

Davey Blaylock had been my best friend. We grew up together. Our families lived six houses apart when we were kids. We played baseball together and were a pretty good double play combo—he a short stop and me a second baseman for a while before I switched to third. As adults, Davey and I lived four blocks from each other. He was the best man at my wedding. One day, I hoped to return the favor.

That never happened. Never will.

Pop and Lee were dead—my brother was in another room where I shot him and covered him with a blanket. At that point, we hadn't been completely surrounded. At that point, we still had a chance to get out of there.

We were in something like a storage facility, a building probably owned by a nice business, a law firm or accounting firm or something along those lines. There were desks and office chairs and useless computers, all in their own section of the large room we stood in. There were wooden shelves — a couple of hundred of them — along one wall. Lamps and light fixtures, a huge fan that looked like it belonged on a swamp boat, tables and tablecloths and a ton of nice plates, glasses, mugs, and silverware.

We had few bullets, and I had my machete. Davey had a baseball bat, the barrel stained red.

There were steps that led to a catwalk that seemed to circle the inside of the large room. There were other offices, smaller by comparison. The main floor windows had been boarded up, and there were a few bodies inside when we arrived carrying a feverish Leland Walker, sweating and delusional. It was just a moment. That's all we needed. A moment to get Lee comfortable.

The moment turned into three hours, and three hours turned into six more. By the time Lee had died and risen and I had put a bullet in his head with tears in my eyes, it had been almost eleven hours, most of them spent in the dark as night passed us by.

It was early morning; the sun wasn't quite on its way up. Unlike us, I'm sure it was well rested. A gray fog covered the land.

"I need to bury Lee," I said.

"Hank."

"He's my brother."

"We need to get out of here."

Davey was right, but I couldn't leave Lee in some room where he would rot and where someone may find him or maybe not. No, I wanted to bury him. I *needed* to bury him.

I went out to my truck as the first rays of sun started to burn off the fog. Davey was behind me. There were a few corpses walking around, but I'm not so certain they saw us.

"Hank, we need to get out of here."

I turned on him. "If you want to go, then go. I won't hate you for doing it. I'll understand. I promise. But I will not leave him like that."

Davey stepped back. His hazel eyes held gray and purple bags beneath them. He had a full beard—something I hadn't noticed until right then. His hair had gotten long and touched his shoulders. It was the hippie revolution all over again. All he needed was a peace sign on the front of his shirt and a lit joint in one hand.

He frowned. "I'll stay. I'll help you."

I wonder if Davey regretted that a couple hours later.

I do.

We hurried, finding a soft spot of land. We dug for all we were worth. It wasn't a deep hole but one that would serve its purpose. We wrapped Lee in one of the long tablecloths in the warehouse and carried him out to the hole. Gently, we laid him in the ground and hurried to cover him up.

By then, the sun was coming up, and the fog was burning off.

"Hank," Davey said as I tossed a spade full of dirt on the grave.

"Yeah?"

"We need to get out of here. Now."

I looked up. *This is it*, I thought. *This is the end.*

The dead came out of the fog in shambling, stumbling droves. My truck was on the other side of the building, and all we had were shovels, the bat, the machete, and two guns that would be useless soon.

We ran.

We were always running.

The building grew closer, but it didn't matter. Around the corner came several rotting corpses that were little more than bones held together by drooping skin. I had the brief thought that they must have risen at the very beginning of the outbreak.

They were on us quick. I swung the shovel at the nearest one then at another one and another and another. We were almost to the corner of the building. Another few steps and my truck would have been in clear view.

I swung the shovel again, connecting with the side of a woman's head. She did a pirouette, her entire body spinning as she fell to the ground. I swung again and…

…and Davey screamed.

I whirled around. Davey leveled what once was a woman square in the face with his fist. Her forehead caved in, and she dropped to the ground, but she had done her damage. There was a hole in his shirt to the side of one shoulder blade. Blood spilled from the wound.

"No!" I yelled and ran for him. I don't know when I dropped the shovel and pulled out the machete, but I swung it in wide arcs, taking out as many at a time as I could.

Most people would have given up. Most people would have let the shock kick in and then let the world end around them. Not Davey. He swung his bat harder and harder, crushing fragile skulls with ease. And he moved away from me, going the opposite direction of the truck.

"Davey, this way," I yelled and took out another three of the dead.

"No! Get to the truck! Leave!"

The world, as it would do so many times after that, slowed down. The sounds became distorted, and everything seemed to brighten and become clearer. The rotting corpses stood out like three-dimensional objects on a video screen.

"Get out of here," he said, but I wasn't listening. I ran toward him, grabbed his arm, and tried to pull him with me. Davey shoved me away, shook his head, his eyes wet with tears and full of resolve. I could see him so clearly. A few strands of gray in his beard, the speckled brains and blood on the front of his shirt and face, the red in his eyes. His lower lip was bleeding, and there was a smudge of dirt on one cheekbone. It was all too vividly clear.

Then the world sped up, and he said, "Get out of here."

"I'm not leaving you."

"I'm a dead man, Hank. I'll lure them away."

I started to argue, but he shut me down and shoved me back toward the truck, back in the direction where there were fewer dead coming toward us. I swung the machete, took out a little kid with dark hair and slack eyes.

"Run!" Davey yelled one last time before doing the same thing but away from me instead of with me.

I stared at him for a moment until the hands of one of the dead touched my arm. I turned, screamed, and swung my machete, taking off the top of the man's head.

"Run!" Davey yelled again.

And I did.

I ran and hacked at the dead. I rounded the building and saw my truck was by itself. The driver's window was slightly down—enough to hear the world as it passed by. It took maybe a minute to reach it, to crawl in and slam the door shut and then crank it up. I floored it, determined to save Davey one way or another. The back wheels spun and then caught traction. Panic set into my chest, and my hands squeezed the steering wheel tight.

The truck swerved around the building. Bodies bounced off the front and sides, blood spattered the windows. The horde lurched away from me. A few turned back, and I ran them down, angry and sad and full of guilt and hoping I would find Davey alive. And then I heard the gunshot.

One.

Single.

Shot.

The truck came to a stop. I could see the dead had stopped as well. There was a crude circle of decaying bodies near one edge of the building. In the center of that circle was my best friend, Davey Blaylock. I couldn't see him, but I knew he was there, and I knew he was the reason the horde had stopped and that they were feeding on him.

The thump of a hand on the side of the truck pulled me away. The woman was missing most of her face. Her bottom lip was barely there, and she was mostly bald. If not for the top she wore, I wouldn't have known she was a woman. I put the truck in reverse and backed over several more of the dead. The truck didn't really bounce over them. It crushed them like soft melons in an overripe field.

I whipped the truck around, shifted into first gear, and mashed the gas. A minute later, I was on the road and speeding away, leaving the dead behind. Leaving Davey behind.

As I lay in that bed later on, the gun in my sweaty hand, my tears soaking into my hair and the pillow beneath me, I thought of Davey. It was my fault he was dead.

...

My fault.

My fault.

...

...

He had wanted to leave, and if we would have, he might have still been alive.

Maybe not. I don't know for certain.

What I do know is if not for him, I would be dead. He led them away, using his bleeding back as bait.

My thumb found the safety on the gun, flipped it on. Then I sat up in the bed. My head sang a chorus of angry lyrics as it thump thumped. My mouth was dry. I stood from the bed and pushed the dresser from in front of the door.

I entered the living room, searched the house, saw the picture of the pretty brunette and wondered if she were still alive, and if so, where was she?

I had been running for so long at that point, like a fugitive from the law, but the law in this world didn't want justice. It wanted flesh. It wanted death. I was tired of running, and if I were going to stop doing so, then I needed to hole up somewhere safe.

I stepped through the back door. The high deck and steps were safer than the ones on the other side. I needed to take those down if I planned on staying there. If I was going to die,

I would do so fighting but not for me. For Davey Blaylock, for his memory.

For his sacrifice.

In the back of my mind, I could feel Lee smile.

Thirteen Weeks (?) After It All Started...

The trailer wasn't safe. It didn't take long to figure that out. I could tear the steps away from the front door and take down the patio deck, sure. But there was the issue of the patio doors, two sliding pieces of glass with just a thin aluminum frame holding them on their tracks and a small lock to keep them closed. It wouldn't take much to get in that way. The ramp leading up to the patio wasn't a good deterrent either. A handful of the dead could walk right up and push in the glass, break the trim-like frame, and crawl in.

Then there were the living threats. The front door was nothing more than a closet door used as an entryway. It wasn't hollow, but it wasn't sturdy. That led me to looking at the back door. It was much higher up, and the steps to it would be difficult for the dead to climb. I doubted many could make it past the third step if they could make it onto the concrete slab at the stairs' base. But the living would have no problems reaching that door or the windows on the deck leading to it.

The bathroom where the homemade wine and shine were wasn't in that good of shape either. The floor felt like it could give out. I certainly didn't need to be taking a leak and have it collapse beneath me. Who knows how many bones would break when I landed?

In the end, the trailer was a death trap for anyone trying to survive in these days.

The brick house on the backside of the trailer was a different story. There was a nice-sized deck at the front and a set of stairs along the side. It dawned on me then that the house was built on a descending hill, and though the front door was only about six feet off the ground with a set of five steps leading up to the porch, the back door was more like twenty feet up, eighteen steps leading to it.

Someone had been careful. The windows were boarded up from the outside with screws, not nails. There were no gaps— the job had been done right, the boards measured and screws put in every twelve inches or so. Wilted flowers sat in pots lining the brown, stone-paved sidewalk.

I rounded the outside of the house, searching for stragglers and found none. A wire fence circled behind it and stretched down to the lake and across a small alcove with wooden posts every six feet or so. It must have been a pen for animals; there was a small house that could have housed a large dog or some goats or maybe even a donkey. The hay suggested it hadn't been a large dog. Back to the front, I went up the steps. A patio table sat in the center of the deck, four chairs around it—one on each side. To the right was another chair. The glass storm door was unlocked. I started to knock on the wooden door beyond it then tried the knob instead.

It turned.

But it didn't open.

It couldn't be that easy, could it?

Around the side, I made my way up the steps, holding tight to the handrail. I reached the landing. There was no glass door here. I tried the knob.

It turned.

This time, the door opened with a slight vacuum sound, a SWOOSH.

I stepped into a kitchen that held a dining table off to the left and a stove, microwave, and cabinets straight ahead.

The first thing I really noticed was the smell. It wasn't stale. It wasn't the reek of decay. It was pleasant. Lilacs.

The house was neat and clean. The living room was off to the right as well as the hall that led to the back of the house. Wood grain furniture right out of the seventies decorated the room. Along the hall was a bathroom and three bedrooms. All the rooms were neat, the beds made. It had that homey feel to it.

It was as if the family left for a vacation and was planning on coming back.

There was soap in the bathroom, towels hanging on the shower rod, toilet paper on the back of the tank. Bottles of water packed a refrigerator that had long ago become warm. Clothes were folded neatly in the dresser drawers.

On the dining room table sat a letter on plain copy paper. When I first walked in, I didn't notice it. Or maybe I did and it didn't register. But on the walk back through, there it was. I picked it up.

To Whom It May Concern,

Welcome to our home. If you are here, then you have managed to survive so far. Feel free to stay a while. Drink the water, eat the food. This house is on a well, and the windmill down by the lake supplies the energy to keep the water flowing. The shower still works.

We have left for the Saluda Armory where my unit is stationed. It is the safest place in South Carolina. If anyone reads this, please, try to make it to the Saluda Armory. It is a safe zone.

Hoping there are more survivors out there,

Jay.

I set the letter down and stared at it. There were people out there. The Saluda Armory—it wasn't too far from there. It was supposed to be a safe zone. The Batesburg Armory was supposed to have been one as well. Honestly, I doubted there was such a thing. Everywhere I traveled had been overrun for the most part.

Lyrics from a band I used to like came to mind. I shook my head. The cynical part of me that had seen little good in this new world refused to trust the words of someone no longer living at that residence. I wouldn't be leaving there for a while. I wouldn't go searching for a safe zone that wasn't there. No need to chase misprinted lies.

Instead, I moved my gear into the house. It wasn't neat at first, but I was more concerned with being stuck outside if the dead came than being neat and proper.

A hangover headache lingered, and the more I worked, the worse it got. I emptied the van as quickly as I could. Hauling everything up those steps wore me out, and my headache intensified. On one of my last trips to the van, I came across the basket of doll clothes I had picked up for Humphrey a while back.

My heart sank.

She had been so much a part of me, of my survival.

Then the anger surfaced. If I'm sure of anything, it's that I felt betrayed. Abandoned, the way Humphrey had been when I found her.

I took the basket and threw it across the yard. It tumbled, end over end, through the sky and then along the ground. A trail of small articles of clothing littered the yard.

I started to go inside. Like so many other decisions in my life, I should have gone with my first instinct. Instead, I made my way back to the trailer and into the bathroom with the homemade shine. I took several of the smaller bottles on the first trip and then went back for two of the larger jugs.

I was stupid.

I made one last trip into the trailer but not for alcohol. I took the picture of the pretty brunette off the wall and carried it with me to my new home.

That was one of the worst mistakes I ever made.

I guess some days passed. I drank. And I talked to the picture. Before I hung it on the wall where another picture had hung before, I noticed on the back was the brunette's name: Cate.

"Looks like it's just you and me, Cate," I said and lifted a bottle of clear moonshine that read Apple Cider on the label. Surprisingly, it had a strong apple flavor to it.

I remember little else about the next few weeks.

Too Many Weeks After It All Started...

Drinking and loneliness are two things that go hand in hand, and they're one bad combination.

Things happened. I know they did. But I don't know in what order they occurred or how true they were in my mind or if they really even happened the way the fragmented thoughts tell me they did.

It was a binge like none I had ever gone on in the pre end of the world days. I know I fired my guns a few times. I think I checked out a few of the nearby houses, searching for anyone or any supplies. Did I build something? I didn't know.

It was like I was asleep and all the nightmares were just far enough into the dark to scare me, but I didn't know why I was scared.

Then I woke up. Someone, somewhere was screaming. I opened my eyes. They felt crusty and stung as if there was salt in them. I had been sitting at the kitchen table when I passed out the last time. I lifted my head a couple of inches off the table. The bottle of whatever moonshine lay tipped over on the table, most of its contents spilled out. I set the bottle upright then placed my head back on the table. It was just another nightmare.

But it wasn't.

It wasn't just another nightmare.

I lifted my head again. The screams were closer, and there was panic and fear in them.

I stood too quickly. My head swooned, and my stomach rolled over. I barely reached the sink before throwing up nothing more than phlegm and alcohol.

The scream. It came again. And again. And again.

My legs were unsteady, and my vision was cloudy at best, but I managed to make my way across the kitchen to the back door. On the way, I grabbed a gun from off the counter and checked the clip. I think it was full.

The sun was bright, and the sky was clear blue. The air outside was cool, and a breeze blew off the lake. It took a few seconds for my eyes to adjust, but when they did, I saw where the screaming came from.

The guy ran up the dirt road, coming from the lake — there was a dock down there. He had just rounded the corner and probably didn't realize he was running back toward the street this road circled back to.

A pack of the dead was behind him. Though they moved considerably slower, they weren't too far away. I realized then that he was limping and not really running at all.

"Hey!" I yelled and started down the steps. My voice was loud in my own ears, and my head begged me to quiet down. I held onto the rail as I stumbled halfway down.

The guy heard me. He started to run toward me and then stopped.

"Come on!" I called to him.

From where I stood, he looked confused. He looked to the horde following him then at me.

"What are you waiting on? Come on."

I went further down the steps, holding tight to the railing. My hand was shaking as I raised my gun. I squeezed off a shot that missed everything.

"Steady there, Hank." I was *far* from steady. I had been drinking for too long.

Then the guy bolted for me. He hopped a ditch and then crumpled to the ground.

I reached the bottom of the steps and ran.

Head pounding, stomach churning, cotton-dry mouth, sweating like a pig, but I ran. All those other instances came back, and my hands became as even as they ever were. I don't know how many shots I fired, but most of them hit home, taking the tops or sides of heads off and dropping the dead where they walked.

The guy struggled to crawl.

I tried to yell for him to get moving, but nothing came out. My voice had disappeared deep inside of me. I reached him as one of the dead was almost on top of him. It was a young girl, probably not too long deceased. She moved quicker than the others. It seemed the young ones always did.

My knife was out by then, and I drove it into her right eye, shoving her backward and to the ground where her head struck with a thud.

The guy was terrified, but as I would find out seconds later, he wasn't afraid of the undead horde after him. He was afraid of me.

"Come on. Let's go."

I reached for his arm, but he pulled away.

"I'd rather die."

I was dumbfounded.

"You don't have that choice," I said. I hate to admit what I did next, but it was the only way to get him off the ground and save his life. I pistol-whipped him in the back of the head, knocking him unconscious.

I turned and fired several times. The closest of the dead fell. Others stumbled over the bodies, some of them tripping and falling as well. It didn't buy much time, but it was enough. I bent down and grabbed the guy beneath his arms and slung him over my shoulder. I wavered for a second as my head spun.

Then I was running.

He wasn't very big and weighed a buck fifty if that, but having been drunk for who knew how long, I wasn't in the best shape to be carrying him and running.

Then I saw...

I saw...

I almost stopped when I saw what the man had seen when I ran up to him. I didn't focus on the scene to the side of the house. If I would have, I may not have made it.

I passed the first of the bodies hanging on crosses—how did I miss that when I ran to his aid?—and hit the steps in a clumsy sprint. I pulled myself up the stairs until I reached the landing. When I looked back, the dead had ceased their pursuit.

Did they see the bodies? Did they smell them? Every part of me said the souls trapped inside *could* see and smell and sense that to go any further was to truly be the end of them.

I went inside and lay the man down on the couch. His head was bleeding, as was his leg. I grabbed a couple of guns, shoved them in my waistband, and...

Where did the machete come from? Mine was gone—left on interstate 26 toward Charleston. But there it was, sitting on the counter like an obscene finger. The blade was crusted with dried blood and there were blackish red spots on the floor, leading away—or to—the door, depending on how you looked at it. I grabbed the machete. It felt right in my hand, like it belonged.

Then I was out of the house and standing on the landing. The dead had come no closer than the first cross. There must have been thirty or forty of them. Maybe more. Some of them had turned around and were shambling away, but most of them just stood there.

I thought about running headlong into them, the machete over my head like a medieval warrior going into battle. There was no need though. They weren't getting any closer, and they weren't really staring at me.

They were staring at the bodies.

Bodies.

It didn't quite click until then.

The side of the house was littered with crosses made from the posts of the fence that had once spanned the backside of the house. The crosses had been placed in the ground like the posts they had once been when they held up the fence. Nailed or tied to the crosses were the decomposing bodies of the dead, each one missing part of their heads.

What the…?

When the…?

I looked further. The crosses stretched behind the house, each one holding a body. Flies buzzed about them, and many of them were nothing more than skin and bones and worn clothing. One in particular caught my eye. It was a child, maybe no more than three or four, bare-chested and barefoot. It was high on the cross, his little arms stretched out, his hands with nails in them. His head also held a nail in it.

I leaned against the doorjamb, stunned from what I saw. Then I went inside, my stomach having sunk into my feet and my heart having leapt into my throat. I closed the door, locked it, and dropped the machete to the floor. I sat down at the kitchen table and stared at the spilled moonshine.

I didn't know what to think or what to feel. I didn't believe I had done those things, but who could have? There were no bodies here when I arrived. The fence was intact. How did I even manage to get the posts out of the ground and cut and made into crosses?

What had I become?

I stood, picked the bottle up from the table, and went to the sink. Its contents went down the drain.

"Why did you hit me over the head?"

I turned. The man was sitting up on the couch, one hand on the back of his head. He pulled away his fingers to look at a patch of dark blood.

"You were being difficult," I responded.

"Difficult?"

Looking at him, he struck me as someone much like myself. He had seen a lot, probably lost a lot of loved ones if not all of them. He had probably put down his fair share of the dead. His hair was thinning but still dark and scraggly. A beard covered the lower half of his face. His eyes were bloodshot, and his clothes were caked in dirt and blood and who knew what else.

"Yeah, difficult. I was trying to help you, and you said you would rather die."

"Gee, Rambo, I guess you haven't seen the graveyard of biters you have around this place."

"Honestly, I hadn't. Well, not until I picked you up and started back for the house."

"Yeah, right."

He stood, grimaced, and limped a few feet. "Are you some kind of drunk?"

I lifted the bottle that was still in my hand, set it on the counter.

"Yeah, I reckon so. I don't remember much about the last few weeks. That mess outside—I don't remember doing it, but I'm the only one here, so I must have."

"So you're not only nuts but you're a drunk as well. Nice. Psycho drunk people are the best. Of all the people to get saved by, I get you."

"Yeah, you got me. But you don't have to stick around. You can take yourself right on out that door. Good luck though. They got us surrounded, and I doubt you're going to get very far."

"It doesn't matter. I'm going to die anyway." He lifted his shirt. There were teeth marks on his stomach—just enough to break the skin and leave a bloody imprint.

"One of them got my leg too." He pulled at a hole in his pants, exposing a deeper wound—one that had already begun to turn gray.

He showed me his hand. A huge gash stretched across three knuckles. "I punched the one that bit my stomach."

I stared at him.

"Where'd all the...what did you call them? Biters?" I asked.

"Yeah. Biters. That's what they do. They bite and tear the flesh off your body."

"Biters. That sounds about right. So where'd all of them come from?"

"I don't know. I just kind of ran into them as I was trying to get out of the area."

"So you ran this way?"

He laughed. "If that's what you want to call it."

"What would you call it?"

"Limping lamely, maybe?"

"Where were you coming from?"

"A house a couple of streets down. It's not much of a place, but I holed up there for a couple of days until my buddy died. Then I left."

"Did you put him down?"

"My buddy?"

"Yeah."

"I think so."

"You think so? You don't know if you put him down? What did you do?"

"Dean had been bitten, and it was all I could do to make him comfortable. He wanted me to go ahead and put a bullet in his head before he died. He didn't want to turn…and I didn't want to kill him."

"You didn't finish the job?"

"I rigged the bedroom door."

"Rigged the door?"

He nodded. "Yeah. With an axe and a rope. If he gets up and tries to open the door, the rope will pull a lever, and the axe will split his skull. It's the only thing I could think to do other than be there when he died and do it then. But I couldn't. I just couldn't."

I thought about that and understood where he came from. I put Lee down, and there is not a day that goes by that I don't think about the way his head snapped back and the way blood and hair and brains splattered the wall behind him.

"I hope it did the trick. If not, your buddy's going to suffer for a long time."

"What do you mean?"

"I'll show you," I said then went to the door. "Come with me."

"Out there?"

"Don't worry. We'll be fine." I opened the door. Minutes earlier, I went out there and noticed the chill in the air, but I didn't notice the brown and orange and yellow leaves on the trees mingled in with all of the greens. Fall had set in pretty good by then, I reckoned.

"What month is it?" I asked.

"Late October if my watch is right."

"Late October?"

More time had passed than I thought. It was mid-September when I arrived here.

"I didn't catch your name," he said.

"I didn't throw it."

Silence fell over us like a cloud.

"It's Hank. Hank Walker, but you can call me Walker."

"I'm Hetch."

"Come here, Hetch. You won't believe this unless I show you."

He looked apprehensive. I guess he had reason not to trust me. I did whack him pretty solid on the head, and there were bodies in the yard on crosses. I went down the steps. Most of the biters—yeah, I liked that term a lot better than rotters—had shambled away. Only a few stragglers hung behind. I don't know if they were waiting for a meal or for the angel of death.

The closest one was a man, maybe in his mid-forties. His brown hair was missing in places, and his eyes drooped in their sockets. I drove the machete into his head then pulled it free. A second male moved toward me, a low groan in his throat that I ended with another over-the-top plunge of the blade into his skull.

The third guy was a big man—not fat, but in life, he had been muscular. The muscles he probably prided himself on were still fairly solid looking and only sagging around his chest and mid-section. If he got hold of you, there would be no breaking his grip. His hair had been cropped short, and his shirt was ripped and barely hanging on by one arm. He had been bitten on the shoulder. For all the weight lifting and being in shape the guy had probably done, he was still like the rest of us: raw meat, and one bite was all it took to spoil it.

"This guy, Hetch. Look at him. You see him?"

"Yeah."

"He was someone's son. Maybe someone's brother or dad. Look at his hand—he was married. He liked to work out. He might have been a jock when he was in high school. His appearance was probably important to him. Are you getting all this?"

Hetch stood at the top of the stairs. He looked ready to run back inside if things got out of control.

"Why does any of that matter?" he asked.

"The body is dead, but the person inside isn't."

"You really are crazy, aren't you?"

"Maybe we all are," I said and then added, "Pay close attention."

I picked up a hand-sized rock and moved toward Muscles. If this were the world that was, I would have probably never approached him. I certainly wouldn't have tried to taunt him. A few feet away, I threw the rock. It hit Muscles in the chest.

It sounded like someone punching a bag of sugar—a heavy *TWHOCK*.

Muscles growled.

"I think I made him mad."

He staggered forward, his right hand reaching for me. I sliced it off with a quick, downward slash of the machete. Muscles leaned to the right and let out a loud moan.

"Did you hear that? That's the sound of someone in pain. He may be dead on the outside, but on the inside, he feels everything." My eyes never left Muscles, and then I spoke directly to him. "Ain't that right, fellah?"

His jaws snapped shut and then opened. He shambled closer to me, this time extending his other arm. I took it off at the elbow. He howled like an angry wolf.

"Now, what are you going to do, Muscles?"

I hated what I was doing, but I had to prove a point. I had to make Hetch understand that there was so much more to the biters than just being reanimated corpses with an insatiable hunger.

I kicked Muscles in the kneecap. His leg buckled backward, and he fell to the ground face-first. His groans were agonized.

"Come here," I said to Hetch.

"You're crazy."

"Come here. I have a headache the size of Montana, so don't make me tell you again."

I thought he was going to bolt. His eyes held that weary stare, that look that if he had somewhere to run or a car to get into, he would. He could have just run in the house. I wouldn't have blamed him if he did.

He didn't.

Hetch limped down the stairs, holding tight to the railing.

"Help me roll him over."

"What?"

"Help me roll him over. I want to show you something."

"Haven't you shown me enough? Just put the machete in his head, and get it over with."

"I will, but you have to see this first. You won't believe me if you don't."

We stood in silence for several seconds before he finally nodded. He pushed from one side as I pulled on one of Muscles' shoulders.

On his back, Muscles snapped his jaws at us several times.

Hetch jerked away and fell on his bottom. "Are you crazy? He almost got me."

"It doesn't matter—you've already been bitten. You'll be one of them soon enough, right?"

I grabbed Muscles by what little hair he had on his head. "Listen up in there. Do you hear me? I know you do. Answer a question for me. Can you do that?"

"He can't understand you, Walker."

I knocked on Muscles' head a couple of times. He growled and gnashed his teeth.

"Hey now, that's no way to act toward the man who's going to end your suffering."

"Walker, that's enough. Just put him down."

I spun on my knee and grabbed him in the leg where the hole was. He dropped to the ground, a scream escaping him. I had my gun out and pointed it at Hetch's head.

What was I doing?

My grip on the world had slipped too far away. But I couldn't reel it back in. Not right then, at least.

"You know what the problem with this world is? It's not the dead. It's the living. We're all too busy being scared of those things, those biters. But you know, maybe they're just as scared as we are. Did you ever think about that? Did you?!"

Hetch had a hand over his head and one forearm at my chest. "No. No, I never figured they would be afraid of us. They just march along, killing and killing and killing."

"They can't help it," I said and pulled the gun away. I slipped it back in my waistband and turned to Muscles. Hetch was right about one thing—I should have just put him down and ended his misery right then. The other biters had begun to turn around, many of them making their way back to us. "Unlike the living, they can't help their impulses."

I stood and pulled Hetch to his feet. "Look at his eyes."

"What about them?"

I chopped off one of Muscles' feet. He wailed.

Hetch backed away. "What the hell?"

"You saw his eyes—they changed, didn't they?"

"But he's dead."

"No. I've told you already. His *body* is dead. *He's still in there.*" I looked to the biters migrating toward us. There were more than a dozen. "They're all still in there. They can't help themselves. But we, the living, we can. I don't know how many living people you've come across, but most the ones I've met have been crazier than the nuts in a nut house."

Hetch gave me raised eyebrows.

"Yeah, I know how I must look to you—like one of those crazies. But I'm not. I'm just trying to survive and not doing a very good job of it."

I didn't know if Hetch believed a word I said. I didn't know if *I* believed it either. To be truthful, I don't know how anyone in this world—the way it is now—could be completely sane. Every one of the living had to be a little off kilter from the things they've seen, the things they've done. Sanity's just a pipe dream.

I turned back to Muscles and shook my head. He looked like he was in pain, like he was screaming on the inside. And me, well, I had caused that pain.

"Nothing personal, buddy," I said to the poor guy. His head split open easy enough underneath the blade of the machete.

To Hetch, I said, "Stay here. I have to help these people."

Help them? That's somewhat laughable if you think about it. In any language, it was murder. Or maybe it was assisted suicide, like that Dr. Kavorkian guy. They called him Dr. Death. He supposedly assisted in the suicides of over 130 ailing patients. He went to jail for murder, though really all he did was help those people leave this world, end the pain they were going through.

At that moment, I was Death—not so much Dr.—to these people. I provided the machinery. No, it wasn't the Thantron or the Mercitron, as Kavorkian called his machines. It was the Machetetron, and it was just as lethal.

"Come on, people," I yelled and stepped away from the house and away from the hanging corpses, which I can only believe I used to keep the dead at bay—if they couldn't smell me, they wouldn't want me. Oh, but they caught my scent right good, and several of them picked up the pace.

I sliced through them with ease, the machete lopping off the tops of heads or splitting them all the way to their noses. My arms grew heavy and ached—but the blood rush and adrenaline kept me going. Finally, the last one went down—a young man with long, tangled hair and wearing only shorts.

Hetch stood at the bottom of the steps, one hand on the rail. Again, he looked like he would bolt.

I walked through the corpses—easily two dozen or more—and stopped a few feet from Hetch. I said nothing as I passed him and went up the steps. At the top, I looked down. The scene from there was worse than up close. I had cut off more than just the tops of heads. There were arms and legs lying here and there, and the blackish red blood painted the grass in splotches.

I was no Dr. Death, but on that day, I was Death all the same to twenty-seven trapped people.

I motioned for Hetch to come in then walked inside.

Seventeen Weeks and Two Days After It All Started...

"Are you just going to leave them there?"

I looked at Hetch. "Close the door, why don't you?"

My arms and legs shook. My clothes were soaked in gore and dried vomit.

The door clicked shut, but Hetch didn't move away from it. Instead, he watched me as if he thought he was next on my list. His eyes were wild, and he constantly licked at his lips, which, for the most part, were covered in a brown beard.

"What?" I asked.

"You're just going to leave them out there to rot?"

I almost laughed at that but managed to hold back. "In case you haven't noticed, they've been rotting since they died."

"You know what I mean."

"Do I?"

He went from scared to angry in a couple seconds. "You're a jerk; you know that?"

"I've been told that a time or two."

Living interaction. I wasn't so sure I wanted it. It had been all too infrequent over the last few months, and what little there had been had ended badly for the most part. Someone always died. So maybe I *was* being a jerk. Maybe I always would be. At least until I die.

Thinking on that now reminds me death isn't that far in the future. Not many people stand a chance of living into the golden years now. And what type of life would that be? Could the world rebuild itself? It first had to figure out how to get rid of the biters.

"I'm going to go shower," I said. "Unless you have a problem with that as well."

"You don't get it, do you?"

"Get what?"

"You're a drunk and you're reckless and—"

That was it. I'd had enough. "Do me a favor," I said.

"What's that?"

"Open the door."

"Why?"

"I said so."

He hesitated but eventually listened.

"Now, step outside."

He frowned, started to speak, but I guess he decided not to. He closed his lips tightly and buttoned them up as pretty as you could want. Then he stepped onto the landing.

"Now close the door."

"Wha... What?"

"Close the door."

"Look, man, it's not safe out here, and I don't have any weapons, and—"

I drew my pistol, pointed it at him, and took the five steps toward him. "If you're still here when I get done cleaning up and changing, then we can talk. If not, goodbye."

He said something else, but I paid him no attention. I slammed the door and locked it. He wouldn't be able to get in—the windows were boarded up, and there were a series of four locks up and down the door, all of which I bolted.

It didn't take him long to start beating on the door. I ignored him as I went down the hall to the bathroom and got undressed. One good thing about that house was it had a well, and it hadn't dried up yet. There was a windmill out on the lake, which supplied the water to the house. I would never drink the water, but showering in it was a different matter. It was icy cold, and my muscles felt like they would turn to stone before getting used to the water. Then they relaxed. I took my time, hoping Hetch would leave. In the short time I had known him, he struck me as high maintenance: someone who would question everything I did and every decision I made. I had been on my own for too long by then to let a stranger question what I did or why I did it.

I dried off, feeling refreshed. How long had it been since I took a shower? I got dressed and went back up the hall.

I listened for a short while. Hetch no longer beat on the door. I waited several seconds, holding my breath, my hands clutched into tight fists. Then something happened, something I didn't expect.

Panic took hold.

I was alone, and being alone was not good for me. Humphrey had kept me sane after everyone else had died. But Humphrey chose to leave. She had been my anchor, and without her, I was nothing more than an abandoned ship with torn sails. I was adrift in an ocean of death, just waiting to sink.

Hetch's screams had awakened me from a drunken stupor. Though he seemed difficult, he didn't come off like most of the nutcases I had met in the dead world. If anything, I was probably the head job with all those biters nailed to stakes out in the yard. What was I thinking?

The door was so far away, and each step I took felt like I moved backward instead of forward. I was having a nightmare within a nightmare, and I knew I would never wake up from it, especially if I were alone again. I slung the door open. I started to yell his name and then stopped. Hetch sat on the top step, his elbows on his knees, hands dangling between his legs. He looked back at me.

"I'm gonna die," he said.

He was right. He had been bitten and not just in one spot. He would die, and it would only be a matter of days. Maybe even just a day.

"I'm gonna die, just like everyone else, and then I'm going to come back and...and...and...I don't want to be one of those things." He pointed to the bodies on the ground. "I don't want to go through what Dean went through. It was hard to watch, and he was delirious at the end..."

"You're not going to die, Hetch."

"Yes, I am."

I waited a minute longer. His eyes were rimmed red. He was scared. So was I. I had a gallon of healing water—touched by God, so the Cherokee say—but didn't I want to use it on some stranger I may not even like after a couple of days.

"Haven't you seen what happens when someone gets bit? They die. They die a horrible death and then they come back."

I nodded. "I've seen—up close and personal. But you're not going to die."

"I've been bit! What part of that don't you understand?"

"I understand quite well. But I have a cure."

"Whatever."

Hetch stood.

"Where are you going?"

"To die."

"You're not going anywhere, and you're not going to die."

"Yes. I. Am."

"Come inside."

"No."

"Are you going to make me slug you over the head again? Come inside. Now. We need to treat those wounds — the sooner we do, the better chance you have of surviving."

"You wouldn't slug a dying man, would you?"

I said nothing. The look on my face must have spoken volumes.

Hetch climbed the three steps back to the landing, passed me, and went inside. I followed, closing and locking the door.

At some point during the drunken haze I had been in, I must have done some reorganizing. All of my supplies had been put away in cabinets, along the counters, and in bedrooms. The healing water had been marked as such with a black marker (from somewhere in the house, I presumed). It simply read, HEALING SPRINGS. I grabbed it and a medicine measuring cup from a drawer by the sink. That wasn't going to work. At least not completely. I took another cup — this one from the cabinet above the sink.

I thought back to what Imeko had done for his granddaughter.

"Take your pants off," I said.

His hands went up defensively. "Whoa. Hold on. I don't swing that way, man."

"Shut up, and take your pants off. You were bitten on the leg, right?"

"Yeah."

"Take your pants off."

He was reluctant at first but finally unsnapped, unzipped, and pulled his jeans down. The wound was small, much like the one on his stomach, but it was nasty. The area around it

243

was gray, turning black. The back of my hand went to it, felt the heat radiating off the skin.

I poured two tablespoons of water in the measuring cup and put a rag under his leg.

"Any water that drips off, catch it with the rag—we don't want to waste this stuff."

"Okay."

I poured the water onto the wound. Some of it spilled down the sides of his leg, and Hetch made sure the rag caught all of it.

Another two tablespoons followed. I did the same thing with his stomach wound, and his knuckles just to be on the safe side. Then I poured him a cup of the water.

"Drink."

"Where'd you get this from?"

"Blackville."

"Where?"

"A little town, well, near a little town, a place called Healing Springs."

Hetch rolled his eyes. "You're kidding me, right? Healing Springs? That's just a myth. Every state has one of those."

"It's not just a myth. I've seen it. It works."

Hetch laughed.

"Drink," I repeated.

As he downed the water, I worked on the wounds, bandaging them the best I could, the leg with a torn towel tied in a knot around his thigh, his stomach with a piece of that same towel and duct tape. Yeah, it's funny when you think about it, but it was all I had, so it had to do. I poured him a second cup, trying to remember what Imeko had done.

"Let me guess, I need to drink this one too?"

"Yup."

I worked on his knuckles next. It wasn't a bite wound, but still, it was a wound he received from a biter.

"How are you feeling?"

"Like I'm going to die."

I glanced up at him. There were bags under his eyes and sweat on his brow.

"Are you hot?"

"My girlfriend used to think so."

I didn't smile, though I probably should have. He was trying to make light of a bad situation. Why not indulge him?

"Do you have a fever?"

"I don't know."

I reached up and touched his forehead. He was hot.

"Do I have a fever, Nurse Walker?"

"I'll nurse you, all right," I said, this time humoring him a little. "And, yeah, you have a fever."

A frown formed. He inhaled deeply. "That's how it starts. The fever. You get it, and then you start throwing up and…and…"

"You're going to be okay, Hetch."

"How do you know?" He pulled up his pants and buttoned them.

"I don't. At least not entirely."

We said nothing. I made him drink another cupful of water and then took him to the back bedroom. From the looks of it, it had belonged to a girl at one time. A canopy bed sat along one wall—which was really the only thing feminine in the room. It would do.

"Lay down. Get some rest."

He shook his head. "I'm not going out on my back."

"You should rest, let the water have a chance to do its thing."

"What are you going to do?"

"Kill the rest of the biters then take the others off the stakes. Burn the bodies, I guess."

"I'll go with you."

"No. You need to rest."

"You mean I need to die." He shook his head, his lips somewhat tucked in. "If I'm going to die, then I'm not doing it in a bed."

There was no need to argue with him. He wasn't going to listen anyway. He thought he was as good as dead. Truthfully, I did too. I couldn't remember exactly what Imeko did to save his grandchild, and I probably did something wrong. At least out there, I could just smash his skull with a rock or the machete and not have to clean up anything in the house. Still, I wanted him to live. I didn't want to be alone again. I believed that rest was the best way to get the healing water to work its magic. Or miracle if that's what it was.

"You mind if I use this?" he asked and picked up a hatchet near the fireplace. It was caked in dried blood.

"No. Go right ahead."

Two hours. That's how long it took before Hetch threw up the first time. If I didn't know better, I would have guessed it was because of the work at hand. Killing the biters, moving the bodies, making a pile in the center of the yard between the house and the road, dousing them with gasoline, then setting them on fire. The stench was worse than I thought it would be, like pulled pork that sat out far too long. My stomach rolled, but I didn't vomit.

"You okay?" I asked.

246

The voice in my head, which had probably been the same voice that had given life to Humphrey, spoke. *He's dying. Of course he's not okay.*

"Yeah. I'm fine," Hetch responded. "Just…" He pointed at the fire and then threw up again. He held his stomach with both arms. His lips were pulled back, exposing blood-spattered teeth.

I walked over to him. At Hetch's feet lay a mixture of who knew what, but the main component was blood. I took his arm and helped him stand upright. His face was pale, and sweat spilled off of him in waves. He was burning up.

"Let's get you inside."

"I'm fine."

"No, you're not."

Panic rose in my chest again, beginning at my testicles and working its way up to my throat, where it caught like a lump. In the back of my mind, I could see Hetch dead and rising, me shooting him and then burying him, just like everyone else. Though I didn't know him all that well, he was, in some ways, like me. He had survived that long, and he had lost everyone he loved. Now, he was going to lose himself.

I was going to lose him.

I had to save him.

I.

Had.

To.

Hetch could barely walk; how he managed to swing the axe or pull the bodies to the pile for the fire is beyond me. He held tight to the rail as I carried him up the stairs. Once inside, I closed the door—always closing the door, always locking it. I didn't believe they could climb steps, but why take the chance? Down the hall, we went to the room with the canopy bed. I thought for a moment to pull the canopy off but chose not to. If there was a little girl with intentions of coming home to this room, I didn't want her to find it wrecked. Thinking about that now, it seems like an oxymoron. I didn't want the room a mess, but I put Hetch in there, who was almost certainly going to die, rise, and be shot right there in that room.

He didn't fight as I put him in the bed.

"Stay here."

"No problem." His voice was weak.

The jug of healing water sat on the table. I took it, a towel, and a cup to the bedroom. My hands shook as I poured a cup. "Drink."

"I can't, Hank."

I lifted Hetch to a sitting position. "Drink the water."

I held the cup to his lips just as I had seen Imeko do. Hetch opened his mouth, let me pour a little in. He licked his lips, opened his mouth again. "More."

By the time Hetch finished the cup, the edge on my nerves began to ease. He was taking water, and as much as this may sound corny, I felt like I was taking care of one of my brothers or Jeanette. Or Bobby. I lifted his shirt and pulled the bandage off. Hetch didn't so much as flinch. The gray had spread up into his ribs and down into his waistband. Those nerves went back on edge.

I poured water onto the towel then squeezed it onto the angry wound. I let it spill over his side and down onto the bed. There was no time to worry with his pants. I put my fingers in the hole the biter had made and ripped the material until the pant leg was almost off. The other bandage came off quickly. Like the wound on his stomach, this one had stretched out along his skin like long fingers reaching for something they couldn't quite get to. The veins stood out beneath the skin as thick, black lines.

"Forget this," I said and poured water onto the wound.

I filled the cup again. "Come on, Hetch, you need to drink up."

"Let me die."

It was a reaction. I swear. That's all it was. I was angry with him, and I reacted.

His head snapped to one side when I slapped him across the face. His eyes popped open; his brows curled down in angry check marks. "Why did you do that?" His voice was a little stronger, but it still sounded terribly weak.

"I'm not letting you die."

He gave a weak laugh. "There's nothing you can do to stop it, Hank. Please, just put a bullet in my head."

Why not? Why not? I thought about that. Why not let him die? I was being selfish. I wanted—no, *needed*—someone else in my life. I wasn't afraid of the dead—that fear ended a while back when I found out Jeanette had died. I wasn't afraid of the living—not anymore though the living were more dangerous than the dead these days. I was afraid of being alone. I didn't want to be alone any longer. I was tired of not having anyone to talk to; I was tired of losing my mind, my sanity, my desire to live. I believed if Hetch died, I would not only put a bullet in his head but probably drink myself to death or at least get drunk enough to put a bullet in my own head.

"I'm not killing you."

Tears spilled from the corners of his pleading eyes.

"Hang in there, and drink another cup of water."

"It's no use."

"Drink the water, Hetch."

"Are you going to hit me again if I refuse?"

"Probably."

He drank the water like an obedient Jim Jones follower. The difference is he had already been poisoned by the Kool-Aid, and hopefully, this was the cure.

I doubted it.

There was no cure. What I had seen was an abomination…or a miracle. Maybe the little girl lived because Imeko believed she would. He believed God had reached down from Heaven with his finger and touched the water, that it had healing powers. I wanted to believe, and I think I did before I needed it to save someone. But doubt is a powerful emotion. Almost as strong as love and courage, but it can destroy both of those just by coming to the surface of thought.

The bandage came off his knuckles next. The wound had puckered, the torn skin no longer covering the actual cut. It was still gray, but it hadn't changed since the first time I cleaned it. Like the other wounds, water was poured onto it. And like the other wounds, this time, I didn't bandage any of them.

I poured him half a cup of water. By then, there was less than half a gallon left—it went faster than I thought it would.

"Drink."

He didn't argue this time.

I set the cup on the end table and stood. "I'll be back," I said and left the room.

Here's a truth I thought I would take to the grave with me: When I closed the bedroom door, I went down in one of the other bedrooms and rummaged around a while. I found some rope at the top of one of the closets. From there, I went outside, taking my machete with me.

My heart was heavy—a feeling I was tired of having. There were several biters roaming the dirt road, but none of them had crossed the little ditch or walked up the easement toward the house. The fire still burned, and that stench of rancid pork filled the air.

I made my way to the back side of the house. Here, the dead on stakes screamed in vivid colors. Arms hung down by their sides. Some of them were on crosses—how I managed those, I'll never know. Wooden stakes, much like what they used in movies to kill vampires, had been driven through their chests. Their bodies were wrapped in wire from the fence, holding them in place. Their feet touched the ground. Each of them was missing portions of their heads. Flies buzzed around their bodies. I told myself I would eventually take the bodies down. That never happened.

I passed the staked biters and continued up the hill, stopping at the woodshed that sat along the tree line. Inside were mostly smaller pieces of wood. I found the longer one sitting along the wall—a four-foot piece of 2X4. I tied a rope around it, grabbed a black toolbox that sat on the floor, and then headed back to the house.

Inside, I entered the room across from the one Hetch lay dying in. I didn't know how much time I had, so I worked quickly. With the toolbox lid opened, I found a thick-tipped screwdriver and a hammer. It took a minute, but I managed to drive the screwdriver through the door, whittling out a hole the size of a nickel. I ran the rope through it and then nailed the board to the inside of the door. I opened and closed the door several times before stepping into the hall and tying the other end of the rope to the knob of the bedroom door Hetch lay behind.

It wasn't the soundest idea I've ever had, but all I needed was a little warning. If Hetch died and rose, he would try to open the door. When he did, the door opposite him would slam shut. The rope attached to the knob would delay him from getting out of the room. By then, I would have my gun ready. I planned on sleeping in the main bedroom, the door locked, just in case.

I untied the rope, checked in on Hetch. He was asleep, his face pale and peppered with sweat. With the door closed and the rope tied back around the knob, I went outside.

I don't know who first coined the phrase, "the world is a cruel place," but that person had no clue. Sure, it could be bad and difficult and people could be cruel, but the world itself? Not so much. Well, not so much back then. Now, the world is nothing but cruel. I lost everything. So did almost every other survivor left out there. I didn't know Hetch's story, but he was about to lose his life after making it so long. The world isn't cruel. No. The world is a real bastard.

There were more biters walking around. They were like vultures that could smell the living. I stood on the porch stoop staring down at them. They seemed to stare back at me. I went back inside, reached for the machete, then grabbed several pistols instead. Screw being quiet.

Back outside, the dead moaned. The party was just getting started. As I went down the steps, the moans grew louder. They worked themselves into a frenzy, but none of them crossed the circle of bodies. It was like a rotting, corpse-laden force field. That was fine. They were about to join the barrier.

I remember the first shot. It split the side of a teenager's head. I remember the last shot. It caused the explosion of an elderly woman's face. The force of the blast sent her sprawling backwards. I don't remember any of the shots in between. But the bodies on the ground told me I had wiped them all out.

And the sun told me it was near dark.

Inside, I sat with a lamp on. It was late. I thought about checking in on Hetch. Then decided not to.

At some point, I fell asleep in the chair, one of the pistols in my lap.

The slamming door woke me.

My heart hammered in my chest. My head buzzed with disorientation. The gun was in my hand and raised near my head. I listened, heard shuffling from down the hall.

"Hetch?" I whispered.

It was dark in the house.

The shuffling stopped, then came another slam. The rope trick worked. Hetch was dead and had been stopped by the rope between the two doors.

I stood. My body shook but not from fear—from sadness. I would put him down, and I would bury him. And I would be alone again.

I eased into the kitchen and caught a glimpse of him standing in the bedroom's doorway. His head was down, as if he were looking at the rope. I wasn't sure, but it looked like one hand was on it or maybe both of them.

"Hetch?"

He lifted his head and looked at me for a long few seconds.

"Walker."

I think I blinked. I think I stopped breathing. I think I almost pulled the trigger at the sound of his voice.

Biters don't talk.

"Hetch?"

"Yeah, man." His voice was weak.

The rope dropped to the floor. He had untied it.

"What's with the slamming door rig?"

"I...I..."

"You thought I was dead, didn't you?"

A small part of me was ashamed at my lack of faith but not ashamed at my will to survive. "Truthfully? Yes."

"I'm not. I'm alive. I feel better. A lot better."

I lit a candle and held it up. He was no more than six feet from me. His face didn't look so pale. He was no longer sweating.

"Let me see your knuckles."

He held out the wounded hand. The wound was pink, the skin around it white. I checked the wound on his stomach next. The gray skin had reverted back to white. The bite marks themselves were red but not angry looking any longer. His leg was the same.

"I can't believe it. It worked."

"I can't believe it, either. I just knew I was going to die and...and..."

"Yeah, I get it. I was about to put a bullet in your brain."

The smile faded from his face. One appeared on mine. My heart didn't feel so heavy. There was a way to save those that were bitten. I doubted it would work after someone died, but there was a way to save them before they reached that point. We didn't speak for half a minute. Maybe more.

"Why don't you take a shower? You smell like death warmed over. I'll make you something to eat."

After he left the room, I lit a couple of candles. The cabinets still had food in them but not a lot. We needed to go on a supply run eventually. But not tonight. Hetch was probably still in no shape to run from biters.

I pulled out a box of crackers that had expired two months earlier. They were still crisp and held no signs of going stale. Two bottles of water went on the table. My mouth was dry, and I could feel my body wanting—craving—the alcohol I had lived off of for weeks. I didn't know if there was any more over at the other place, and I had no real desire to find out. My body, however, begged me to search. There had to still be some over there.

I held onto the edges of the table, closed my eyes, and took deep breaths. In and out. In and out. In and out.

The urge passed, and I sat down. I could see the jug with the Healing Springs water in it. There wasn't much left—maybe a third of a gallon. I wished I had known about this...

...before Pop died...

...before Davey died...

...before I sat in that warehouse holding Lee's hand as he threw up and sweated and wasted away, greeting death with a touch of humor and a lot of tears and begging me not to let him turn...don't let him turn...please, Hank, don't let me turn...

. . .

. . .

...before Jeanette...

A crushing blow sank my spirits. Hindsight and all that aside, my family was dead, and there had been a cure all along. Somewhere in the background of the world around me, I heard the sound of water running behind a closed door. I lowered my head to the table, the weight of truth crushing me all over again.

I cried…

Twenty Weeks (?) After it All Started

Hetch was sometimes a pain in the rear, but he was one of the living and one who wasn't Hell bent on feeding me to his dead wife, or raping a pretty biter, or blinded by an overzealous preacher-man. He was normal—for what that was worth. Normal was relative in the old world. It was unheard of in the dead one.

We're all just a little messed up in some way or other.

And maybe that's what made him Hetch: being normal in this screwed up world.

It took almost a full week before he was strong enough to do anything besides lie around and nap. There were times where he acted like a little kid, whining about not feeling well and wanting me to bring him his meals. I watched his temperature like a doting mom to that whiny kid, checking it often.

Two weeks after Hetch's arrival, I made a run into Batesburg for medicine, passing the armory of dead soldiers along the way. There were biters outside of town but not as many as I expected to see so close to the town proper.

The drug store was empty of life of any kind. And there were plenty of bottles of medicine—Tylenol, Ibuprofen, Aleve, Excedrin, and a whole host of generic brands as well. I took as long as I could, gathering medicines in plastic bags I grabbed from the front counter and throwing them in a buggy. There was water and Gatorade and chips and crackers and some canned goods, and bandages and…and I realized then that the little town had no survivors. It was a startling epiphany that made me cold all the way to the bone.

I had never before felt like someone was watching me even though there was no one else around.

Until then.

I looked around the immediate area, saw no one in the gray shadows of the store. I pulled out my pistol and pushed the buggy toward the front. One wheel didn't want to cooperate and rattled along the floor instead of turning quietly. The hairs on my neck stood on end, and I couldn't shake the shiver that had crawled up my spine. It was like someone had taken a piece of ice and touched me on the back of the neck.

Outside, there were half dozen biters roaming the streets. I shoved the gun back into my waistband and slid the machete from its sheath. I had to be quick. To let them notice me before I could take a few of them out meant running for the truck before I was ready. Though I was almost positive I would never return to that drug store or even that little town, I still needed the supplies I had stashed in the buggy.

I moved quietly, sneaking up behind the first few and bringing the machete over the tops of their heads with ease. Two or three others noticed and turned toward me. I took them out before they grew too close to each other and then made my way back to the van. In the driver's seat, I exhaled and put my head on the steering wheel, my hands gripping either side of it. I never get used to the feeling of the dead being around—they are like venomous snakes waiting to strike, and yeah, their venom will kill you.

The air of the town gave me the creeps, as if the ghosts of all the dead surrounded me. My skin crawled as if hundreds of tiny hands slid along my body. I almost turned the key in the ignition and put the van in gear. Getting out of there was all I wanted even if it meant leaving the buggy of supplies on the sidewalk.

I looked around again. There were no more biters to be seen. Honestly, I don't think it would have been so terrible if there had been a thousand of them right then. At least the dead were physical—I could *see* them. I could *hear* them. I could react to them. The way I felt right then, getting out of the van was more dangerous because I *couldn't* see anything that could harm me.

I opened the van door and got out. I went to the buggy. Its wheels were loud on the concrete, shaking the metal frame as they hit each crack and bump along the way. The side door opened, and I tossed supplies inside haphazardly, not caring if anything spilled out. I shoved the cart aside. It bumbled a few feet before tipping over, crashing with a loud clatter of metal on concrete.

I hissed, suddenly angry with myself for the extra noise. Then I saw it. Out the corner of my eye. I turned, my hand already pulling the machete from its sheath. It was a biter. It had to be.

But it wasn't.

I stared at the dog. It was brown and white and thin. It was small and scruffy and dirty and pathetic looking. Its ears hung down, a clear sign it was scared. It was probably as hungry as I was.

"Hey," I said. "Hey, little dog."

I hadn't seen many animals since the end of the world began, and this one looked as lonely as I had been—as I still was. I took a step forward. It took a step back. Both hands went out in front of me.

"It's okay. It's okay. I'm not going to hurt you."

Another step forward and the dog backed away again, its tail between its legs.

We stared at each other a while longer.

"Stay here," I said as if the dog was going to listen. It had probably been through as much as any person had. I went back into the drug store. It took a minute, but I found the pet food section. It was close to the back, near the pharmacy. I grabbed a bag of dog food and made my way to the front. The dog was gone by the time I got back outside with the bag open.

"Doggie?" I called softly, not raising my voice too loud.

I made my way around the corner of the drug store.

"Doggie?"

The backside of the store held nothing more than garbage and a rundown car that probably wouldn't crank up in an emergency. I made my way to the front, turned, and walked down the street a little way. I didn't get too far before I heard the dog growling.

On the other side of a parts store was the dog. His fur was on end, and his tail was tucked between his legs. But he wasn't running, and he wasn't cowering down. He growled then barked and then backed away, his nails tapping on the crumbling blacktop. Standing in that little alleyway between the parts store and another store were several biters. At first, they didn't notice me. I wasn't sure if somewhere in their brains they recalled how dangerous an angry dogs could be. Or maybe they were just as dumbfounded as I was to see a living animal. It didn't matter one way or the other. The dog was food for the dead. As I think about it, many people would have considered him food for the living. Yeah, maybe that's why he didn't let me near him.

In this world…in this crap hole those of us that remained still lived in, seeing a dog was like seeing the past. It was Fido and Rex and Lassie saving little Timmy. It was man's best friend trying to survive without man and man trying to survive without dogs. It was Scooby Doo, where are you? It was Sam from *I Am Legend* taking on vampire dogs and saving Will Smith's behind. It was everything that was right about the old world and everything that was wrong about this new one.

The stalemate ended when the biters started shambling forward, some of them going after the dog, some of them coming for me. I dropped the dog food and had the machete out in as quick of a motion as I could. I swung it in a wide arc, taking the tops of two biters' heads off. I swung again.

And again.

And again.

With each biter I took down, another one replaced it. What was going on? That alleyway wasn't that big. Where were they all coming from?

I drew my pistol and took the nearest one out. The biter's head snapped back with the force of the blow. The bullet exited the back of his skull and struck a woman behind him in the forehead. They both fell, like dominoes, one bumping into another, and then they struck a couple more. In seconds, half a dozen biters were on the ground.

I pulled the trigger a few more times. The dead fell, their bodies like matchsticks or kindling, forming a barrier that the others couldn't quite get through without falling over. For them, it was a final death sentence, and I was their executioner.

One.

Two.

Three.

Four.

Five.

Six.

How many more? So many in such a tiny space.

Seven.

Eight.

Nine.

Where were they coming from?

I heard growling from behind and spun to see the dog crouching, as if it were about to strike. There, at the mouth of the alley, were several more biters. Coming to the party, I guess.

"Crap!"

With a wall of dead bodies to one end of the alley, I started for the entrance. Before I got there, the dog lunged at one of the biters, hitting it in the stomach. He ripped at the woman as she fell to the ground. He jerked his head from side to side, tearing rotten flesh from her body but not killing her, not like I guess the dog thought it would.

I couldn't risk a shot, so I turned the gun to those still standing. Three shots and the gun was empty, but the biters at the entrance were down, and they would never get up. The dog was gone again, but the female biter was still alive and struggling to stand. She struggled no longer after the machete's blade split the top of her skull down to her neck.

Behind me, the wall of flesh had held the remaining biters at bay. I stood for a moment, looking, watching. Then I realized the alley I was in lead to the entrance of another building. Or maybe it was the EXIT to the building and the entrance was on the other side. Either way, the door was open, and the dead had piled out of it.

I watched. It's all I could do. Everyone who had survived in that little town must have gone to that building as a safe house, somewhere they could conjugate or…no, that wasn't it. I was wrong in so many ways, but the biggest of those was how many people would have survived the initial outbreak. This town might have supposedly had a safe haven in the armory just outside of its boundaries, but within…within, there was no way this many people survived.

Unless.

"They are the people who came here to escape."

Suddenly, I had hope. Just as suddenly, it was gone.

If Bobby and Jake were in there, they were dead. They weren't in the armory. They weren't at the Table Rock cabin. If they were there, they were dead.

I was sapped of energy. In the span of fifteen seconds, I went from hoping I would find someone from my family to knowing there was no way they could be alive, not in that building where biters still filed out of.

My shoulders slumped. I left the wall behind me, stepped over the biters at the mouth of the alley and stopped on the street. The dog was a few buildings down. He had pulled the open bag of food away from the alley and now had his head buried in it. I couldn't blame him.

Back at the van, I grabbed a gas can. I hated wasting the fuel, but I had to take care of the dead. Bobby or Jake could have been among them. I hated the idea that if they were in that building, then they would suffer unbelievable pain before they died. But I couldn't go in after them. It was the only way.

It was the only way.

The ghosts were all there, and they begged to be silenced.

I doused the wall of corpses with fuel. I went back to the mouth of the alley and cut away the shirt of one of the biters there. I found some stones and bricks and wrapped them in torn strips of cloth before soaking them with gas. I tossed them into the crowd and then went back to the front of the buildings. The parts store was on my left. I smashed the window with one of the stones and went inside. There were no dead there, only the specters of their lives.

More gasoline went onto the floors and counters and shelves. I made sure and doused the oil shelves as well as I could. With the can empty, I left it on the floor, went back to the van, and got a lighter.

The dog was gone, the bag of food ripped open, most of it still lying on the sidewalk. I guess he had his fill.

I took another piece of clothing from the dead and dipped it in the gas in the middle of the floor of the parts store. I went back outside, lit the arm of the shirt, and watched as a flame quickly engulfed it.

"Bobby, Jake, if you're in there, I'm sorry."

I tossed the shirt into the store. There was a loud *WHOOSH* even before the shirt hit the floor. Flames raced through the building. I backed away and watched. Soon, the entire store was burning. When the flames leaped from it to the stores on either side of it, I walked away.

I got in the van and closed the door quickly. For good measure, I locked it. Even inside the van, I felt out of sorts, as if at any minute, the boogey man from under some kid's bed was going to grab me and pull me from the vehicle.

I shook my head, trying to rid myself of the feeling. It didn't work. I sat there for the longest time, watching as flames hopped from building to building. A few biters appeared from shops or from around corners, their bodies on fire. Most of them didn't get very far before collapsing. Those that managed to get away from the buildings still didn't make it beyond the road before they too dropped to the ground where they died—in agony, I suppose.

My heart hurt as I watched them die. Deep down inside, I hoped none of them were Bobby and Jake, though honestly, I felt somewhere in that mass of rotting corpses they were there.

I also hoped that I would see the dog again. Man's best friend and all that. I didn't.

As day began to give way to dusk, I cranked up the van and left the small town behind.

Twenty Weeks and an Afternoon After it All Started

The drive back to the lake felt like it would take years. In truth, it was only twenty or so minutes. By the time I reached the house, the creepy feeling I had in Batesburg was gone, but it never really left my mind for the remainder of the day. Neither would the burning corpses I left behind, many of them still shambling about inside or around that building.

I thought about the dog. If only he would have let me get near him. I guess I get it—the dead and the living alike had probably scared him in some way or other.

I got out of the van and took a look back in the direction of the small town. Black smoke hung in the sky off in the distance. I wondered if the entire town would burn down, and if so, would the flames end there? Or would they follow me to the lake or head off in another direction altogether? Maybe the world burning itself to the ground wasn't such a bad thing, all things considered.

Leaning against the van's side, I closed my eyes. Behind those lids, I saw Bobby and Jake in better times, and then I saw them burning, their skin flaking off, their bones crumbling to the ground, hands seeking something to grip hold of, something to pull themselves along.

Tuck and roll. If only they could.

Hetch lay on the couch while I brought things in and put them away. Then I sat at the table and tried to control my shaking hands.

"Hank, are you okay?"

He had stood and crossed the room at some point and was only a few feet from me.

"Hank?"

"What?"

"What's wrong? What happened?"

I didn't answer right away. Instead, I stood and grabbed a bottled water from the counter. I uncapped it and drank half of it down. It was cool and refreshing. I leaned against the counter, staring at and through him, not really seeing anything.

"Hank?"

"I saw a dog," I said.

"What?"

"A dog. You know, man's best friend?"

"Yeah, yeah, I know what a dog is. What about it?"

"It was alive, and it looked like it hadn't eaten in months."

"What did you do?"

"I got some dog food from a store and took it to him, but he ran away."

"And you're upset about this?"

"I heard him growling, and I went to investigate. There were biters in the alley—dozens of them. I took a bunch of them out with the machete, but they kept coming and coming and coming. Then I realized…all those biters were the townspeople and probably others who had gone there for safety."

I took another long swallow of water, almost finishing off the bottle. Hetch said nothing.

"My brother, Jake… He took my wife and son and several other family members, and they went to this cabin we had in Table Rock. When I got there, they were all dead except for Jake and Bobby. Bobby's my son. Jake left a letter for me on the door, saying he was heading to the Batesburg armory. I went there not long ago. It was overrun with biters.

"But the town…when I got to the town, I didn't see the first person, dead or alive, at least not at first. It was a ghost town, Hetch. Just the souls of the dead crying out for peace."

I finished the water off and set the bottle on the counter.

Still, Hetch said nothing.

"I set fire to several buildings, and I watched as the dead burned and collapsed and died, and I mean really died.

"I watched it until half a dozen buildings were engulfed in flames. The sound of the fire was like the rushing waters of a waterfall."

I licked my lips. I was still thirsty, but I wasn't going to get another bottle—it had to last longer than a couple minutes.

"As I sat in the van watching the town burn, I had this feeling…this feeling that Jake and Bobby were in that building, just as dead as the other biters, bumbling around, hungry, and on fire."

"Hank, listen," he started.

"Where's your family?" I asked, cutting off whatever sympathetic bull crap he was going to say.

"I'm it, Hank."

"You're it?"

"Yeah. I never married, and I don't have any kids that I'm aware of." He paused as if pondering whether or not this statement was true. "And if I did have one, well, it's probably best I didn't know."

I nodded.

"Yeah, probably a good thing."

"Do you really think your brother and son were in that building?"

268

I shrugged. I didn't know for sure—I never saw them, after all—but the odds were good if they made it there, then they are as good as dead.

"If you're not sure, then how can you say for certain they were?"

"I just feel it in my bones. That's all."

"In your bones?"

"Yeah, like a gut feeling, you know?"

He nodded.

It was time to change the subject, and I knew very little of the stranger standing fifteen feet away from me.

"Where are you from?"

"Charleston," he said.

"Big city. Lots of people. How many biters?"

"Too many. When things started going down, things went bad in a hurry. That place is so compact in certain areas—not a lot of folks stood a chance. Those that didn't get sick were pretty much done in by their dead loved ones. It was bad."

"How'd you make it out?"

Hetch gave me a sad smile and looked down at his own bottle of water as if it was a beer and there were answers to be found at the bottom of it.

"I got lucky," he said and took a swig. "My buddy, Dean, and I went fishing down at Wateree, you know, a weekend thing. We left that Thursday just before things went bad. By the time we started back…well, there was no going back."

"Where's your friend now?"

"I told you, remember? I left him in a house a couple blocks away. That's why I was running away from all those biters."

"That's right. He was bitten. And you said you put him down, right?"

"Yeah. Well, I think."

"You think?"

He nodded uncertainly.

I chewed on that for a while.

It would be another few days before Hetch was at full strength. In that time, we talked a lot—more than I would have liked before. But in that world, I guess humanity didn't just lie in a living person but in their lives before the world died.

When he was better, we went on our first foraging trip.

"Where are we going?"

"I figure Prosperity or Newberry—one of them are bound to have some food or water. Maybe even some gas."

"Are you sure?"

"No."

Why start lying then?

We loaded the van with guns and ammo and some food, but not a lot—enough for a bite to eat while we were out.

I stared at Hetch when he got in the passenger's side of the van. He wasn't Humphrey, and it felt like a gut punch when he sat down.

"What?" he asked.

I shook my head. "Nothing. Just…just a memory."

"What of?"

I thought about it for a moment. How do you explain this to somebody?

Oh, a teddy bear used to sit there, back before you came around. We had nice conversations and killed a lot of biters together, but she's gone—yeah, she. Her name was Humphrey and…yeah, I know that's a boy's name, but that's what she said to call her. Yeah, she

270

said to call her that. Yeah, she talked to me. What? I'm crazy? Really?

I shook my head. "An old friend."

I turned the key. The van's engine rumbled to life, and I put it in gear. Half an hour later, we passed a Wal-Mart close to downtown Newberry. The college was just down the street. I thought about pulling in, checking out some of the dorms, but what good would that do? Most college kids didn't have all that much money, and Ramen noodles and beer were gourmet dishes for the higher educated.

Instead, I turned around and drove into the parking lot of the Wal-Mart. The dead were plenty here. I wondered if there were other people holed up inside. With that many biters, there had to be some sort of living meal there, right?

I drove close to the building, and the biters turned toward us. They followed the van as we circled toward the front of the store.

"There's too many," I said.

"Do you think there are still supplies in there?"

"I don't know, but it's not worth finding out—not right now."

We drove off, the dead following us the best they could. There was a CVS not too far away, but there were plenty of biters there as well. Unlike Batesburg where the ghosts were plenty and the biters were nonexistent at first, Newberry was overrun with them.

"This whole place is a dead zone."

"Are we just going to turn back?"

I nodded. "That's what it looks like."

We made our way back the way we came, passing the Wal-Mart on the right.

"Hey," Hetch said. "What if they were distracted?"

"What if they were?"

"One of us can distract them. The other one, well, maybe the other one could get inside and look around, maybe find supplies."

"How do you propose we do that?"

"Turn around. Go back to Wal-Mart, and I'll show you."

I thought he was nuts, but we needed supplies. I did a U-turn. I pulled up along the front of the parking lot but didn't pull in. The dead—there were so many of them. One wrong move and we were both on the menu.

Hetch pointed. "Over there."

I looked at the small store in the same parking lot as the Wal-Mart. It was yellow and white and made of brick and mortar and glass. In front of it was a propane tank.

"Do you see it?"

"The propane?"

"Yup."

"What about it?"

"One shot to the center of it and *BOOM!* that building goes up like a bomb went off. The noise will attract the biters to the building, and we can make a run for supplies."

I thought about it for a moment. It was worth a shot.

"How good is your aim?"

He frowned. "Eh…not all that great."

"Even with a rifle?"

"I'm not that great of a shot—you would just be wasting your ammo if I did it."

"Can you drive?"

This time, his expression was less of a frown and more of a silly, *I deserved that* grin.

"I'm pretty sure I can still do that."

We traded places. He pulled the van into the parking lot. The dead began to converge on us. I grabbed a rifle from the back and settled it on the edge of the door.

"A little closer," I said, fully aware the biters were approaching quicker than I wanted them to.

"Take the shot."

"Get a little closer."

He eased the van forward, taking us toward the ever-growing horde.

"That's good."

He put on the brakes, and I steadied the rifle. The window was completely down, and the dead grew closer by the second.

"Take the shot."

"I will."

Another few seconds passed, and I could hear them. Their moans were deafeningly loud.

I pulled the trigger.

Bullseye.

And the tank didn't explode. There was no big boom and a roaring fire to accompany it. Instead, a cloud of white vapor erupted from it and spilled around the tank about twenty or so feet. But it did draw some of the biters away. Just not enough of them.

I pulled the rifle back into the van and put the window up.

"Get out of here," I said.

"We can still do it."

"Get out of here."

"Hank, listen—"

"No. You listen—get us out of here!"

273

By then, the first of the horde was on us, their hands smacking the sides of the van, the hood, the windows.

"Yeah, okay, getting us out of here."

He put the van in reverse and mashed the gas. There were thumps and bumps as he crushed several biters along the way. Back on the street, he started to speed away and then stopped.

"What are you doing?" I asked.

"They're following us."

"Not if you go. We'll be long gone before they can walk a hundred yards."

"No," he shook his head. "I mean, they are following us *away* from Wal-Mart."

"Yeah. I get it. Let's get out of here."

Hetch rolled his eyes. He actually rolled them. I wanted to lean over and punch him in the head, but he was behind the wheel, and I didn't think that would be too bright. Then he explained.

"You don't get it, Hank. If they follow us away from the store, we can get inside easier. The less of them that are near the front of the building, the better chance we have."

"Is this anything like your exploding propane tank trick?"

"I thought it would work. It did in one of those James Bond movies. Bond just pointed his gun and fired, and the tank blew up all the bad guys."

"You saw it in a movie?"

"Yeah."

The thump on the front window brought us from our discussion. Again, Hetch backed the van up, this time along the road. The dead followed him, their bodies rotting and their moans much like an angry mob's yells.

"Did you see that in a movie too?"

He laughed, which is more than I could do.

"No. It's a diversion, a tactic used all the time. Kind of like when some women I used to know wanted the boss to notice them, they dressed a little differently, more seductively. It always distracted the men—all of us—and pissed off the other girls in the office. For a while, though, the distraction worked in getting those women what they wanted."

"Does that mean you're a woman and you're going to use your wares to distract them?" I pointed at the steadily progressing horde.

"No—you're going to distract them."

"I am?"

Again, he laughed.

"You're going to go right up to the store. I'm going to hop out, and you are going to drive off—slowly. This will lead them away from me. Shoot a couple of them. If noise is as much of a distraction as movement, then that could draw a few more of them away as well."

I understood his thinking, but I wasn't too keen on it right then. This was his first time out in the world since almost dying. What if he wasn't ready? It was like pushing your kid on a bike and letting go before he had his feet peddling. The kid was usually ready, but the parent never was.

"I don't know about this. It's too risky."

"We need more than what you brought back, and unless wherever you got it from still has more, do you have any better suggestions?"

Wherever I got it from? It did have more before I burned the place down. I was certain of that. But I wouldn't tell him. No. That secret was mine.

"Fine, but I'm only giving you a few minutes in there. You look around. If it appears too dangerous, get out of there. You got it?"

"Got it, boss."

He gave a cheesy salute and then sped up, pulling away from the dead as they gave chase. Fifty yards away, if that, he slammed on the breaks. The tires barked on the blacktop.

"Trade places," he said, opened his door, and got out.

I rounded the van and got in the driver's side.

"Now, turn around and go back."

The road was a four-lane. It was easy enough to make a U-turn. When I did, I saw the biters. There were so many more than I expected. They marched toward us, a shambling mass of rotting limbs. I cracked the window enough to hear the chorus line of moans and groans, the sounds of pleading coming from the souls trapped inside.

"Walker, go."

I don't know why I listened to him, but I eased off the break and pressed onto the gas. The van picked up speed, and I swerved off the road to keep from hitting them. We passed them on my right. There must have been hundreds of them.

"This isn't going to work," I said, my nerves tingling and my stomach fluttering with millions of butterfly wings.

"It's worth a shot."

"Not if one of us—or both of us—gets killed."

Hetch said nothing, which was probably a good thing. He had to be thinking the same thing. But he was willing to take the risk, take a chance that we may not survive so that we may, well, have a *chance* to survive. I still wasn't so keen on the idea, but I also wasn't the one who had almost died because of a bite from one of those things.

I inhaled a deep breath and mashed the gas harder.

We reached the parking lot, and I swerved in, striking a biter and knocking her over in the process. She landed hard against the sidewalk, her head splitting open. There were still plenty of them swarming the place, but we had a clear path to the front of the building. I floored it, reaching the doors in seconds.

"Take this," I said and handed him my pistol.

He glanced at the gun, hesitant to take it, I guess.

"Hetch, take the gun."

Finally, he took it, though I'm still not too sure he wanted to, and then he got out of the van and hurried to the doors. I watched him run, feeling like the dad dropping his kid off for his first day of school. I suddenly felt very lost and alone inside. My stomach knotted, and sweat began to bead along my forehead. The van felt stuffy and small and confining.

Hetch had to shove one of the doors open, but then he was gone. I sat there for a few seconds more, hoping he would come back having decided he wasn't quite ready for school yet. Then the dead began to beat on the back of the van. I drove off and back into the street but much slower than before.

On the road, I led as many of them away from the parking lot as I could. In the rearview, I could see a couple hundred biters straggling behind the van.

"This is taking too long," I said to no one. "I need to get back." With that, I did another U-turn, but the dead walked the width of the road. There was no plowing through that many biters. A moment of nervous tension welled up in my chest. I would never make it around that mass. We were going to die there, me inside the van and Hetch somewhere in Wal-Mart.

But there was a break in the bodies along the edge of the road. I turned the van toward that gap and then eased onto the shoulder. I gave the van enough gas to keep from bogging down in the grass. I hit several of the biters but not enough to slow me down. When I was able to get back on the road, I realized I had gone a lot further from Wal-Mart than I had intended.

Back in the parking lot, I pulled up where I had left Hetch. I started to get out, to run inside and see if I could find him. But if the biters came back, we would both be stuck. As it was, we still had a fighting chance. There weren't as many biters still in the parking lot, and the few that were there, I could easily take down with a machete or the front end of the van.

A minute passed. Then another. My chest tightened. My mouth became dry. Four minutes passed, and I was on edge, looking in the mirrors and checking the front of the store. I began to sweat not because I was hot but because I was worried. In the fifth minute, the dead began to make their way back to the parking lot. I started to get out of the van.

There was no need to.

Hetch pushed a door open. He pulled a buggy full with all sorts of things and then went back inside. One of the biters started for the door. I got out of the van and pulled the machete free. Hetch shoved the door open a second time, pulling with him another cart.

The biter, a grizzled-looking old guy with wisps of gray hair on his head, shuffled forward. He was close enough to Hetch to get a good chomp down on him. Then he did something I didn't expect. He stopped and turned away. He came toward me, his eyes a horrible white, his bottom lip torn free, exposing black gums and gray teeth. His nose was nothing more than flat skin. I brought the machete across his head, where it sank into the side of his skull. I pulled the blade free as the old man dropped to the ground.

"Come on," I yelled and rounded the van. I pulled open the side door. By then, Hetch was there with the first buggy. I unloaded it quickly as he ran back for the other. It rattled on the concrete, one wheel spinning and bumping along.

I looked back. The biters were getting closer.

"We have to hurry," I yelled and slung bag after bag after bag into the van.

We shoved the carts away and hopped in. The dead converged on us. They slapped at the windows and the doors and the sides and back of the van. It was like a sea of dead, and we were stuck in the middle of it, drowning as the waves tossed us about.

"What are we going to do?" Hetch asked. His eyes were wide and wild. He was breathing hard, and I thought he would hyperventilate where he sat.

"We have to get rid of some of them."

"How?"

"Shoot them. Stab them. We have to get out of this crowd before the rest of them get on top of us."

We rolled down the windows just enough to shoot the first few surrounding the van. They crumpled away, each one taking a couple with them when they fell. I gave the engine some gas, and we lurched forward, knocking over several biters in the process. The back tire spun on one of the bodies, caught traction, and then we were moving across the lot. Out on the road, we circled around the coming horde, Hetch with his window down and firing away when one of the biters was too close. He missed more than he hit.

I don't know how we made it out of there, but we did. Back on the road out of Newberry, we sat quietly for a few minutes, the adrenaline rush of the previous hour slowly calming down enough for us to think things through a little.

"What happened back there?" I asked.

"We got supplies."

"No. Not that. That biter had you. You were a goner. Then it stopped and turned for me. What was that all about?"

"I don't know." He sounded like a child. His face seemed to become small, his eyes grew distant. "But it happened in the store too."

"What do you mean?"

"There was a kid. I don't know, maybe a teenager."

"Was he alive?"

"No. No. He was very dead. Probably had been for some time. He was near the back of the store. I didn't hear him at first, but when I did…he was almost too close to do anything. Then, just like the old man, he stopped and turned away. I was so startled at first that I did nothing, just kind of watched him limp away. Then I got mad and knocked him down and kicked his skull in."

"He didn't try to bite you?" I asked.

"No. He just turned away."

"I wonder what that's all about."

"You don't think it has anything to do with me being bit, do you?"

I shrugged. "Why would it?"

"Maybe I'm still infected, but since I didn't die…I don't know."

"Me neither."

Whatever the reason, Hetch had survived not one but two close calls that day. We were done gathering supplies, hopefully for a while.

That lonely drunk from a few weeks earlier, now completely sobered up, realized one important thing about this new world: Being a loner was a deadly thing. Having someone in your corner, someone who can create a diversion or do the dirty work, was a salvation unlike any other.

Twenty-Nine Weeks and Three Days After it Started...

We never talked about that day at the grocery store again. We may have thought on it, but discussing it was off limits, an unwritten and unverbalized agreement between us. Instead, we focused on protecting the house, keeping the biters at bay. But one thing we didn't do, one thing that I had held sacred until it became too dangerous to worry about, was bury the dead. We left them around the yard. They made a sort of barrier that protected us from the biters. Maybe they could smell the rotting bodies, and that was enough to keep them at bay even when they saw us out there, which wasn't too often as it grew colder.

Still, burying the dead was the right thing to do, but I could no longer do it. Sometimes, I would look at the bodies, the flies buzzing around them, the stench of them clotting the air, and feel a heavy guilt settle on my shoulders. I wondered about their lives, who they were before they died, how they died, if they were with loved ones or alone, like I had been for so long. I wondered if they had been in a group, and if so, was there anyone else left from that group? I wondered who they were.

I would stare out the window at them when Hetch wasn't looking. I would pick one of the bodies out and try and imagine their lives before the fall of the world. I would try and look into their lives if that makes any sense. What were they like before death claimed them the first time? It was a maddening thing to do, but it was almost an obsession, one I kept to myself.

Occasionally, we ran into other survivors, but the world had become a wary place—strangers weren't to be trusted more now than before the world died a collective death. They weren't to be trusted at all.

For the most part, we eased into a systematic schedule—*a life* if that's what you would call it. Defend the house and scavenge when needed. We made several runs to Newberry, the tactic always the same, the results far better than the first time around. We tried to take out more of the biters each time around in hopes that the next time we went, it would be easier. It wasn't a bad life, all things considered.

That all changed two days ago when I remembered something we had talked about when we first met.

"Get your shoes on, Hetch."

It was early morning, and it was cold outside. Winter had arrived, and she came with a vengeance. He was lying on the couch, a cover pulled up to his chin.

We were thankful for the fireplace, but even with it burning low, it was still somewhat cool in the house.

"What?"

"Get your shoes on."

"Where are we going?"

"To check on your friend."

His eyes came fully open. "My friend?" He swung his feet off the couch, shoving the cover aside.

"Yeah, your friend. What's his name? Dean?"

"Dean's dead."

"Are you sure?"

He hesitated.

"You said as much when we talked about it before," I said. "Get your shoes on."

Hetch was wrong about one thing. He said the house he left Dean in was a couple blocks over. It wasn't. It was around the corner of the U-shaped neighborhood, just beyond the gated boat dock. It was then that I noticed the odd-looking windmill sitting near the water's edge of the cove. It was around forty feet tall. Its six blades moved slowly.

"What's wrong, Hank?"

"Nothing."

"Seriously? You stopped cold. Is it the windmill?"

"Yeah."

"What about it?"

"That's how we still have water."

"Are you sure?"

"Positive. Without electricity, there's no water. The windmill pumps when the wind blows. There's probably a rod down the shaft that traps the water and pulls it up as the water pumps."

"How do you know that?"

"I grew up in the country—it's similar to the concept of a hand pump near a well."

"So as long as there is water and wind, we'll be able to take baths?"

"Yeah," I said then added, "but I wouldn't drink the stuff unless it's boiled."

And there was a lot of truth to that—who knew how many biters were in that water? Thinking about it now, I don't know how I didn't see it before or why I didn't even question why there was actual running water in the house. I guess I just trusted the letter that had been left behind. But to never actually see the windmill—as if it were a background prop in a movie—I don't see how I could have missed it.

We moved on and dispatched of what few biters we saw along the way.

"Right there," Hetch said and pointed to a yard with no fence, the house a quaint little structure with three steps up to the porch and a wooden door painted white. The windows weren't boarded up—the inhabitants of that particular house either fled early enough or died way before they had a chance to run.

"Come on," I said.

"I'm not going in there."

I started to argue but bit my tongue. I had seen loved ones change, and I understood how he felt.

"Okay," I said. "Stay on the porch. If you see any biters, let me know."

Hetch stared at me, blinking several times.

"What?" I asked.

He gave a shrug. "What if he's…?"

I lifted my machete. "Then I'll take care of it."

I went up the steps, tried the knob.

"I locked it behind me," he said.

I have to give him credit; he was thinking when he left his buddy behind.

Back to the door, I kicked it hard just to the right of the knob. The jamb didn't splinter, but it gave. The next kick split the wood, and the door snapped open, striking the wall hard enough to make it bounce back. I stood in the doorway, listening, waiting. Nothing moved from inside.

Dust motes swirled in the sunlight. A slight breeze blew in off the lake, sending a shiver along my spine. I stepped inside, the clops of my boots echoing off the hardwood floor in the silent house. Three steps in, I stopped and listened. Nothing. No sounds at all.

The house was neat and clean, and the furniture wasn't dusty—it looked like the family would come home that afternoon as if nothing happened.

I peered down the hall. An axe hung from a bar in a doorway. There was a small splotch of blackish red blood beneath it. A few steps later and I was by the door, my heart beating hard. I felt like a crime show cop, one about to break in on the bad guys, gun drawn, except I had a machete.

I silently counted to three, spun into the doorway, machete above my head. A biter lay dead on the floor, his head split open. I gathered he had been Dean at one time.

I let out a slight chuckle, one of relief.

Back outside, Hetch looked at me with raised brows. "Well?"

"Did you rig that hatchet?"

"Yeah."

"It worked." I clapped him on the back, a "good job" gesture.

We started back toward where we were staying. In my mind, it was my house. The owners would never be back. That much I was certain of. But it was still just where we were staying, a rental but for free and with no eviction date.

We were barely passed the boat ramp when the screaming started.

I spun around. Across the water on a road not too far away was a child. She was running from a mass of biters. The road was a hundred or so yards away by boat, but I had no clue how far on foot.

"Come on," I yelled and pushed the gate to the boat landing open. The houses didn't butt up against the water, and I made my way through the backs of the yards, stumbling and almost falling several times. The embankment circled around into a cove. I could see the road going in the same direction—they would eventually meet at some point.

The girl's screams grew louder. I looked up. She was so small, maybe five or six. I thought of Humphrey, of the little girl I never met who had loved that little bear so much that it appeared in a family portrait. And the girl's screams held me in desperation.

I ran harder. I could see the last yard coming up on a street. Then I realized I could have run up the road Hetch and I had been on, and I would have run right into the same area.

Hindsight...

My boots hit the road, and I had my pistol out. The girl had slowed, and they were gaining on her.

I fired my pistol...

...

...

...

...and her screaming stopped.

...

...

Her screaming stopped.

...

...

...

Like so many times before, time slowed. I saw the girl's head snap back. Her arms went out to her sides and then trailed behind her as she fell. She had long, brown hair that probably hadn't been brushed in months. She wore a pair of stained pink pants and a white shirt that was more dirt than anything else. Her skin was just as dirty as her clothes. If not for her screams, I would have mistaken her for a biter.

And that's what my hand and eyes had done.

I'm almost positive of that.

Almost.

I stared at the little body lying on the ground, red blood pooling beneath her head like a halo. My heart stopped. My brain stopped. My breathing stopped.

I believe I dropped my gun before I fell to my knees.

The little girl was dead.

I had killed her.

...

...

Not for the first time, all I wanted was to die as well.

Tears welled up in my eyes, making everything blurry. But I could still see that red halo around the little girl's head from a hole I put there. Seconds earlier, I took aim and fired. Seconds before that, she was a living, breathing child who had somehow made it this long through the end of the world.

And she was dead.

...

...

I didn't see the biters descend on her, each one taking a pound of flesh for what it was worth. It didn't register that those who couldn't get to her were coming for me. I didn't hear Hetch yelling my name—or maybe I did, but it didn't get past my ears.

I did hear the gunshot.

It was enough to drag me out of my sudden stupor.

Another gunshot followed, and one of the biters dropped beside me.

They were near—so close several of them had dropped to their knees and were crawling toward me.

I tried to get to my feet, fell back on my butt. I scrabbled away like a crab but not putting much distance between the biters and me. I had to stand. I had to run. I had to pull out my gun and shoot as many as I could. But there was no gun. I had dropped it.

The machete was in my hand, like an extension of my arm. I didn't realize it until the first of the dead were right on top of me. I went to punch him. The blade split right through the old man's skull. I pulled the machete free. I'm not sure if I was more surprised I still had it or that I had just split open the skull of another biter who had been inches from me. It didn't matter.

I tried to stand again, but something was wrong. There was a pain in my thigh that screamed at me—like being hit by a baseball coming at you at ninety miles an hour. I swung the machete, clipping the dead at the knees and then slicing off the tops of their skulls after they hit the ground.

There were so many of them, coming in droves, their groans so loud I could hear them in my skull.

"Get up, Hank," Hetch yelled. He sounded so far away. Part of me wondered why he wasn't helping me. Why was he sitting back while I got swarmed?

Somehow, I managed to get to my feet. The pain in my thigh intensified. The biters kept coming.

I swung the machete.

There were a few gunshots, but really, what did I expect? Hetch only had a pistol with fifteen rounds in it. There were a lot more than fifteen biters. And, as he said before, giving him a gun was just a waste of ammo.

My arms grew tired, but I swung and swung, felling as many of the dead as I could. Somehow, I managed to get further from Hetch than closer to him. I had gotten turned around with each swing and thrust of the machete. I struck something with my foot as I turned to take down what had been a young man in life but was just another soul-trapped, rotting corpse now. The metal sound of my gun skittering across the hard scrabble road caught my attention. I drove the machete into another skull and limped toward the pistol.

Pain caught up to me, and I stumbled and fell to the ground inches from the gun. It was all I could do to grab it, turn, and fall onto my back. From there, I emptied the pistol into the dead as they approached.

One. Two. Three. Four. They went down, my aim true, the bullets as deadly as ever. I sat up and spun on one knee. Another went down by the blade of the machete. Then another one. I fired another shot and then circled around the bodies and the thinned-out group of biters. The hoard was manageable, but still, there were a dozen or so left. Six shots took out the closest to me. My machete took out the rest.

But there were still two more. Two more…

They crouched over the little girl, the terrified little child who might have escaped if not for my intervention.

Bile rose up in my throat, and heat filled my face. Anger flushed through my body. I stepped over the corpses, now forever at rest, and came up behind the closer of the two leaning over the girl's body. It had been an older woman in better times. I brought the machete down across the back of her head. She collapsed onto the little girl. The other one—a teenaged boy with just a shirt and underwear on and missing half his face—looked up at me, his eyes completely white. He growled and made to stand. He fell back to the road. I pulled the machete from his skull.

I was tired. Forget that. I was exhausted. My arms felt like rubber bands. My legs were weak. My body ached, and there was that throbbing in my thigh. I didn't care about any of that. I cared about the little girl.

I moved the old lady from on top of her. There was still plenty of flesh on her bones, but there were chunks missing from all over her body. Most of her face was gone as well. All except for the bridge of her nose and up. I could see the bullet hole in the center of her forehead.

I knelt down, fresh tears falling from my face. One of them landed in the mangled mess of one of her cheeks. I shook my head.

"I'm so sorry. I'm so sorry. I didn't mean to… I'm sorry. I'm…"

On my knees among the bodies of dozens of the dead, I cried. It was an ugly cry. I can only imagine how bad I looked, my face all screwed up, snot rolling from my nose, my shoulders hitching up and down, wails coming from my throat.

I looked up at a sound I thought—I know—I heard. The groan of a biter. I looked around, spinning on one knee, a pebble from the road grinding in it through my jeans. There was no biter there, but the groan…I still heard it in my ears.

I looked back down at the ruined child. Slipping my hands beneath what was left of her body, I picked her up, and then I stood. I stumbled up the road, which was a steady incline, the little girl held tightly to my chest, her blood soaking into my clothes.

Hetch was there, and I could see then why he had not rushed to my aid. There were probably a dozen or more corpses at his feet. He held a hammer in his hand—it was bloodied (as was Hetch), and there was still a piece of scalp on the claw end.

"Hank," he said as I walked by him.

I said nothing and continued up the hill.

"Hank, listen to me."

Again, I continued to walk.

"Hank!"

I turned, nodded toward the dead. "Do me a favor," I said. "Get my gun and machete for me."

Then I started walking again. I wouldn't stop until I reached the house. There, I lay the girl on the ground and made my way to the tool shed in the back.

I dug my last grave for the dead that day, and I buried a little girl…one I had killed. Hetch tried to help, but I wouldn't let him.

"Come on, Hank. Let me dig a little."

"No."

"You're exhausted. Just let me help."

"No!"

"Why not?" He was in my face. A sneer crossed his lips. I reckon he was pissed. I was taken back to my high school days where boys would feign wanting to fight, daring the other guy to take the first swing, too chicken to do it themselves.

I had never been that chicken.

I swung, clipping Hetch's jaw and sending him to the ground.

"It's my burden," I said.

Nothing else was said about it. Hetch stood watch as I finished digging the grave and placed the little girl in it. I put a sheet over her body.

"I'm sorry," I said again before tossing the first spade full of dirt onto her little body.

When I was done, I drove the shovel into the ground next to the little girl's grave. I stared down at it for several minutes before walking off. The day had gotten colder, and there were clouds rolling in. The weather was about to turn bad. If I had been thinking straight, I would have noticed that right away, and I would have known we needed more wood for the fireplace and needed to make sure we had plenty of supplies for winter.

Hetch spoke, something about "it was an accident."

Whatever.

I was an accident. Everything I had ever done was an accident. Even the way I met my wife had been an accident—if not for her bumping into my truck, I would have never known her. I tried to avoid them as much as possible, but somehow, they always found me. Or I always found them.

I made my way back to the house, went up the steps, my thigh throbbing. It was difficult making it up the stairs, but I managed.

It's amazing how time can crawl by so slowly that you swear you could see whiskers turning gray while other times, it passes so fast that if you blink, an hour or two or three is gone. By the time I made it up the steps and inside, it was dusk. How long had I fought the dead? How long had it taken me to dig the grave and then to fill it in? How long did it take for me to get up the steps and inside? Time...

I lit a candle in the bathroom and stripped out of my clothes. I thought about burning them the first chance I had. The shower was cold but a welcome feeling on my skin all the same. The bar soap was little more than a sliver, but when the suds ran down my stomach and onto my right thigh, the stinging was instant and intense. I rinsed my leg quickly and touched the area. I jerked my hand back as if I were shocked by a jolt of electricity.

"What the...?"

The shower went off, and I stepped out of the tub. I toweled off the best I could before tamping down the area on my thigh that was sore. When I was done, I held the towel to the candlelight. I saw blood.

My hands were trembling as I picked the candle up from the sink basin where it had been sitting. I held it down toward my leg.

...

...

...

I wrapped the towel around my waist and left the bathroom. Hetch was sitting on the couch—the very place he had spent the last couple of months. He sat up immediately.

"Hank, listen. I know you feel bad..."

"I've been bit," I said, cutting off anything he wished to say.

Twenty-Nine Weeks, Three Days and Seventeen Hours After it Started...

"Where's the water?"

Hetch was in the kitchen, pulling bottles out of a useless refrigerator. I stood in the living room, the towel draped around my midsection, a thin trail of blood seeping down my leg. It had surpassed my knee in a map-like pattern and made a line down my shin. The blood was almost to my foot.

"Where's the water jug, Hank?"

"There's not enough," I said.

He popped his head up. "Where is it?"

"Under the cabinet beside the stove. I didn't want to accidentally drink it by mistake. You never know when you might need it."

"We need it now," he said and slammed the refrigerator shut without putting all the water bottles back inside. He took a couple of steps to his right and turned around. The cabinet door came open, and Hetch emerged with the jug of Healing Springs Water. He grabbed a cup from one of the top cupboards and set it on the counter. Hetch was careful in pouring the water, letting none slosh out onto the counter or floor.

"Drink," he said and held the cup out to me. His hand was shaking.

I took it, downed it, and then handed it back.

Hetch poured another cup. I could see desperation in his eyes when he held it out to me. "Drink."

I knew that feeling. I still do, now more than ever.

He held the jug up. There were maybe two cups left. If I were lucky, there would be three.

The wound wasn't terribly deep, but it was wide. It looked like a chunk of muscle had been pinched in a vice, but the teeth marks were unmistakable. The torn skin—three inches in length and just as wide—was still red, the exposed tissue as pink as it could be. Blood still dribbled from it.

"Drink," Hetch said and again held the cup out to me.

I felt the desperation running through my veins. It was the same desperation I saw on Hetch's face. I didn't want to go out like that. I didn't want to wilt away and then wake up dead one day. I didn't want to be trapped in a decaying body with little control of what I was doing. I didn't want to die, but I wasn't afraid to either. I had seen plenty of death. I lost all my loved ones, all of my friends. Really, there wasn't much left to live for.

I had been bitten, and there wasn't near enough of that holy water to keep the infection at bay for too long.

I drank the water anyway.

"Come on. Sit down. Let's put some water on the wound."

"I'll get a rag," I said.

"No. I'm just going to pour it on. Just like you did with me."

He was careful. He tried to keep as much of it on the wound as possible. Not more than a few drops spilled down my leg. He tore a dishrag into strips, put one on the wound, and wrapped the other piece around my leg, knotting it at the side to hold the bandage in place.

We sat quietly, both of us staring down at my leg. Blood had already begun to seep through the bandage. Hetch rocked back and forth in his chair, his hands rubbing together as if he were cold. I was already planning my leave, thinking of how to get away from Hetch and head home. If I was going to die, I wanted it to be in my bed with a bullet in my temple. Better yet, I could go to Table Rock and lie down by Jeanette's grave. We could be together in death.

Yeah, that was what I would do.

"Where did you get the water from?" Hetch asked, bringing me from my thoughts.

I shook my head, shrugged. "I told you. The Healing Springs."

"Where is it?"

I had to think for a moment before I recalled. "A little town called Blackville."

"Where is it?"

"I don't know. I just kind of ended up there one day."

"Do you have a map?"

I nodded. "Out in the van."

He went outside, a flashlight in one hand, a gun in the other. He was quick about it, only gone for a minute or two. When he came back in, he dusted himself off as if he had fallen down.

"It's snowing," he said.

"Snowing?"

"Yeah."

I got up, winced when I put weight on my right leg. An odd burning sensation clung to the wound and radiated outward. At the door, I looked out. It wasn't a light snow dusting the ground like I had expected. The flakes were thick and fat, and the world was quickly becoming a sheet of white.

I turned around to see Hetch hunkered over the kitchen table, the map unfolded, the flashlight shining on it. One finger traced along the map.

"What are you doing?"

"Trying to find Blackville."

"You're going to try to make it there in the snow? You'll never get there and back in time."

He looked up from the map. "I'm not going alone. You're coming with me."

"No, I'm not."

"Hank, you will die if we don't get some more of that water."

I sat back down, my hands in my laps. "I'm okay with that." And I was, honestly, okay with it.

Again, he looked up from the map. "I'm not giving you a choice. Isn't that what you told me?"

"Things were different then."

"How? How were they different then than they are now?"

"I hadn't killed that little girl then."

How do you argue that? Hetch didn't know either. All he said was, "It was an accident, and I'm not going to let you commit suicide over an accident."

"She needed our help, and I killed her."

"You tried to save her."

"I shot her in the head!"

Again, there was no argument.

He went back to the map, his finger tracing the route he planned on taking.

"We can take 378 to 391 and then hit 178…"

"Yeah, I know—through Batesburg. I know."

"You know how to get there?"

I shrugged. I guess I did know. "I took the same route from Healing Springs to here, so, yeah."

"Let's go."

"No."

"Don't be stubborn, Hank."

"Let it go, Hetch."

"No. We're going to get you to this Healing Springs place and get some of that water."

"I'm not going."

"You're going."

I walked to the kitchen counter, picked my pistol up from on top of it. "I'm not going. I'm done. I accept it. Get over it. Get on with your life. Do whatever you want to do. I don't care. I'm going home—at least close enough to it so I can be with my wife again—and I'm going to die, but I'm not going to flame out and wake up again. I'm going to eat a bullet and end this whole mess. I ain't coming back as one of *them*."

Hetch's hands went to his hips. "Why?"

"Why not?"

"Don't, Hank. I've spent the last three months here. You saved my life."

"The water saved your life. Not me."

"Why did you take care of me? Why did you use that stuff on me instead of keeping it for yourself?"

I wanted to punch him. I wanted to put the gun to his head and pull the trigger. I wanted him to leave. But I didn't want any of those things. He had been a stranger three months earlier. But he wasn't then. He was the closest thing to a friend that anyone could have these days. And I *had* saved him. Me. Why?

I was tired of being alone. I needed companionship. I *needed* a friend.

"That was different," I said.

"Don't change the subject."

"You sound like my wife."

And the argument went cold. The world hit me hard between the eyes. I set the pistol on the table. My towel dropped to the floor. My head spun, and I felt nauseas. No, the infection wasn't getting to me. My comment did. I couldn't believe I had said that.

You sound like my wife.

Jeanette had been a great woman, and sounding like her should have been a good thing, a compliment. Instead, I made it sound horrible, like she was someone hard to live with, a difficult person.

"Hank?"

Hetch still stood by the table.

"I'm sorry," I said. "I shouldn't have said that. I…you're a good guy, Hetch."

My head was still spinning, but I was aware the towel was on the floor. I bent down, holding tight to the counter, picked it up, and wrapped it around my waist. I looked at Hetch. He could have been one of my brothers.

"I was tired of being alone," I said.

"What?"

"I saved you because I was tired of being alone. I would be dead already if you hadn't come along—I would have drank myself to death, and if I ran out of alcohol, I would have went out searching for more—a death sentence if there ever were one.

"You were my redemption."

We stood in silence, two men who had lost everything they had ever loved, and now…now one of us was going to lose the last shred of hope he had, and the other one was going to die.

"You were my salvation too—literally," he said.

I pulled a chair out at the table and sat down. "When I die, I want you to forget me. Okay? Just forget I ever existed. It'll make things easier for you."

"You're not going to die. And I'm not going to forget you. Why would you want to be forgotten?"

"I just do."

"I want to be remembered," Hetch said. "It probably won't happen, but that's what I want—to be remembered as a survivor. As someone who made it through the worse, and came out on the other end."

"You want to be remembered?"

"Yeah," he said and took a seat across from me. "I want someone—anyone—to remember me."

"And how are people going to remember you?"

"I don't know. I might write a book about the end of the world, about the dead and about surviving."

I nodded, my jaws clenched.

"I'm not going with you," I said.

"Come on, Hank."

"I'm not going to stop you from going. But if I start getting along in a bad way, it could be worse for you. You go, get the water. I'll wait here."

"Are you going to be alive when I get back?"

"Do you mean am I going to kill myself while you're gone? No. If I'm dead, the infection will be the reason."

"Can I take the van?"

"Yeah."

"Can I have the keys?"

I pointed to the coffee table in the center of the living room. "Right there."

"If the map is right, it shouldn't take but a couple to four hours to get there."

"It's snowing, Hetch. It might take a little longer than that."

"I'll be back real soon."

"Okay."

"And Hank?"

"Yeah?"

"Don't die on me."

"I'll try not to."

With that, Hetch left. I didn't stand to watch him go, but I listened. I heard each step as he made his way down the stairs. The van door opened then closed. There was the roar of the engine when he turned the ignition. The motor revved, then came the sounds of the tires crunching rocks and snow and ice as Hetch pulled away. The sound eventually died off, and I was left to myself, to the silence of the nightmare I was in.

As I sat there, I realized how terrible of a mistake it was not to go with him. The creeping loneliness started to fill the room, taking the places where dark shadows hadn't loomed yet. The candle on the table flickered, doing its dance, but I thought the darkness would get it as well, extinguish it the way the infection had all but extinguished mankind. I licked a thumb and first finger, reached across the table, and put out the flame. Complete darkness filled the room.

And I sat.

Thinking.

Dying.

Hetch wanted people to remember him. He wanted to tell people of the future—if there even is a future—about the world today, the dead, the living, the destruction, the bodies of the truly dead lying and rotting, the flies buzzing about them, the snakes and rats taking what they could, the buzzards conjugating and pulling apart what was left of the dead like an open buffet. He wanted to let someone know that he had been alive, that he had been a person who had a life before the world got fed up with humans and decided to eradicate them.

Maybe it wasn't such a bad idea.

Maybe it was a great idea.

I stood from the chair, my eyes having adjusted to the dark room. I went over to the couch Hetch had recovered on, reached beside it, and picked up my backpack, the one Humphrey had ridden in during all of our little excursions for food or gas or while looking for other living people.

A touch of sadness reached out to me, grabbed me and held me for a few moments. Then it was gone, and I pulled my flashlight out. I flicked it on and began my search of the house. It didn't take long to find what I was looking for: a pen and some paper.

I sat back at the kitchen table, relit the candle with one of several hundred lighters I had collected over the months, and began to write.

Twenty-Nine Weeks, Five (?) Days and Some Hours (?) After it Started...

I'm tired.

Hetch is gone. I'm not certain he will return. He headed out shortly after the snow began to fall, but he hasn't returned yet. That was almost two days ago.

I think. It's getting harder to focus, harder to make thoughts into coherent sentences. I hear the moans of the dead, but when I open the door, all I hear is the wind and tree limbs cracking and popping under the weight of snow and ice. I don't even see any biters... You would think I would see them since I hear them so clearly...

I've been writing...as much as I can ever since Hetch left. My fingers keep cramping up. My knuckles on my right hand are swollen, making it difficult to hold the pen. I have to stop often to rest my hand...and my thoughts. I've left so much out but have somehow managed to catch up to this moment in time.

This moment in time? At this moment, I'm dying.

There. It's out there now.

I'm dying. It's a truth I haven't wanted to admit, but now, as death nears...well...I've come to accept it.

The fever has been here for over a day. My skin stings. The more I rub it, the more I want to pull it off. I realize now that the scratch marks I've seen on biters were not inflicted by the dead but by the living as they were dying, their fingers clawing at and peeling away their own skin. I've scratched at my arms and chest, leaving marks behind. Beads of blood trickle from self-inflicted wounds, but I can't stop rubbing and scratching at my burning skin.

...

...

My stomach cramps. It's like someone yanking on my intestines every few seconds. The first few times...the first few times, I doubled over so far as to fall on the floor until the cramps eased off a little...enough to stand or get back in my chair...

...I want to pull my guts out and cut them from my body with one of the knives...in the...kitchen.

My eyes boil...

They are dry, and I swear there is sand in them...

I want to say a few things before...

...

...before I go.

It's still snowing. It doesn't snow like this in South Carolina. Hetch...he left to find the...Healing Springs...my God my stomach...

...

...

...

...

Hetch said he would be back...be back in a few hours. Hours? No. The snow slowed him down. He might have ran out of gas...or ran off the road...or maybe the biters got him...

It's probably...probably...just as well. By the time he got back...gets back...if he gets back...I'll be dead.

Sweating from the fever, my body on fire.

My lungs feel so full...so hard to breathe...

Must finish this.

Focus, Hank. Focus.

Focus…

I drank the last of the Healing Springs water yesterday. It's not enough. The wound on my thigh is gray. It's turning black. The veins are thick and bulging against my skin. The bandage is no longer blood-soaked but green and brown with pus. I can smell the infection. My fingernails are yellow and crusted with blood.

I've already begun to rot.

While I still have a little strength…

When I was a kid, my brother, Lee, once fired Pop's shotgun. It had a name…I can't remember what it was right now…something like an animal or…that's it. It was Ox, like Babe the blue ox, but without the Babe, the blue. Lee broke his shoulder. I think I might have wrote that already…

I've never fired the gun. I always wanted to…but after what happened…to Lee, well, I never got up the nerve to touch it much less shoot it. That was before the entire world died. I've held the shotgun several times since, staring at it, wondering how it would feel to pull the trigger. Before this gets me, I'm going to lose my socks—it's not like I need them to keep warm or anything.

I went outside yesterday. The snow was six inches deep if it was one. There's probably more now. I did my best…but the hole I dug wasn't that deep—maybe just enough to cover up my body and leave a mound of dirt, or snow, in its wake.

Something happened while I was out there. Something…odd. Several biters appeared out of nowhere. I didn't hear them, but they must have heard or seen me…I don't know. When I finally saw them, I lifted the shovel and prepared to defend myself. They stopped their approach when they got within about ten or fifteen feet of me. They stared at me through their cataract white eyes, their jaws slack and their skin grayish-green. Then they all shambled off, their feet dragging along in the snow, leaving ruts behind.

They moved so slowly... The cold must slow them down. That's fine information to have now...

"Where are you going?" I yelled. "I'm right here."

One of them turned back. I'm not sure if it was confused or not, but the look on its face was just that: confusion.

"Yeah, you!" I yelled. "I'm talking to you. Come and get me, you rotting bag of bones."

The biter turned away and joined its companions as they left me there.

Anger.

That's all I felt.

Anger.

I've been chased and chased...by these things...and now that I'm right there, no gun in hand...wanting an end to it all...they just walk off.

I stumbled up behind the male, who looked back at me. He had scratches on his arms and face, and he was missing an eye. I wonder if he plucked it out when he was still alive. The shovel connected with his skull. It split open. I drove the spade into the back of his head after he hit the ground. Then I went after the other two men. I smashed the first one, swinging the shovel like an axe. The second one turned back to me, as if attracted by the commotion behind it. I screamed as I bashed its head with the spade. I continued to scream and yell and beat the biter long after its head had ruptured like a rotten watermelon.

When I was done, I stumbled backward and fell into the snow. I dropped the shovel as well. I lay there, staring at the gray sky, snow still falling, my clothes steadily becoming soaked…

When I was a little boy, I loved to make snow angels. Making them was like doing jumping jacks while lying down. Lee was always really good at it…so was Jake.

I lay on the ground, my arms weak and body tired. I wanted to go ahead and die. Maybe I could freeze to death…but that wasn't happening. I was too hot to freeze. The snow melted around me…

I didn't make a snow angel.

I thought…

Hetch almost died that first time we went scavenging together. That old man…that old man had been right on top of him. Then he turned around and came for me… Hetch said there was a kid in the store. That kid…did the same thing. They could smell him…they could smell the *rot* inside of him. They didn't go after him because he's infected…

Maybe the water heals the wounds and lets you live…maybe…maybe…

Then the second odd thing happened.

I felt something licking my face. It was wet and like sandpaper. I wanted to swat it away but was too weak to move all that fast. I shifted my head to the side, and there stood the dog from Batesburg. He was kind of scrawny, and he might have been sizing me up, hoping he could make a meal out of me.

Go ahead, I thought. *Eat me, and get it over with.*

He didn't eat me… He licked me, and there was no joy in what he did. I think he knew.

308

I struggled to stand and threw the shovel aside when I was halfway up. I fell back into the snow...

...

...

My stomach feels like it's going to explode...

...

...and spill my intestines all over the floor...

...

...

The dog ran away the best he could in the growing snow. I watched him go, his tail tucked between his back legs.

...

...

I hate myself for scaring him away.

I crawled back to the house...and up the steps. On the landing, I leaned against the door. My eyes were heavy. I wanted to sleep...sleep and never wake up...never wake up.

I don't remember opening the door...or crawling inside...or getting back to the table... I woke here, my head down, the pen still gripped in my hand...

My fingers hurt... I can barely move them...

Hetch should have been back by now...

...

He's probably dead...

I think I've looked at the picture of the pretty brunette for the last time... I think her name is Cate... I hope she's alive and safe... She really is a beautiful woman...

Thinking of her makes me sad...and I feel...

...guilty.

...

My Jeanette is dead, and I miss her terribly…but it won't be much longer now…not much longer at all…and I will be with her…forever…

I won't be traveling to Table Rock…I won't die at her grave…

I'll find her though… In death, I'll find her…

…Maybe, I'll find Bobby too…and Jake…and Pop…and Davey…and Lee…maybe they're all waiting for me.

We can all be together again.

That's comforting…like the images of Heaven Momma always talked about…

How many times did she tell us boys, "Fly right, and go to Heaven. All your departed friends and family will be waiting there for you when you get there"?

I can see them now. Pop with his bald head and dry sense of humor, his way of saying things that made you think even though you didn't want to. Lee, with his unkempt hair and scraggly beard…always quick with a smart remark. Jake with his boyish smile and big heart…Rich and his family. Wilson will be there…oh yes he will…Jeanette with her pretty smile and soft skin and loving arms and…

…

…

God, I miss her…

…

…

I can't cry anymore. There are no tears left…

My head began to hurt sometime in the night.

Thumping…thumping…throbbing. The veins along my skin feel thick…as if they were growing and would burst from the swelling. The pain…the pain is like a migraine…a vice on my skull, squeezing my temples and cheeks and running down into my jaw and neck…stiffening…

…

Focus, Walker…

Jeanette was—*is*—my soul mate. We did things together that I probably wouldn't have done otherwise. Spontaneous things. Like getting donuts in the middle of the night or going to the beach at midnight so we could watch the sun come up. One time we ran through the sprinkler system at the old baseball field at two in the morning. We laughed and slipped and got soaked and got turned on, and that led to…well, you get the picture…

When Jeanette told me she was pregnant, we had only been married for three years. She had wanted babies sooner. Shortly after we got married, she asked, "When are we going to have children?"

She caught me off guard…she was good like that. I looked up from the book I was reading—yeah, I used to read—and said, "Why don't we wait until we've been married three years and we'll talk about it. Okay?"

She agreed. Reluctantly.

On our third anniversary, September 6th, it was…she came out of the bathroom with one of those pregnancy tests. Her eyes were glassy, her bottom lip trembling…just a little…and she said, "I'm pregnant."

"Seriously?' I said.

Her face crumbled… It was the wrong response…

…

…

I wish I had said something else…

I wish I could change that.

When Bobby was born, and I held him for the first time, I knew then that, yeah, seriously…I'm a father…

…

…

I feel like I've been hit in the head with a hammer. Yellow dots dance in my vision…

…making it hard to write.

I would lie down…but I need to finish…need to tell my story…

It's not that I don't want to be forgotten. I don't care about me…I want my family to be remembered…

…remember Jeanette…

Baby, I'm so sorry I let you die. I'm sorry I wasn't there for you when the dead came… I'm sorry I told you to go…to leave our home… It would have been safer there…

I love you…

I love you…

I love you…

Remember Bobby Henry Walker…

I never called him Junior. I wanted him to have his own identity.

Bobby…if you're still alive, stay safe, be strong. I'm sorry I wasn't there to protect you and your momma… I'm sorry you had to see her die. Please, know that Daddy loves you…

Daddy loves you…

Remember Leland…

…

…

…this hurts…

My stomach is in knots. I reek of death. The wound on my leg has spread lower than my knee and up into my hip. My

312

bones are stiff. The blood in my vomit tells me I don't have much time…not much time at all…

Everything is growing fuzzy around the edges…

Hang on, Hank. Just a little while longer, old boy.

Remember my brothers. Leland Rex Walker. Richard Clark Walker. Jacob William Walker. The best brothers a guy could want…

Did I ever tell the story of Jake riding his bike and trying to jump over a hole he and the neighbor boy, Billy, dug?

They were ten, I think… I can't remember now. I probably won't remember much longer…

They dug a hole—a deep one, maybe four feet wide and three feet deep…

They built a ramp—a crappy one. Three cinder blocks and a piece of plywood. For a skateboard, that might have been okay. For a bike, it was a disaster waiting to happen.

…Cramps…

Hold on, Walker…

Focus. Focus…

"Hey, watch this, guys," Jake said and straddled his bike. He went around Billy's yard several times, picking up as much speed as a ten-year-old could. Then he hit the ramp.

…

…

The front tire didn't go up like it should have. It went down and hit the other side of the hole. Jake shot forward on the bike, racking what little manhood a kid his age has.

…

…

That's probably not how he wants to be remembered…

Remember Pop.

Pop, I tried to make it. I tried to make you proud. Like most of my life, I failed again. But you always saw the possibilities with me... Where everyone else thought I would fail, you never gave up. Thank you, Pop.

Remember Davey Blaylock...

The best friend a guy could ask for. Thick and thin, to the end... It's my fault you're dead, Davey. I've had to live with that ever since...I still can't believe it...

Remember them all.

Remember them all...

Remember...

Remember...

...

...

...

Breathing...is so hard now. Lungs are full of nastiness. It took almost all the energy...the energy I had to reach the side door.

I made a note... I'm not sure I spelled the words right, but I tried. The note...the note says, HETCH, STAY OUT. I'M DEAD. I think I taped it to the door...then I locked it...

It's almost time... I can hear Death knocking on the door. You just come on in, Death... Just come on in. I'm...in the back...bedroom...the one I thought Hetch would die in...

Hetch...

He wanted to be remembered...

Remember Hetch.

He never married. Never had kids... He had a gal, but they called it quits before...the crap hit the fan...

He survived two bites and a nasty cut... He went for help. He was a good guy...

314

Yeah, he must have died too…never came back… Get away while you can…from the crazy man…

…the crazy man with the dead on stakes around the house…

…Don't blame him…don't blame him at all…

I can't

quite see all that

well right now…

Mine eyes have seen the

glory of the coming of the Lord…

He is trampling out

the vintage where the grapes of

wrath are stored;

He hath loosed

the fateful lightning

of His terrible

swift sword.

His truth

is marching

on…

The wrath? Did I just write that? The wrath…is the dead…so many of them…the world ends…the world ends because of the wrath…like that preacher man said. The dead will eat the living…something like that.

My eyes don't see much of anything right now…

Everything…everything…

…is a haze.

I hear the dead…they're coming for me…

I can hear them over the roar of the trains…in my ears…I can hear them…over the forever…sounds of gunshots in my soul, thumping…thumping with my rapid heartbeat. They pound at the door…I can hear them…

Coughing…

Blood…so much…

blood…

I'm tired.

Fingers hurt…body hurts…mind…

mind…is numb…??

I hear them… I hear them…

The door…how did they…how did they get up…

…steps…

They're here…I hear them…

…the dead…

Hetch, forgive me…

Thirty Weeks and Two Days After it Started...

I woke up.

You have to understand that.

I.

Woke.

Up.

I shouldn't have.

Everything was blurry, and there was light—bright and white—that hurt my eyes when I opened them. A raw pain like that of staring at the sun for far too long on a hot summer day ripped through them. I clenched them shut.

"He's awake."

The voice sounded excited. And familiar. But muffled as well. It was definitely a voice I knew, but my ears felt clogged, and there was a slight buzzing in them.

One hand went to my face, shielding my eyes when I opened them again. The light was still there but not directly in my field of vision.

"Hank?"

That familiar voice again. I shook my head, opened my mouth to speak. All that came out was a wheezing croak.

That familiar voice spoke. "Hetch, get some water."

Hetch? Hetch? He's still alive? No. I must be dead and this is...wherever it is.

And who was the familiar voice?

"Turn down the lights, will you?" the voice said. It felt odd to hear that. I hadn't seen real lights that weren't powered by flames in a long while.

The lights dimmed, and I lowered my hand. Things were still blurry, but I could see in the gray of the room that I was not home. I was not in a hospital, and I wasn't at the house at the lake. The room was nothing more than a square box, no windows to be seen, and a door across from where I lay in a bed. There were several chairs—the type that belong in a dining hall or cafeteria and not in a place being used as a caregiving room. A sheet covered me from midsection to toes. My head lay on a soft pillow.

My skin no longer burned.

My stomach was no longer in horrible knots.

My head didn't hurt.

My lungs no longer felt full. I could breathe.

The fuzziness in my vision faded as my eyes adjusted to the room's light.

"Hank? Drink this."

The voice was in front of me, just off to the right. A hand touched my arm. It was rough, a hardworking man's hand. I could see a white cup. There was a straw jutting out the top. The person who spoke lowered it to my mouth, and I drank. The water was cool and fresh and felt like Heaven as it went down my throat, filling my chest and stomach with its sweet relief.

My vision cleared a little more, and the person who stood by me wasn't Hetch. I rubbed my eyes, blinked several times.

It was impossible.

"Jake?"

"Yeah, Brother. It's me." He laughed. Tears streamed down his face.

I reached up. I was so weak I could barely grip his hand. His skin was real, his touch was real. It *was* my baby brother…and if he were there…

My eyes opened fully then. My heart sped up. "Bobby? Where's Bobby?"

"He's okay, Hank. He's asleep."

He's okay. He's okay. He's okay. He's okay.

That's all I could think for several long seconds. My head dropped to the pillow as if I were completely exhausted though I was more relieved than anything else.

"Where is he?"

"Down the hall. I'll wake him in a little bit. The poor kid's had a rough few months."

"Haven't we all?" I asked.

"Yeah. I reckon so."

Another thought dawned on me, and I tried to sit up, tried to scoot away from my baby brother. "You have to get out of here. I'm dying. I should already be dead… I…"

"You about scared the life right out of me is what you did." Hetch came up beside Jake. His beard was gone. He wore clean clothes. His left arm was in a sling, and there were several fading cuts on his face.

"We beat on the door, and you didn't answer, and that note you left…I just knew you were dead. When we found you…" he shook his head, tucked his lips in on each other. "You were sitting on the floor in the back bedroom, your shoes and socks off, that stupid shotgun by your side. If I didn't think you were already dead, I would have killed you myself."

"I was dying," I said. "You never came back."

"I did," he argued. "If I wouldn't have, you really would be dead and probably stumbling around that house you locked yourself in."

"The biters. They were trying to break down the door. I heard them."

"The only thing you heard were me and the soldiers."

"Soldiers?"

"Yeah. The military—it's still around. At least, what's left of it."

There were still soldiers. I chuckled.

"I thought you were dead."

Hetch laughed this time. "I thought I was too. The van skidded off the road. I was an idiot—driving way too fast for conditions. I hit a patch of ice and spun out, went right off the road and into a ditch. Knocked me stone cold out. When I came to, the door of the van had been taken completely off, and a soldier was pulling me free from the wreckage."

"Soldiers? Seriously?"

"Yeah. Seriously. They thought I was crazy when I told them of the healing water. But one of them knew the place and took me there."

"Was there anyone there at the Healing Springs?"

"One man—an Indian."

"Imeko?"

"Yeah, I think that's his name."

"Where were the others?"

"Others? It was just him and a stuffed teddy bear."

"A stuffed teddy bear?" I smiled a little.

"Yeah. The old guy was sitting on one of the picnic tables with the bear in his lap."

"The bear, was it wearing any clothes, maybe some bunny pajamas?"

Hetch's face scrunched up, his brows creased down. "Yeah. How'd you know?"

"Humphrey." I didn't realize I spoke aloud, but Hetch responded.

"Yeah. That's what the old man called it."

"Called *her*."

"What?"

"Humphrey's a girl."

"A girl?"

"Long story," I said. "Is Imeko okay?"

"He's alive and well, or as well as he can be. He was covered in snow. We thought he was frozen, but he looked at us when we drove up. We got what I needed and then tried to get him to come with us. He fought us every inch of the way, saying his people died there and he wished to do the same."

"His people died there?"

"That's what he said."

"Is he here?"

"Yeah, but he's not happy about it."

"What about his granddaughter?"

"I told you, it was just him. There was no one with him. Just him and the teddy bear."

This bothered me. I started to ask if he were sure but bit back the question.

"How long have I been out?"

"Six days."

"Six days?"

"Yeah. I didn't think you were going to make it. I had to keep one of the soldiers from putting a bullet in your head when we found you."

"Thanks." I meant it.

It was all so much to take in. Hetch being alive. Jake being alive. Bobby...Bobby being alive. I wanted so bad to get up from that bed and find him and hold him in my arms. There were other things I wanted as well. Questions filled my brain, threatening to make my head explode. Then he set a notepad on my bed. It was the same one I had written in as time ticked away the seconds and minutes of my fading life. I looked up at him.

"I thought you might want that."

"Thanks," I said. I opened it and flipped through the pages. My handwriting grew worse and worse as I got sicker and sicker. Some of it didn't make much sense, and a lot of things were left out. I closed the notebook and nodded. I guess I did want there to be a record of me after all. (This is also the notebook I currently write in. This, I think, will be the last entry.)

"Where am I?" I finally asked after a long silence with me staring at a blood stain on the notebook. It had to be mine.

"Fort Survivor S.C. #3."

"What?"

"That's what they call this place. Fort Survivor S.C. #3."

"Where are we—not the name of the place, the town?"

"Century Falls—it's a little town in Lee County."

"Is it safe here?"

"Safest place I've been in a long time."

"We're at the high school," Jake said. "They built walls around it, dug a huge moat. There's a little bridge—like a drawbridge—on one end. It stays up at all times except when someone comes and goes. Security is tight. No one comes in until they have been thoroughly checked over, strip search and all. Even then, they are quarantined until the docs can look them over. Hank, it's safe."

"How long have you been here, Jake?"

"Five, six weeks. Something like that."

"And it's safe here? You're sure?"

"Hank, the dead can't get in. I can show you if you like."

"I'd like that."

It was another couple hours before I was able to get out of bed. They told me it was four a.m. when I woke. By seven, I had eaten a bowl of oatmeal and showered—hot water and all—and was dressed in clean clothes. My stomach felt odd at first, probably from having actual food in it after being so sick.

"Can I see Bobby?"

Jake smiled. "Let him sleep, Brother—we'll see him soon enough. Are you ready to see how safe this place is?"

Hetch and Jake led me out of the room. My legs were still unsteady, but after a few minutes of walking the halls of the high school, they began to feel stronger.

The sun was just coming up as we made our way outside. It was cold, and there was plenty of snow on the ground.

"It snowed a lot."

"Too much," Hetch responded.

We trudged across the ground, the snow crunching underfoot. I pulled my coat tight and shoved my hands in the pockets. My breath came out in plumes of white vapor. It was good to breathe.

The walls loomed higher than I expected. In my mind, I envisioned cars or trucks or maybe buses and semis surrounding the entire school, each one bumper to bumper but with enough gaps beneath them to allow a few biters to get through from time to time. What I saw was nothing like that.

The walls were concrete—prefabbed or otherwise didn't matter—and easily twenty feet tall. There were ladders anchored to those walls. Every ten feet or so, a soldier stood, weapon in hand. They didn't talk to one another. They stared out at the world beyond the school grounds.

"Come on," Hetch said and made his way to one of the ladders. I followed, but I moved much slower than he did. My legs and arms were tired by the time I reached the landing. The soldier said nothing to us as we moved closer to the edge of the wall.

From where I stood, I could see the moat. It was wide— thirty or forty feet—and maybe just as deep. Inside of it were hundreds of stakes; one end of each one was buried in the ground, the other end sharpened and pointing toward the sky. There were plenty of corpses in the moat, their bodies impaled on the stakes. Some of them still moving their arms and legs. I think I heard a couple of weak moans as well.

Beyond the moat and the stakes and the bodies was what was left of the town, which wasn't much. Many of the buildings were destroyed, fires having done the bulk of the damage. I wondered if they had been burned down on purpose. Snow covered a lot of the black soot around the ruined buildings. There were hollowed out husks of cars lining the crumbled streets. It looked like someone had dropped a bomb on the town, and all that was left was the school.

A few biters shambled around but terribly slow, the cold weather hindering their movement.

We walked the wall the entire area around the school, coming up on what could be considered the front of the compound. The drawbridge was there in the up position. There were four men standing guard here, each with a rifle and all of them looking straight ahead.

Like the rest of the area around the school, the buildings and cars on that side were nothing more than rubble and shells, the skeletons of a previous life and time.

"Let's go in," Jake said. "You're probably starving."

I hadn't noticed at that point, but he was right. I was more than starving. I was famished. The small breakfast I had eaten consisted of a bowl of lukewarm oatmeal and water.

Inside, we hung the coats on pegs near the entrance. The warmth of the building immediately began to thaw my frozen face and hands and feet. We made our way along the halls, all of them painted white, the lights brilliant in their glow. We passed a few people heading the opposite direction, mostly in groups of three or four but even a few loners who looked as content as full church mice.

A family of four walked past us. The older of the two children—a girl with red hair down to the middle of her back—was a teen. There was no mistaking that. The other child, a boy who was probably not quite to his teenage years, looked away as we approached. The man had dark hair and sunglasses, and he held the hand of the young woman he was with.

I did a double take. Her hair was long and brown. Her eyes were brown as well. She was tall, and there was something vaguely familiar about her. I stopped and watched them walk away.

"Hank, come on," Hetch said. "Besides, that gal is obviously taken."

I ignored him. "Excuse me, ma'am," I said and took a few awkward steps toward them.

They all looked back at me. Though I couldn't see the man's eyes, I knew there was suspicion in them. He stepped in front of the woman—on instinct, I'm sure.

The woman put her hand on his arm. They exchanged looks before he moved out of the way and let her approach me.

"Can I help you?"

I hesitated. It was her. It had to be her.

"Can I ask you something? I promise I'll let you go on your way, but just let me ask you one question."

She looked back at her man. He stood there, hands in his pockets. He looked like he could pound me pretty quickly if he felt like it. He shrugged and then nodded.

"What do you want to ask me?"

My throat felt very dry. I licked my lips, but that didn't wet them the way I had hoped.

"Your name. Is it Cate?"

Her face said everything. Her mouth hung slightly open, and she cocked her head to the side just a little. "How did you know my name?" Her voice was like honey from the comb, sweet and smooth.

"I saw a picture of you—a wedding picture. It was in this house. A trailer. I took up shelter there for a few days. Your picture comforted me."

Again, her face spoke volumes. Her brows creased down, and her eyes thinned. I wasn't sure if she were angry or confused or what.

"My picture comforted you?"

"Yeah. I know it sounds crazy, but I was alone and talking to your picture...ummm...you know what? Never mind. I sound crazy. I know I do. But you saved my life. And I'm so happy you didn't end up like most of the world."

There was a long silence between us. Then Cate leaned forward and put her arms around me. "You're welcome." She let go and stepped back.

I nodded, a little shakily, before turning around and letting them go about their lives. My face was hot, and my heart felt good. It was like seeing an old friend you had lost contact with over the years.

The cafeteria was large, and there were maybe fifteen people there. Fifteen? Just a month ago, I thought I would never see that many people again in my life—all total. Now, it was a reality, and adding the three of us into that made eighteen. Eighteen people in one room. Unfathomable. And they were all sane.

They led me past the lunch tables and to the serving kitchen. There were four people in there, three men and a woman, all with nets on their heads and gloves on their hands. One of the men, a tall fellow with a gaunt face and glasses, stepped up to the counter.

"What'll you have, mister?"

I looked to Jake and Hetch.

"Try the chicken noodle—it's great," Jake said. "Just like Mom used to make."

Just like Mom used to make.

"That sounds good."

And it was. Though it didn't taste as good as Mom used to make, it still tasted better than anything I had in months. I ate the soup, drank down every last bit of the broth.

"That was great."

"Why don't we go find Bobby," Jake said.

"Yeah. I'd love that."

We stood from the table. I took my bowl back to the kitchen, handed it to another one of the workers—he wasn't much bigger than the guy who had served me, but he had a warm, engaging smile.

"Thank you," I said.

He obliged with a, "You're welcome."

My stomach rumbled but not from hunger. It cramped, and I let out a small grimace.

"What's wrong, Hank?" Jake asked.

"My stomach's not used to food, I guess—at least not good food."

He left it at that, satisfied with my answer.

We were more than halfway back the way we came when we passed a door to the right. Inside sat an old man, his hair as white as the snow outside, his skin like brown leather. He sat on the floor, his legs crossed, hands on his knees. He rocked back and forth and hummed.

"Imeko?"

I stepped into the room, repeated his name.

He stopped humming and looked in my direction. His eyes were two coal embers peeking out from layers of eyelids and age.

"Walking man," he said to me.

I didn't understand what he meant. If he had said, "Walker, man," I would have gotten it. But I wasn't even sure he remembered me. He looked more fragile than when I had left him.

"Imeko. It's me. Hank."

"I am aware."

"Where's Alaya? Where's your family?"

"Dead. All dead."

"How?"

Imeko looked beyond me to Hetch and Jake in the doorway.

"Give us a minute," I said.

Jake nodded and pulled the door closed.

"Imeko, how did your family die?"

"I killed them."

"*You* killed them?"

"I killed them. If the dead didn't get them, I did. It was all I could do."

"What about Alaya? You wouldn't have killed your granddaughter. You went through too much to save her."

His hand shot out and grabbed my wrist. His grip was firmer than I thought it would be.

"Especially Alaya. She…she was not right…" he tapped his forehead. "In here."

He released my wrist and then looked away.

"She was not the same."

With that, he stood, though it was a great effort for him. I tried to help him, but he pushed my hand away. Imeko walked an old man's walk to the bed against the wall. I hadn't noticed until then, but Humphrey sat on the bed, her bunny pajamas still on, the blood from Alaya's wound dried and ground into the white material. He picked Humphrey up and held her out to me.

I took her with no hesitation. She didn't speak to me at all. Not even when I spoke to her.

"It's been a while, Humphrey. It's good to see you."

When she said nothing, I looked back to Imeko. There were tears in his eyes.

"Why did you keep the teddy bear?" I asked.

"To give back to you. Now, you be gone. Be gone from this place."

"I don't plan on leaving. Not for a long time."

Imeko rounded the bed. He pointed at me and spoke angrily. "You leave this place. You...you're not right in the head. You leave, and never come back. For your own sake."

"Imeko, I just arrived."

His face was fierce, his eyes like hot coals. "I've been given a vision from the gods. They said the walking man must go. If he stays, many will die. You are the walking man, and you must go. You belong out there, out with the dead souls."

I backed away and shook my head. "I don't know what happened to you, but you've lost your rocks, Imeko."

"Leave me be. Leave us all be," he said and went back to the middle of the room where he sat back down, crossed his legs, and began to rock forward then back, forward then back, humming as he did so.

A minute passed before I turned and left the room. I gave one last look back to Imeko, and sadness filled my heart.

"What was that all about?" Jake asked.

"Nothing important. He's lost everything, including his mind." We walked down the hall together, me with Humphrey in one hand, determined to forget Imeko and desperate to see my son. We rounded the corner to see a group of kids standing in the hall. One of them had blond hair that could use a good cutting. He was talking to a couple of others, mostly girls.

"Bobby?" I called, my voice quaking.

He turned. He looked so much like Jeanette. It was as if she chewed him up and spat him out. The blue eyes were hers. The blond hair also. He had my chin, but that was about it.

It may have been just me, but I thought I could feel Jeanette in that hall with us. I could almost picture her leaning against one of the cinderblock walls, her head tilted, her arms crossed over her breasts. She was smiling, and there were tears in her eyes.

Then he noticed me—*who* I was. And as the world slowed down again and he began to run for me, I heard him yell…

"Daddy!"

~Hank Walker
Date Unknown

Dear Faithful Readers,

If you wouldn't mind staying with me for a little while longer. I'd like to tell you a tale (but not of a fateful trip). If you don't get that reference, then you're probably too young to remember *Gilligan's Island*. If that's the case, it's okay.

A few years ago, back at the end of 2009, I was part of an online writers' group. In that group, we discussed various points of writing and the merits of the rules that go with it as well as publishing successes and their counterparts: the unsuccessful attempts. One thing this group was good about was challenging each other. We would throw out prompts to help with creativity. We often held contests that lasted several months and dwindled the participants from around twenty to one lone writer—the champion. It was like a writer's Survivor challenge. It was no small feat to go deep in the competition, but it was even tougher to win it.

When not competing against each other, we often threw out random things to discuss. One day, the topic turned to zombies. Remember, this was the end of 2009. *The Walking Dead* comic books had only been around a few years at this point, and the television series was still almost a year away.

"It's an overdone subgenre," many of my fellow writers said. "It's cliché, and there is nothing new out there."

One person even said, "There is only so much you can do with a zombie story." I can't remember exactly how I got involved in the conversation. At the time, I wasn't really interested in zombies. Sure, I had seen my fair share of movies and read a couple of books (David Moody's *Autumn* series had been my favorite), but I had no interest in *writing* a zombie story. What I was interested in was character development, and at that time, my writing was going through a significant change, one that would eventually create the voice and feel of my stories today.

A suggestion was made and then a challenge issue. Surely, I couldn't write a story based on human character and emotions. Surely, the story had to be zombie-driven. Everyone would get eaten, and mankind would go out in loud screams and deafening moans. The group knew I was all about challenges. Surely, I wouldn't let a challenge go without at least giving it a try.

Christmas came and went, and on January 20th of 2010, I sat down and wrote this line: *The rifle was light, unlike Pop's shotgun.* I stared at it for quite some time, trying to figure out why that line was so important. Then I said, "Screw it. I'm just writing one scene." Those seven words turned into just under 2400, and the story of Hank Walker was born. But that's not where this story ends. Oh no. This is where it began. You see, originally, Hank's tale was called, *My Brothers and I*, and I had no intentions of writing beyond that one story, that one scene. That's what I thought. Some of my writer friends thought the story was okay, and a couple of them liked it. One of them — a wise man by the name of Eric, who totally hated zombies and was one hard critic to please — said he thought it was cool, but he didn't like the title.

"What's wrong with it?" I asked.

"I didn't see any brothers. Where're his brothers?"

He had a point. If I was going to call it *My Brothers and I*, then it needed to have Hank's brothers in it. Remember, at this point, I had no intentions of continuing on with this storyline. I just wanted to prove I could write something somewhat emotional and have zombies in it as well. I thought I had succeeded, especially with this particular line close to the end of the original piece: *The children, they're always the hardest to kill.*

Then a curious thing happened. Out of nowhere, the title came to me, three words that sent my brain into hyper drive with thoughts of a bigger story. *Dredging Up Memories*. I thought on those words hard. As a writer, I tell stories about people. All of these stories are memories, whether mine or the characters'. And by telling their stories, I dredge up their memories time and time again. All writers do this whether they realize it or not. We tell stories of memories.

Though he seemed to stay on my mind, I didn't write anything else about Hank for a while. That changed when I found a website dedicated to stories about the zombie genre. The website, *Tales of the Zombie Wars*, had a lot of cool stories on it. I wondered if I could get *Dredging Up Memories* published there. I subbed it, not really expecting much. Then on April 9th, 2010, it appeared on TOWWZ. I couldn't believe it. I must have gone to the site a dozen times in the first two or three days. Why? Because people could post comments about it. As much as I wanted to see good comments, I really thought it would receive more negative than positive.

Then I saw this comment: *I like the story very much. It really finds the balance between having a John Wayne who shoots at everything without mercy and a total coward who starts crying for anything as a main character. I'm only somewhat missing a closing to the story. Wouldn't surprise (or disappoint) me to see this story continue...*

It was followed by another one: *A great lead in— One thing I really like about this piece is how you portray a guy trying to deal with the insanity of his situation. You portray him, his thought process, in such a realistic, connectable manner —the details are killer, such as the Spiderman T-shirt and his thoughts about his 6th grade teacher. Most of all, I think you do a fantastic job of relaying his doubts—are they really 'dead' in the old sense? Does little Tommy still feel pain in that state? So well delivered; really looking forward to where this goes!*

I was hooked. Yeah, there would be more to this story. And there was. Plenty more. Though the story is clearly a zombie story, I tried to layer it with a simple question: What if the souls were trapped inside the bodies of the biters? This would make the story less about surviving the z-pocalypse and more about having mercy on the people trapped in the rotting corpses shambling around the world. And what if one of those souls was in the dead body of a loved one? If it were you, could you pull the trigger and end the existence of someone you love even if you knew beyond a shadow of a doubt that it would be what they wanted if they could speak? I honestly don't know if I could do it. It would almost be better to find out the loved ones had died and someone else helped them find rest, or peace, or true death than to have to do the deed myself.

If you live in the South Carolina area, you may recognize a few of the places mentioned here. Table Rock, Sommerville, Blackville, Columbia, Batesburg, Saluda, Newberry, and a few other places are all real. I did take a few liberties with scenery, but some of those places are as authentic as they come. Like Healing Springs. The legend about the location is just as I wrote it. The way it looks is just as I wrote it. The healing abilities of the water? Well, I don't know if they can cure the bite of the undead, but I do know it was the perfect solution to the nastiness that is the zombie bite. Obviously, there are a few settings that are completely made up though they are based on real places.

Like many of my stories, *Dredging Up Memories* has a lot of me in it. However, only one character is patterned after someone I know. That person would be Jake, Hank's baby brother. He was influenced by my own baby brother, Andy. You see, I truly believe that in the situations that Jake was put in, Andy would know what to do even if he was scared and unsure of how to go about it, or even if he could actually go through with it, but in the end, he would. He just would. This is Andy. He's a good ol' boy who does right by folks. If push came to shove, Andy would do right by those who were dead and needed to be released. He would also persevere where so many others would just give in and take the out a bullet provides. Sounds crazy, I know, but sometimes, you just feel something so strongly it has to be true.

If you've come this far, I want to say thank you for sticking with me into the darkest hours of the night. Thank you for reading about Hank Walker and the heartache he goes through. This may be the end of *Dredging Up Memories*, but it's not the end of Hank Walker's saga. There is more. Hank has blank spaces in his memory that need filling in. Being drunk for weeks at a time will do that to you. Those blank spaces need to be explored. I've already started looking into them, and what I've discovered is Hank doesn't recall those events for good reasons—some things your mind hides away in the depths of your soul because you simply can't handle the truth of those things. For Hank, death may be better than the truth. Ahh, but that story is for another time.

Again, I thank you for reading *Dredging Up Memories*. I hope you enjoyed Hank's story. Until we meet again, be kind to one another.

A.J.

The Great Big Page of Thankfulness

I'd like to thank a ton of folks, but that list would be longer than this book is. Still, there are some I wish to thank personally:

To my old writing group, *Liquid Imagination*, where Hank Walker's story was birthed. Many of the stories I have written over the years have direct connections to you guys and gals. Without y'all, well...let's not dwell on that.

Justin Dunne, your constant encouragement and questions about Hank and his story helped keep me going when I started to lose enthusiasm with it. Sometimes you just need someone pushing you onward. In my case, this was you. Thanks, Mate.

A special thanks goes to the administration of the *Tales of the Zombie Wars* (TOWWZ) website. If not for you guys, Hank's story would have ended at that opening chapter.

For all the folks who commented on *Dredging Up Memories* on TOWWZ, thank you. Your comments, as much as anything else, played a huge part in this story continuing and even finding its end. It was always good to see a chapter posted, but the real thrill came from the comments of you fine folks.

As always, a great big thanks and a huge kiss go to my wife, Cate, for constantly telling me I can do this writing thing and for not letting me give up when I felt nothing was going well.

Finally, to all of you, Faithful Readers. You are the driving force behind many writers. To be read, to have your work enjoyed by you, is one of the biggest thrills a writer can have. Thank you.

A.J.

About the Author

A.J. Brown is a storyteller who pens emotionally charged, character-driven stories that often include a touch of the dark paranormal.

If you would like to learn more about A.J., you can check out his blog, **Type AJ Negative**. You can also find him on Facebook at his personal profile (ajbrown36) or his author page (www.facebook.com/typeajnegative).

You can also find his other books, *Along the Splintered Path*, *Southern Bones*, *Cory's Way*, and *A Stitch of Madness* on Amazon. You can get the print versions of all of those books on Amazon as well, but if you would like to purchase one signed and for a significantly lower price, contact A.J. directly through his e-mail address, ajbrown36@bellsouth.net. Or you can visit his online store at: https://squareup.com/market/aj-brown. A list of all of his publications can be found on his blog, **Type AJ Negative**.

Made in the USA
San Bernardino, CA
10 May 2016